Forever Mine,

A BBW Romance

Forever Mine,

A BBW Romance

Shelli Marie

www.urbanbooks.net

Urban Books, LLC
300 Farmingdale Road, N.Y.-Route 109
Farmingdale, NY 11735

Forever Mine, A BBW Romance

ISBN 13: 978-1-64556-728-8
EBOOK ISBN: 978-1-64556-740-0

First Trade Paperback Printing November 2025
Printed in the United States of America

10 9 8 7 6 5 4 3 2 1

*This is a work of fiction. Any references or similarities
to actual events, real people, living or dead, or to real
locales are intended to give the novel a sense of reality.
Any similarity in other names, characters, places, and
incidents is entirely coincidental.*

Distributed by Kensington Publishing Corp.
Submit Orders to:
Customer Service
400 Hahn Road
Westminster, MD 21157-4627
Phone: 1-800-733-3000
Fax: 1-800-659-2436

The authorized representative in the EU for product
safety and compliance
Is eucomply OU, Parnu mnt 139b-14, Apt 123
Tallinn, Berlin 11317, hello@eucompliancepartner.com

Forever Mine,

A BBW Romance

by

Shelli Marie

Acknowledgments

To God Almighty, I give the glory.

To my family support team:
Jeremy & Tiffany, Jessica & Daqwan, Danielle, Vassie Jr. and Maya, Jaden, Tianna, Kaylen, Journey, Thalia, DJ, JaKoby, Marlee, Wynter, Deklen, Kairo, and Sofia.
Thanks for all of your encouragement.
I love you guys! Always!!
To the rest of the Dishman Klan: Jennifer Dishman, Kim Dishman (R.I.L.), Marlo and Devin Dishman, Daddy, and Genora Dishman, Krista, and Christopher Dishman.
I love you all dearly!!
To my extended support team: My sissy Teruka B, my pen sisters: Lady Lissa, Summer Grant, Marina Jefferson, and Destiny Henry, my sister Sheila James, my bff TonYelle Reese, my soul sistahs: Cyndy, Andrea, Quaran, Regina, Priscilla Cole, Lenwand, Junanya, Kendra, Tanya Gary, and Helen! I love you all!
SPECIAL THANKS TO ALL MY DEDICATED READERS!!
MUCH LOVE . . . ALWAYS!!

Preface

Oaklyn Jones

Spending time with my mother during our Saturday summer walks had always been the highlight of my week. Not only did we love exploring and sharing ideas, but we often came across something or someone that left us feeling incredibly blessed. This time, we just happened to stroll by a couple of homeless folks who were standing on the sidewalk with a mic, some sort of box, and a grocery cart full of miscellaneous items.

"That's so messed up. Two grown-ass men out here performing for coins when damn near every company in the city is hiring. I don't see why they can't just get a real job to make enough money to get up off these streets. It ain't safe. In fact, those are the same guys that have been squatting in the vacant house up the block. You ain't seen them before, Oaklyn?" My mother whispered as we passed the strangers on our way to KISS Coffee over on Ainsworth Street. It was a Black-owned company that was really popular in our thriving neighborhood.

"Yeah, I've seen them a few times, but dang, Mama, you ever think that maybe they're just down on their luck right now?" I asked in a low tone as my heart went out to the two men.

Being the caring and sensitive nineteen- year-old I was at the time, I stopped near the rose bushes, dug deep down into the zippered compartment of my soft brown leather crossbody bag, and drew out three single dollar bills and two quarters. Holding tightly onto the only cash I had on me, I backstepped a bit and flashed a friendly smile. Bending down with my eyes still glued to the handsome stranger with the mic, I dropped the money into the big, brown pressed wool cowboy hat placed upside down on the ground before them. As I drew my hand back and began to turn away, the young guy gently held onto it and stopped me from leaving. Normally, I would've started swinging if a stranger touched me without my consent, but it was different with this guy. His vibe was actually inviting.

"Excuse me, sir," I whispered and stared into his cap-tivating brown eyes. They were slanted just enough to make you believe that Asian genes flowed through his bloodline.

"I'm sorry for putting my hands on you without permis-sion, but I just wanted to ask if I could sing you a song for your generous donation," he said kindly.

"Three dollars and fifty cents was all I gave. I'm really sorry I couldn't give more, but unfortunately, that's all I have on me," I shyly admitted, but I couldn't seem to turn from his gaze.

"Then it was indeed a generous donation, and that means you are a very special person to give your last," he replied with a wink.

As my chest pounded with anticipation, I thanked him before silence held me captive. There was something exceptional about this young man, and I could feel it.

"My name is Braxton, and this is my Uncle Pete, who raised me after my folks were killed in a house fire," he explained.

"Oh, I'm so sorry for your loss, Braxton." After I gave my condolences, I introduced myself along with my mother. "I'm Oaklyn, and this is my mom, Draya."

"Nice to meet you folks." Braxton spoke politely with his eyes deeply on me. "And . . . Oaklyn, huh? I like that name. It's really unique."

"Thanks." I blushed a bit.

"How about I sing you a little something?"

"A'ight then. Go for it," I anxiously urged with a grin.

With his eyes still on me, Braxton picked up the mic connected to a raggedy PA system. I prayed that the thing worked.

"You have any special requests, sweetheart?" Braxton asked.

"Whatever is on your heart at this moment."

My mother noticed the extended eye contact that Braxton and I continuously made, then quickly nudged me with her shoulder and gave me a smile. "Under all that filth and roughness, he's actually a cutie pie."

"Stop it, Mama!" I hissed playfully, in fear of her embarrassing me.

As we stood there, giving each other a hard time, the music began to play and stole our attention. It sounded excellent until the feedback from the mic screeched loudly. The sudden, powerful surge of annoying noise caused us to jump and desperately cling to each other.

"Sorry about that." Uncle Pete laughed and adjusted the knobs to make the music come back on clearly.

The wink he gave his nephew prompted Braxton to get into character. On cue and swaying with the rhythm, he held the microphone tightly in his grip and then belted out the lyrics from one of my favorite songs. "This mind, ooh, will never neglect you."

With all my focus on him, I allowed his voice to hypnotize me and draw me into a daze. No matter how hard I tried, I found myself hopelessly staring at this giant, caramel-complected stranger. Even with the tattered clothing and the wild hair growing on his head and face, I could still see the potential in this young man. My mother was right. With a little cleaning up, he could be very handsome.

"Thank you so much. That was amazing! Your voice is amazing," I excitedly complimented him when he finished his song. By this time, a small crowd had gathered around us, and several of the spectators were recording. This made me blush even more.

"How beautiful!" one of them yelled out.

"The way he serenaded that girl brought tears to my eyes," another one said.

"Wow! Looks like you have fans already," I teased and patted his arm.

"The only one I see is you," he whispered as he came into my personal space.

My heart skipped a beat behind those seven powerful words, and if it weren't for my mother dragging me off, I probably would've made a fool of myself. Thank goodness it didn't happen that way.

"Why did you pull me away like that, Mom?" I asked curiously.

"Because I just had the best idea."

"What is it?"

"Well, I was thinking that after we get coffee, we could stop by the store and pick up a few things. That way, once the basketball game goes off, we could make some food, then take it to the guys over at that vacant house they've been staying in. It has to be after the game, though, because you know I can't miss it. This NBA summer league has been so entertaining."

"I know. I know, Mom, and that's a great idea. While you're watching the game, I can even make some of my famous red velvet cupcakes with the cream cheese whipped icing. Oh, and maybe we should take them some extra blankets and clothes and stuff like that. I know it's summer, but it's been getting pretty cold at night."

"You're right. Make a list on your phone while we're walking so that we won't forget anything," she instructed with a smile.

Although my mother was tough as nails, she could be just as soft as I was. She proved that to me right after the Blazers whooped on the Lakers, and she cooked a bunch of food. Taking extra special care of the meal, she placed it all neatly inside the disposable containers with lids that she had purchased while we were out. She even dug out an old cooler on wheels that we had and filled it up with ice and drinks.

When we showed up at the abandoned property later on that evening to take Braxton and Uncle Pete some food, my mother took the lead. Without being prompted, she whipped out some extra candles and a tablecloth, then set up all the food. My mother's display of kindness touched me deeply. While I had only expected to feed them and give them the things we gathered, she had something else to shock them with. She surprised even me.

Thirty minutes into the visit, she mysteriously drew out the clothing vouchers from her job, along with the information and a personal reference to get them immediately placed into transitional housing. My soul jumped for joy, and so did my body. I couldn't contain my happiness. Neither could Uncle Pete and Braxton.

Things moved rather quickly after that, and within three days, their application was approved the following Tuesday. My mother and I were so excited that we offered to give them a ride to the apartment complex they were being placed in. The brief walkthrough, signing of the lease, and receiving their keys took all of an hour, and now they were housed free of charge for at least a year. Who could ask for more?

Uncle Pete definitely couldn't. He gasped. "Look at the stainless-steel appliances and marble countertops. This shit right here is nice." That man was as happy as a kid on Christmas and wasted no time taking his things out of his bags as soon as he finished his second look around the fully furnished apartment. Braxton, on the other hand, didn't want to unpack a thing.

Carefully searching for the right words without sounding too nosy, I asked him why he wasn't getting settled in like his uncle. Before he answered me, he scrunched his face up and turned to me.

"No need to unpack and get too comfortable because I don't plan on staying here long."

"Oh, you got somewhere else to stay? Because last time I checked, you and your uncle were living in an abandoned house with no electricity or running water. This is a blessing, Braxton, and those things don't come by too often. Believe me, I know."

"My blessing was meeting you, and that's why I wanna do better. For myself and for my future."

"Is that right?" I pressed him.

"Don't you think that us meeting on Saturday was something more than a coincidence? Look around you, Oaklyn. You changed the lives of two total strangers in less than a week. Don't you think that's a sign?"

"What makes you think it's a sign, Braxton?"

"Well, ever since we met, I can't stop thinking about you. It's been like my whole world is going in slow motion, and you're in the middle of it, bringing the sunshine to my life."

"Boy, stop it!" I cracked so I wouldn't end up blushing or feeling insecure with my size. "Why would you be interested in big ol' me when there are millions of chicks out there with a Barbie shape?"

"Those wide hips, thick thighs, and perky boobs are sexier than a muthafucka! I don't know about the rest of the guys around here, but baby, you're just my size."

"Stop it, Braxton!" I giggled.

"I'm serious, and I plan on showing you how much I'm diggin' you, girl."

"What ya gonna show me, Braxton?"

"Give me three months, and I'll be a totally different man. Now that I have a bathroom at my disposal, I can shower, shave, and get myself together. I'm ready to get a real job and get a real place for us."

"*Us*?" I checked. "We're eighteen, Braxton, and we don't even know each other. You're talking crazy."

"Just give me three months."

"What can you do in three months?"

"Make you fall in love with me."

Shit, little did he know, he already had my nose wide open. Oh, but falling in love? That may have been pushing it. Personally, I didn't think that a serious relationship was in the cards for me. Growing up as a heavy girl hadn't brought me any luck in that department, but I still decided to humor him. I couldn't resist.

"Is that right, Braxton? It seems like you have it all planned out," I teased with a smile.

"Yes, I sure do. I can already see it. We can get our own place and live happily ever after."

"Okay, Mr. Fairytale Man," I clowned and laughed even harder.

"You got that right. I mean that shit, too. All the way down to the happily-ever-after ending for us," Braxton repeated with a genuine grin.

"Okay, I'm not gonna bust your bubble. I'll just sit back and watch how you move because right now, what you're saying is nothing but a bunch of words. The proof is in the pudding, baby."

"I'm gonna prove it to you, too, Oaklyn. Just wait and see."

That day, Braxton made a bunch of promises that I took lightly, until he did just as he said, and within three months, we had ourselves a nice little apartment on the north side of Portland. It wasn't much, but it was ours.

The first four or five months of living together were filled with fairytale magic, just like he had promised—both in and out of the bedroom. Braxton tended to my every need physically, while emotionally supporting me through my college courses. In turn, I managed my man's wants while pushing his music on every avenue possible. From the corner store to the radio booth, I handed out samples of his newest single. In no time, our relationship blossomed into something beautiful, and Braxton's career began to take off. His following even tripled.

Well, with fame came fans, and my man, like many other entertainers, fell quickly into the trap. Letting the hood celebrity status go to his head, Braxton walked high on a cloud, looking down at others—including me. The honeymoon phase had obviously expired, and the loyalty no longer existed, so where did we go from here? Did I leave him and run back to my mama? Or did I stay and stick it out?

As my mind spun with a bunch of questions, a series of answers silently showed me that the truth hurt. Not as much as my heart did, though.

Not even close.

Chapter One

Oaklyn Jones

A Decade Later . . .

My life slowly went from sugar to shit, but I persistently fought for my relationship. No matter how much it drained me, I did everything in my power to make things work until I ran out of options. After ten years of heartbreak and disappointment, all I had left was hope, and that too began to dwindle.

Had I been foolish to think that Braxton would change? That same question had been floating in my mind for the past few years while he continuously cheated on me. True enough, I thought for sure he would straighten up after I got pregnant and gave birth to our baby girl, Brazil, but it only got worse. So bad that I had to quit more than a dozen jobs and got evicted several times, all because Braxton couldn't be reliable or responsible. Why didn't he have time to help me with Brazil, but he had plenty of time to visit the mall? Why couldn't he get us a place to live instead of carelessly spending his royalties on unnecessary shit? Ugh, that man made me mad!

"You must have something really heavy on your mind, Oaklyn, because I've been yelling your name for the past couple of minutes. You didn't hear me?" my best friend, Koola, hollered in my face.

"No, I didn't. I was busy looking at all these receipts from the crap Braxton has been buying. You know how much he paid for that diamond grill?"

"I don't even wanna know, and stop worrying yourself. Things will be different once he gets signed. That's when the real dough is gonna come. Just watch."

"I've been watching for the past decade, Koola, and I'm tired. I'm tired off all his bullshit."

"Please don't tell me Braxton is cheating again. I'll be so disappointed in him."

Koola sat down beside me and frowned. She was over-protective and hated it when anyone hurt my feelings.

"Well, get ready to get disappointed because I know he's exchanging numbers with at least half the females he meets while he's at these places performing, and I don't wanna know how many he's fucking out of those. Ugh."

"Why did you stop going to his shows, Oaklyn?" Koola probed. "I never could understand that."

"I'm not built for that shit," I explained. "It bothers me when all these women throw themselves at him. All that hugging and kissing shit for the pictures and autographs gotta go."

"Did you tell him that?"

"Hell yeah, but he insists that he has to be nice. Says that if he's rude or mean, it would taint his image with the public. What about me, shit? It's tainting my image of that muthafucka!"

"Oaklyn!"

"No, Koola, I'm serious. It's like I don't even matter anymore. Ever since I moved into housing and he ain't gotta be responsible for bills, he does what the hell he pleases. If we ain't arguing about him cheating, I'm fussing about him slacking on his responsibilities. He's barely been helping me with Brazil. She be beggin' that nigga to take her to play basketball or even to the park, and he can't even do that shit. He's either too tired or too busy. I'm telling you, girl. I'm tired. Fed up and tired. Thank God for my mama."

"Girl, for real, but why you ain't been telling me this shit?" Koola fussed angrily. "We are like sisters, Oaklyn."

"I just wasn't ready to admit that we may be better apart." The thought of calling it quits with Braxton broke my heart, but it was his deception that crushed it. I wasn't sure if there was any coming back from this pain.

"Give him one last chance, and if you find out he's actually cheating on you, give his ass the boot, Oaklyn. I don't care how famous he thinks he is. He is foul for doing you wrong. Fucking bastard!"

"Maybe he's tired of fucking with a fat girl," I grumbled, trying hard to face reality.

"Fat girl? Where?" Koola gasped. "I wish I had your flawless chocolate skin and beautiful, curvaceous body. You got ass, hips, and tits, while I'm stuck with this little flabby fupa, size B-cup titties, flat ass, and these scarred-up legs."

"Hush!" I said, then laughed.

"No, seriously, Oaklyn. Please tell me that nigga ain't been tryna fat shame you."

"*No,* never that."

"I was about to say." Koola had become more upset than I was. She was cussing Braxton out, and he wasn't anywhere around. "Ugh, I hope he walks through that door."

"Don't worry. He ain't. He done already called me to tell me that he had some type of rehearsal at Chachi's place."

"What happened to the studio he was recording at?"

"Koola, that dude was a fake. He bought that building with stolen identification, and they seized it."

"Damn, that's messed up," she warned playfully. "God don't like ugly."

"Sho' don't," I agreed as my mother came knocking on the door to bring Brazil home.

As always, she entered the apartment with an arm full of bags. When she set them down, I noticed the scratches on my daughter's face and immediately questioned her about them.

"Leave her alone, Oaklyn. She is okay," my mother answered before Brazil got a chance.

"What happened, Brazil? Who put their hands on you?"

"I didn't even start it, Mama!"

"What happened?" I repeated, losing my patience with this little girl. Brazil wasn't but six years old and already kicking up dust. I'd had it with her grown tail.

"Amy talked mess about my daddy. Talking about he was at her house singing to her mama."

"What?" I gasped while my mother stood there shaking her head.

"She said Daddy was kissing on her mama and everything," Brazil snitched and nearly gave me a damn heart attack.

"Are you kidding me?"

"Nope," my mother answered. "Soon as I went inside her school to pick her up, her teacher informed me that the principal needed to speak to me."

"Why didn't they call me?" I gritted and went to check Brazil's scratches. "I sent you to the school in your nana's neighborhood thinking it was better, but shit, you over there fighting too."

"Did you whoop her, Bitty B?" Koola teased, making Brazil giggle and clown.

"You know I did! Ain't nobody about to be talking about my mama or daddy."

"Get yo' ass in the bathroom and run some water. I don't even wanna talk to you right now. Fighting at school!" I sighed heavily and cut my eyes.

As Brazil ran off, I walked Koola to the door. After we said our goodbyes, I turned around and shot daggers at my mother. She had to stop babying my daughter.

"You are turning that little girl into a real B.R.A.T.," I fussed. "She gets in trouble at school, and you still bring her home with a bunch of gifts? Mom, you gotta stop."

"While you're worrying about how I'm spoiling Brazil, you need to check her daddy for sleeping around. He's the one to blame, Oaklyn," my mother fussed. "I can't believe he's the same person we met out on them streets. He used to be so sweet and such a gentleman, and now I look at him. I don't even know who he is anymore."

"I don't care who you wanna blame right now, Mom. You still should've punished Brazil for her actions," I complained.

"Well, I did take her basketball."

"Wow, really? Like she ain't got five more of 'em."

"Well, I took her favorite one. Shit! Little heffa broke that thousand-dollar vase I got in China last year." My mother sneered and jingled her keys. "I'm leaving, and I'll see you Sunday because when I pick Brazil up tomorrow, she staying the weekend with me, right?"

"Yeah, Mom, but you gotta be stricter with her. That attitude of hers is getting to be too much."

"I'm gonna stay on her, Oaklyn."

The promise that my mother made went right out the door with her because I knew better. There wasn't a thing she wouldn't do for Brazil, and although I loved and appreciated her for that, she still needed to tighten up those reigns.

"Little girl! We need to have a talk," I yelled out as I locked the door and went into the bathroom. Filled with questions about what my daughter's classmate had said to Brazil, I started to ask but quickly refrained when I heard her daddy coming through the front door. Like clockwork, he began hollering my name.

"Oaklyn?"

"You wash up, get out, get your pajamas, and get yo' tail in the bed, Brazil. I'll come check on you in a minute," I told her before going out to the living room to see what Braxton was screaming about.

"Why didn't you answer me?" He frowned.

"Because I was talking to Brazil about getting in trouble at school today."

"That mouth of hers, Oaklyn. I done told you."

"For your information, she got in a fight."

"Please tell me shorty whooped whoever it was."

"Hush that shit up, Braxton," I hissed lowly, then cussed him out about what was said about him.

"You know what? I ain't even gonna entertain some shit a kid said, and you're crazy if you do." He laughed to downplay his foul actions, but I knew better. That nigga's excuses were faker than a three-dollar bill. "Now, I'm tired and I'm about to go to bed, Oaklyn. I got a busy weekend coming up, starting with this private gig."

"Whatever, Braxton. Ugh!" Yes, I cut him off again. No need to listen to his lies and explanations. I'd had quite enough of that mess. What that man needed to do was hurry up and pull it together. If he didn't, he was about to lose his family.

That was for certain.

Chapter Two

Braxton Carter

Two days later . . .

Right when I was trying to earn back Oaklyn's trust, Brazil got in a fight with Jen's daughter, Amy. The altercation between the first graders caused the tension to tighten. Oaklyn stayed on me, bringing up shit from ten years ago.

"Braxton," she yelled through the bathroom door. "I was just out here thinking. Remember that shit you did when we got our first apartment? Remember that bitch Stacey?"

How the fuck could I forget the chick when Oaklyn beat her ass for pushing her way into our apartment? That was the very first time I got busted for cheating.

"Remember how I snatched her when she called herself coming up in our place to get you? Then you wanna try to hop up and help her, but I had that bitch in a chokehold and wasn't no getting out of that shit! She broke the window and the door off the hinges."

"And they took her ass to jail?" I added.

"And *we* got kicked out. Remember that shit, Braxton?"

"Whatever, Oaklyn!" I hollered while I adjusted my ass on the toilet before my leg went to sleep. "Can a nigga get some peace?"

"What the hell are you doing in there?"

"Damn, I can't take a fucking dump?" I hissed.

"You've been in that fucking bathroom thirty minutes, Braxton. You better not be in there on your phone being sneaky and shit."

With her, it was always something. She was tripping for real. "I'm coming. Damn, Oaklyn!"

After I rose from the toilet, flushed, then washed my hands, I thought about the high-paying singing gig that I had that night, and I couldn't help but feel a bit leery. Shit, I really thought it was a scam until dude sent me a thousand-dollar deposit via CashApp and told me that I would get another nine after his daughter Teagan's surprise party. That was more than I had ever made in my life for one performance. For this muthafucka to pay ten racks just for a couple of songs and a bunch of autographs for the guests, he had to be rolling in the dough. How could I turn that down?

With the gig heavy on my mind, I walked out of the bathroom and damn near ran over Oaklyn who was standing there with her hands propped on her wide hips. "Damn!" I huffed with a frown, then backed up to walk around her.

"Why were you in there so long?"

As I turned to her and silently searched for an answer, I got caught up in Oaklyn's beauty. The sight was truly breathtaking. The fresh twists she sported looked damn good on her, but then again, she could have a fucking mop on top of her head and dressed her thick, shapely body in rags, and she would still be the most beautiful brown girl in the world. Why couldn't I just do right by her?

"You ain't got shit to say, so I'm gonna assume that I was right."

"Right about what?" I grumbled, becoming irritated all over again.

"Right about you being in that bathroom on your damn phone, Braxton."

"If we had two bathrooms—"

"Let me cut you off before you even get started, because how dare you even come at me like that? Have you forgotten so quickly, sir? It's because of your careless decisions that I'm staying in housing now."

Oaklyn was right, but she didn't have to keep rubbing that shit in my face. I fucked up, and I couldn't change the past.

"Now, tell me. What were you in there doing, Braxton?"

"Damn, baby, I was taking a shit," I snapped harshly and shook my head. "If you don't believe me, take yo' ass in there and get a whiff."

"Nigga, no!" Oaklyn clowned and went to shut the bathroom door behind me. As soon as she did, she used her fingers to plug her nose. "Damn, stanky ass."

"Well, it ain't supposed to smell like roses."

As I went to get my shoes, Oaklyn was right on my heels. She wanted to know where I was going.

"Well, since I can't leave all my shit over here, I gotta go over to my uncle's to get dressed for my gig."

"If you get us another place so Brazil and I can move out of housing, then it wouldn't be a problem."

"It's coming . . . slowly but surely, and you can believe that."

"You always say that shit, and every time you make a decent amount of money, you either spend it on some flashy shit like that diamond grill in your mouth or all that damn jewelry you're sporting. Then, when you're not spending it on yourself, you're giving a nice chunk of it to Uncle Pete," Oaklyn complained.

"If it wasn't for him looking out for me, I would've been in the system when I was ten. I'm just returning the favor, baby. Don't trip."

"Trip? Shit, Braxton. What more do you need to do for him? I mean, you already helped him get on disability and got his veteran benefits going, and we even got him a nice place. Hell, he's doing better than we are."

While Oaklyn was correct, she still didn't get it because she grew up in a home with at least one of her parents. I had no one except Uncle Pete, and he had always been there for me. Aside from her, her mother, Draya, our daughter Brazil, and my boy Chachi, he was the only family I had.

"I'm not about to argue with you, Oaklyn, because I gotta go. I'll be back after this gig. Is that cool?" I checked just in case she was on that bullshit and didn't want me back over there.

"You got a key, don't you?"

"Yeah, but—"

"But nothing, Braxton. Just make sure you bring yo' black ass home after this party you're doing."

"I am," I replied, knowing damn well that it wasn't my home, and it was all my fault just like she had stated. If I had kept my job while pursuing my career, we would have had another place by now, but no. I was too stubborn and hardheaded to make it happen. Now, I had another chance to do it by using the money I was about to get. It was definitely enough for a security deposit and the first and last month's rent, but not much more, considering the current rental rates were extremely high. On top of that, how was I going to guarantee that I would have the rent each month when I didn't have a steady job? Folks were out here charging over two grand a month for a simple two-bedroom apartment. It was ridiculous, but also the very reason I wasn't confident that I would be able to support Oaklyn once she got out of housing. What would I do then?

As I sat there trying to work things out in my head, my thoughts were interrupted. Once again.

"What time is this party over, and exactly how much are you making tonight, Braxton?" Oaklyn questioned as she walked me to the door. "I'm only asking because I wanted to get Brazil a few things. She's been bugging me about some new sneakers."

"I'm not sure what time it'll be over, and I gotcha on that dough, baby." Without giving her a specific amount, I promised to take care of them, then sealed it with a juicy kiss. Just like the first time, her lips against mine gave me an indescribable feeling, one that always put a smile on my face and made me a little giddy on the inside. Oaklyn was the only chick that could make me feel that way.

"Okay then, babe." She giggled and hugged me. "I'll see you later, and I love you."

"I love you too," I reciprocated as I walked out the door, then jogged to my olive-colored Dodge Charger. That bad boy took me four years of forking up a grand a month in order to finally obtain full ownership. It was a hefty price to pay, but it was well worth it.

"This is my baby." I laughed to myself when I climbed into my ride and patted my camouflage-designed padded leather steering wheel grip.

After I tapped my push-start button, then pulled out of the space in front of Oaklyn's apartment, my boy Chachi was ringing my phone. As soon as I connected the call, he was yelling loudly.

"What's good wit' ya, playa?"

"Cut that shit out, nigga. You know I'm tryna be faithful, Chachi," I clowned. "I'm tryna stay straight."

"That's what you would want to do if you wanna keep yo' family together."

"You got jokes."

"Nah, I'm just fuckin' with ya, Brax. I was just calling to see if you still had that gig tonight. I know you were worried about the folks not paying you."

"Yeah, ol' boy shot me the deposit. I'm about to go get ready now. Why, you wanna roll with me?"

"Hell nah! I'm good."

"Why?" I asked Chachi.

"I don't feel like being around a bunch of bougie folks. You can have that shit, bruh. I just wanted you to call me if there were any bitches there worth fucking with. I could use a rich chick to finance me right now."

"Stick to yo' day job, nigga."

After all the shit he had just talked to me, I had to clown him about his position over at the Frito Lay warehouse in Vancouver, Washington. Chachi didn't like that shit.

"At least I got my own crib. You won't even buckle down to get one for you and yo' baby mama. You be too busy splurging on unnecessary material shit and taking care of Uncle Pete, while he's spending his money over at Viewpoint."

"The strip club?" I laughed loudly. "You gotta be fucking kidding me."

"Nah, I wish I was, Brax, but I saw that shit for myself last night when I walked up in there and caught him getting a lap dance from Trixie."

That was it. Me and Uncle Pete needed to sit down and discuss some things because if he had money to go to the strip club, he definitely didn't need the extra five hundred that I had been giving him every month. I had to make it quick, though. I didn't want to be late to my show.

"Let me go, Chachi. I'm just pulling up at my uncle's spot."

"A'ight, one."

When we hung up, I parked and ran up into Uncle Pete's and let him have it. Funny thing was, he wasn't even bothered by it. In fact, he found the shit hilarious.

"I didn't tell you to give me no money, nephew. You do that shit out the kindness of your heart, and I'm thankful because without it, I wouldn't be able to get me no ass on the regular."

"That's enough, Unc. I gotta go," I replied as I ran to the bonus room he had and got my black slacks, black blazer, and a white button-down shirt. After I showered and slipped into my suit, I headed to this chick Teagan's surprise party to perform. That was the only thing on my mind: Money, money, and mo' money.

Chapter Three

Teagan Hoffman

My thirtieth birthday was right around the corner, and honestly, I didn't feel like celebrating. Not after recently experiencing several near brushes with death, beginning with my routine trip to the 24-hour gym. That particular Wednesday night, I was forced to park across the road from Anytime Fitness. Normally, I would leave my fully loaded BMW in the adjacent lot after dark, but this particular time, the area was blocked off with orange cones and yellow caution tape.

Given the upscale neighborhood in which I resided, I felt completely at ease as I stepped off the curb to use the crosswalk. However, this sense of security rapidly dissipated when I noticed two black SUVs with darkly tinted windows approaching quickly in both lanes. Just in time to avoid a potentially fatal collision, I managed to leap behind a parked car, sustaining only minor cuts, bruises, and a mild concussion. Although I felt well enough to go home, the medics who showed up several minutes later insisted on transporting me to the hospital, where they ended up admitting me for observation. Stressed me the hell out.

The anxiety that began to fill my body only heightened when a nurse allegedly administered penicillin into my IV without prior authorization. My chest tightened, then my throat and tongue became swollen, which made it difficult for me to breathe.

How could she miss that important note in my medical file?

I was well on my way to meeting my maker, until the doctors miraculously caught the dangerous mishap just in time to save me. That shit was mad weird, and I had no choice but to call my mafia-affiliated parents. Once they found out what happened, they became suspicious of foul play and immediately put tight security on me until the doctors released me weeks later. Overreacting, as usual.

This whole ordeal wouldn't have been so bad if my boyfriend, Walter, was there by my side to go through this string of bad luck with me. Unfortunately, he had been nowhere to be found since before all the odd things began happening. It had now been a couple of months with no show or call. Walter's absence made me depressed enough to want to skip my birthday festivities. Fuck that extravagant party my mother and father planned. I mean, who wanted to kick it with a bunch of people that I barely fooled with, when my heart was in shambles? Two entire years with Walter, a man I gave my heart to, and he just up and disappears? I thought we were all good.

"Please tell me you're not in here pouting," my best friend, Eva, huffed.

"Just fantasizing about how I thought I had Walter securely bagged, as well as our future all planned out, starting with the candlelight proposal and elaborate wedding ceremony, all the way down to the power move into a huge new estate. Maybe even have a couple of kids down the line. Who knows?" I sighed heavily.

"Girl, please."

The same enchanted tale that had continuously played in my head had now abruptly come to an end, and I was having a hard time getting over it. Maybe it was because the breakup with Walter wasn't a normal one, where we fought over something minor, then called it quits. It was like this dude pulled a whole disappearing act. The only trace he left was a long, drawn-out text informing me that he had moved on, not only with another woman, but to another location that he failed to disclose before he suddenly changed his number and shut down all of his social networks.

"Where could he be?" I whined.

"After exhausting all possible ways of reaching him, including hiring several private investigators, you found nothing but a bunch of dead ends, Teagan—"

"Yeah, it's like Walter dropped off the face of the earth, but there's no way, Eva. He has to be somewhere hiding, and that's disturbing."

"He's disturbing," Eva mocked. "I'm going to the bathroom, and when I come out, those tears better be dry."

"Ugh, whatever," I hissed and waved her off as she disappeared down the hallway, leaving me to my silent rant.

The more I thought about how dirty Walter did me, the angrier I became. It had gotten so bad that I even contemplated hunting that man down and shooting him on sight. Him and his fucking dog, Jemma. Sad that he loved that bitch more than he loved me. Ugh!

"I can't believe this shit!" I cried and threw my face into my cupped hands as I plopped down on my white tufted sectional that sat dead center in my huge formal living room. When I became strong enough to lean back, I lifted my smooth, thick, chocolate legs and rested them on the matching chaise. I needed to pull myself together before Eva came out of the bathroom and clowned me again.

All she kept repeating the past couple of months was, "Stop crying over that loser, boo. Stop allowing a nobody like that to disrupt your life, Love, you have all the money and possessions that you could ever want in life, Teagan. You're too strong to let this keep you down, honey."

That shit wasn't as easy as that chick made it out to be. If it was, I wouldn't still be angrily pouting. You see, everyone wasn't as strong as Eva. I know I wasn't, and that was what she failed to understand. We were nothing alike. While I threw my all into a relationship, my friend stayed more carefree in hers. Unlike myself, she vowed never to let anyone come close enough to penetrate that precious vital organ in her chest. That was precisely why Eva had never gotten dumped like I had. How could she, when she never had a real relationship to get dumped from? In fact, I had never met any guys she messed around with. She stayed secretive, and I didn't bother her. I had problems of my own.

"Ugh, I'm so tired of feeling like this," I grunted as I fidgeted on the sofa and dried my tears the best I could. No matter how much I rubbed them away, I couldn't stop them from falling. All the while I wiped my face, I kept wondering if I had done something to cause the breakup. Maybe it was the way Walter got upset each time I got really pushy when I wanted something. Maybe I was too much for him. As a matter of fact, I probably was. Come to think of it, I couldn't recall one time I took no for an answer, and that was unsettling. Yeah, maybe I had been a bit over the top.

If that were the case, all Walter had to do was tell me. Not just leave a bitch for dead. *Damn.*

As I listened to Eva's footsteps in the hallway, I tried to sit up straight. I forced a grin, but I still couldn't stop the sniffles or the warm liquid flowing down my flushed cheeks.

"Teagan, come on now, boo. You have to cheer up and dry them tears." Eva tried to reason as she came back into the living room and sat beside me.

"I'm trying to."

"Look, Walter was just your first love. That li'l fling y'all had was just a small taste of what's out there, hon."

"*A small taste*? Girl, that was two fucking years of my life that I can't get back."

"Look at that shit as two years behind you, Teagan," she insisted then got to barking. "Now that you're fully recovered physically, you need to work on your mental. That means you need to get up off yo' ass like you promised me. *We* are going out tonight."

"I know what I promised, but now I'm having second thoughts, Eva. I don't even know what I would wear, and I don't have the energy to look."

"Teagan, go and slip into that bomb-ass white outfit you bought not that long ago, and wear those white leather boots to match your cropped white leather jacket."

"Are you talking about the same outfit that I bought to wear to the birthday party next weekend? The same one I had to cancel because Walter won't be there to ask me to marry him?"

"Bitch, you act like the nigga died."

"It almost feels like he did, Eva."

"Well, he didn't, Teagan. He left you for no apparent reason, with no valid excuse, as if he didn't give a flying fuck. He didn't even show up when you really needed him, so evidently, he didn't care. I say it's time to get over it and get over him. You know what? I'm gonna show you how, too."

"How, Eva?" I questioned with a sniffle. "And please don't start that shit about the best way to get over an old nigga is getting up under a new one, because I ain't ready for all that."

"It's been months, boo, and your parents finally got those unnecessary security guards up off you. Now, get yo' ass up. Start doing shit for you, not to make another muthafucka happy. To make you, Teagan, happy."

As badly as I wanted to admit that it really made me happy to take care of my man like my mama did for my daddy, I didn't dare confess it to her. That shit right there would've stirred up a whole different argument, and I didn't have the strength to have another verbal battle with my bestie. Especially when she never thought she was wrong.

"Okay, I'll get up and get dressed, Eva, but wherever it is you think you're taking me better not be a damn setup for no blind date," I warned as I finally pulled myself from the sofa. "I really don't even feel like being around a bunch of folks right now."

"I gotcha."

After Eva promised that we were going to a small, private gig to hear some live music, I went and got dressed. Although it was a difficult task to complete through tears, I managed to tackle it, and within the next hour, I was following her to her brand-new, mint-green Kia Sorento parked outside.

"Who is it now?" I mumbled as I felt my cell vibrate in my lap as we pulled out of my driveway.

The second we left my house, my mother called. While I thought something was wrong because she dialed me after I had just spoken to her earlier, all she wanted was to be nosy, asking me about who I was with and where I was going. Sheesh, what was the interrogation for?

"Mom, I'm fine. I'm going out with Eva, and I'll call you tomorrow."

Once I got her off the line, I exhaled and laughed to myself. I really needed a break away from everything and everybody. "Thanks for getting me out the house, boo," I finally spoke once we hopped off the highway. "I was about to go crazy in that house. Between you and my mother calling or dropping by just to nag me about any and everything, I swear I was gonna lose my mind."

"Teagan, hush! I already told you that we worry about you. Ever since Walter disappeared, you haven't been the same. That's why I wasn't about to let another weekend go by without dragging you out of that big-ass palace you stay in all by yourself. I don't see how you do it. What the fuck you need five bedrooms and six bathrooms for? Huh? Hell, when I stay the night in the guestroom, it feels like I'm in a fucking hotel . . . at the Four Seasons or some shit . . . especially when yo' housekeeper, Venezuela, is here asking if I need anything every five damn minutes," she teased as we pulled up in the crowded parking lot of the Grand Ballroom.

"Why are there so many people? I thought you said that this was a private affair," I scoffed and ignored Eva's sarcastic remarks as I watched her drive around to the back of the building where security was waiting. As she veered into a reserved parking spot, I questioned her again about what was going on. Like before, she told me that it was an intimate showcase for up-and-coming singers.

"I hope it's R & B because I don't feel like hearing all that rap shit tonight."

"What? No ass-shaking tonight, boo?" Eva asked playfully.

"None, girl. Tonight, I just wanna sit back, chill, have a couple of glasses of wine, and not think about nothing except for getting my damn life together." I sighed heavily as I climbed out of Eva's Kia. As soon as I did, a cute, brown-skinned guy dressed in black opened the door for me. "Oh, we're getting service like this?"

"This is only the beginning." Eva smiled and switched her hips from left to right in the form-fitting red dress she sported. It looked amazing against her caramel skin and golden-brown box braids that were neatly pinned up in a bun.

"What are you up to?" I whispered as the same handsome fella escorted us through the rear entrance.

"This is all about you," the guy said, then looked me up and down. "Now I see what all the fuss is about."

"What do you mean by that?" I asked with confusion written all over my face.

"Those alluring amber eyes and those long, smooth, cocoa brown legs are . . . damn! Oh, and all that white you're sporting got you out here lookin' like a real-life angel. Maybe you can be my—"

Eva interrupted. "Excuse me. We gotta get going . . . Harold, is it?" she questioned as she checked the security tag hanging from his muscular neck.

"Yeah." He smiled showing his perfect set of teeth. Damn, that man was gorgeous.

Truthfully, if he weren't the help, I would've given him my number to hook up with him later. He was just my type on the outside—big, tall, brown, and had exactly what I craved between his legs. I could tell by the large bulge in his tight-fitting black dress pants. Now, don't judge me. It had been months since I got me some. That was the last time I was intimate with Walter, and it was so good. Probably because it was goodbye sex, and I didn't even know it.

"Teagan!" Eva yelled, drawing me out of my daze. I'm glad she did, too, because I was about to get lost in my thoughts and become angry all over again.

"Yes," I answered calmly, then forced a grin.

"Come on. Everyone is waiting on you," Eva said as she grabbed my hand.

"Waiting on me? For what?" I interrogated while my heart rate rapidly increased.

As my friend led me through a black door and we entered into the darkness, I clenched her palm tighter and drew myself nearer to her. "What is going on, Eva?"

I whispered loudly as I listened to the loud chatter in the distance. Before Eva could answer me, a huge set of red satin curtains rose, and the spotlight hit us both.

"Come on," she repeated as she pulled me to the mic.

While everyone cheered and my whole body broke out in a serious sweat, Eva released my hand and then announced that it was my thirtieth birthday celebration. Yeah, they got me with this one. A surprise fucking party. Who would've thought? Definitely not me.

"Instead of us ruining her whole night by singing happy birthday to her, I'm gonna have Braxton Carter do it for us." As soon as Eva mentioned Braxton's name loudly into the microphone, the yelling erupted. All the guests acted like he was some big star when he was actually just a local celebrity who had a nice little following on social media. Nothing big. At least not to me.

"This is for you, boo," my friend hollered over the crowd. The music began playing as Eva gave me one last hug. When she released me, she yelled my name out again, then eased me forward from behind and headed off stage. Without me.

Standing all alone with the spotlight on me made me panic. My stomach bubbled, and I wanted to run off with her, but my legs were locked. I couldn't move them. Without a clue what to do next, I did what came naturally. I closed my eyes, bowed my head, and prayed in a whisper, "Please, Lord." As I lifted my head, comfort immediately spread over me, and the melodic voice of Braxton Carter belted through the speakers. It actually sounded better live than it did on YouTube.

To get a closer look at this guy with the incredible voice, I slowly turned to face him. Magnetically, our eyes connected, and once again, I was frozen in place. Not even the Tupelo, Mississippi tornado that my grandma used to tell me about could move me.

All I really wanna do is wrap you up in the groove.

Braxton belted out the lyrics of a popular R&B birthday song from 1998 and made it his own, while leaving me in a fucking trance. I didn't even realize that I was crying until he finished and hugged me.

"Thank you," I sobbed onto his muscular chest.

I highly doubted that my waterworks did damage to his nice black suit because it was already sweaty. Oddly, it still smelled delicious enough for me to hold onto him a bit longer than I anticipated.

"My pleasure and happy birthday, beautiful." Braxton spoke to me through the mic as the crowd went crazy.

Instead of leaving me there on the stage like Eva had, this fine, talented man escorted me off with him. "Wow! Thanks!" I told him again as we made it to the back hallway where I had initially entered from.

"My pleasure, and now I know what all the fuss was about." He grinned at me as he repeated the familiar phrase.

Ignoring his half-ass compliment, my eyes immediately zoomed in on his perfectly groomed facial hair and partial gold-trimmed grill. It was country as hell, but it looked damn good on him.

"I don't know what you mean by that, but thanks for serenading me with that classic. A lot of people probably ain't never heard it before, and if they have, they surely ain't heard it sung like you sang it. I absolutely loved it."

"Thanks a bunch, and I wasn't talking about the song. I was talking about you, beautiful. You seem so humble. Most rich chicks be all uppity."

"How you know I'm a rich chick?" I asked curiously with a raised brow.

"Because yo' family paid me ten Gs to sing that one song to you and stick around here for a couple of hours to mingle, take pics, and sign autographs," Braxton confessed. "But now that I met you, I think I'll sing a couple more selections. By then, you should be done greeting all your family and your gangsta guests. After that, maybe you'll have a few minutes to chop it up with me. When I'm done performing, I'll be backstage waiting."

"Gotcha." That sounded like a great plan to me, but who the hell was he referring to when he called some of my guests gangsta? Curious to find out, I disregarded his comment and decided to go and see for myself. To join the crowd, I walked around the partition and proceeded down the ramp. When I rounded the corner, the first group of people I spotted answered my question. It was my dad's brother Amelio's family, including his daughter, Amari, with whom I rarely got along. Unlike my father, Armando, Amelio and his kids still conducted family business. In other words, they were active Mafia members who engaged in illegal dealings, and I didn't like it. Not one bit.

Placing the irritation that I felt from his presence to the side, I faked a grin and briefly greeted him, then the rest of his family, bypassing Amari. Flashing a frown her way, I cut my eyes and left their table, then went around and personally thanked everyone for coming. Lastly, I wound up in the area where my parents sat. After I hugged and thanked them while Braxton performed his final song, I opened all my gifts and then took the dough off the money tree that was on the gift table. Wrapping it up as quickly as possible, I said one last thanks, then headed backstage to meet up with Braxton. I was anxious to find out what he had in store for me. It had been a good minute since someone had made me feel as special as he made me feel that night. So much so that I forgot all about my ex breaking my heart. For real.

Walter who?

Chapter Four

Braxton Carter

It was crazy how money could make a person act funny and nearly lose their damn mind. That was exactly what happened to me after the birthday party, when I got paid the rest of that ten grand. Before then, I hadn't told a soul how much dough I got quoted for the performance because I didn't want to jinx it. I just wanted to make my money, go home to my girl, Oaklyn, and shock her with it. Well, that was my initial plan. Too bad that shit went out the window soon as Teagan offered to pay me a thousand dollars per song to come back to her parents' yacht to sing to her. How could I say no to that?

While my heart urged me to turn this beautiful, wealthy woman down, the hustler in me couldn't resist the lucrative opportunity. It was like an angel was on one of my shoulders, telling me to be good, while the devil was propped up on the other one, pressing me to go and see what it felt like to be on a fancy boat with a rich chick. As I tried my best to listen to my conscience, the praises that Teagan sang about my talent continually drowned it out. In the end, I was stuck long enough to disregard how Oaklyn would feel about me staying out all night without a call or explanation. That was something I had never done in the ten years we had been together. Instead of just ringing her line or shooting her a text, I simply powered off my phone and decided to worry about it once I left the yacht. That was, if I could shake off the alcohol and get my damn clothes on.

"Shit," I huffed, sat up, and felt my head spinning as the sun shining through the small round window temporary blinded me.

"Hangover?" Teagan laughed loudly as she handed me some type of drink concoction, then gestured to me to lie back on the bed with her.

After I drank it down, I set the glass on the night table and leaned back until my head touched the double set of fluffy pillows. As I wiggled around to get comfortable, my stomach bubbled with anxiety. All I could think about was how Oaklyn was feeling.

"What's on your mind?" Teagan probed.

"Not shit, really," I lied and tried to think of an excuse to get off that damn yacht.

Before I could come up with something, Teagan began to ask me about the comment I made the night before pertaining to her gangsta guests. Without hesitating, I mentioned the strapped, shady cats I saw getting out of a fleet of limos in front of the venue.

"That was my uncle, and my cousins. I hate to admit it, but you were right. Those muthafuckas are gangsta, but my father has nothing to do with that lifestyle anymore. When my mother had me, he got out of the game and invested his money in real estate. He flips houses and owns over thirty Airbnb properties."

This chick's family had some serious dough. From what she said, they had money so long that she had never had to work a day in her life. *Ain't that some shit?* Honestly, I couldn't even imagine how life could be if I never had to worry about finances again. An unlimited source of funds? That was like a dream come true.

"Now, I told you about my upbringing, Braxton. Why don't you tell me about how you got started singing? Like, how long have you been doing it?"

For me, this had always been a touchy subject, and it usually pained me to talk about it, but oddly, I felt like I owed her a brief explanation. No hard details. "I started singing when I was around five years old. At that age, I already knew all the songs that played on the radio. It was crazy."

"Wow! I bet! You were actually performing at that age?"

"Well, not in public or anything like that until I was ten."

"Where did you perform?"

"On the streets." I sighed and rubbed the top of my head, suddenly feeling a little embarrassed.

"Really?"

"Yeah."

"By yourself?"

"No, with my uncle, Pete."

"Your parents let your uncle take you out that young?"

"My parents died in a house fire when I was ten, and my mother's younger brother, Uncle Pete, who had just gotten out of the military, took care of me so I wouldn't go to the state. We were doing good when he had money, but when it ran out and he couldn't find a job, we got kicked out of our apartment. After that, we barely had food to eat and couldn't keep a constant roof over our head, but we made it in those fucked-up times, and truthfully, I hate even talking about the shit," I said, cutting it short.

"I'm so sorry," Teagan whined, and then came the comforting. It went from her rubbing my back to sucking my dick and within seconds, thoughts of the past were just that: in the past.

"Don't let that shit get you down, Braxton. You have a raw talent that nobody can take from you," Teagan reminded me after she finished topping me off. She rose from the bed to wrap her naked body in a black silk robe. "I'm gonna go freshen up. Feel free to join me if you like."

As my eyes tracked her shapely frame toward the bathroom, showering with her was the last thing on my mind. I had already tapped that ass in every position I knew, so I was cool in that department. The only thing that I was thinking about now was getting to my phone so that I could check my messages.

To keep my movements discreet, I waited for Teagan to disappear behind the closed door before I reached over to the night table, grabbed my cell, and quickly turned it on. Not for a second did I think to cut the volume down.

"Fuck!" I gasped as the alerts loudly sounded off one after the other—all messages from my girl. Oaklyn went from threatening to change the locks to keeping our daughter, Brazil, away from me. Now she was going too damn far, but there was nothing I could do about it at the moment. That shit had to wait until I could get off the fucking boat.

As my chest tightened from worry, I climbed out of the big platform bed and stared down at the box of Magnums that were flipped upside down on the floor. When I reached down to pick the package up to toss it, I felt something rattling inside.

"Oh, hell nah!" I gritted as I opened the box and realized that I had only used two of the condoms out of three. It wouldn't have been a big deal if I didn't remember going three rounds with Teagan. "I gotta do better."

Feeling guiltier than before, I rushed to get dressed without taking a shower. Just as I finished, Teagan came out of the bathroom with a makeup-free face and her head wrapped in a towel. Through it all, she was just as gorgeous as she had been the night before. *Damn.*

"Why are you looking at me like that, Braxton?" Teagan giggled as she stretched the pink towel around her, looking like a thick-ass Black Barbie. "I'm the one starstruck."

"Stop that." I laughed as I slipped my shoes on. "You gonna get a nigga's head big."

"If you're talking about that one down there, it don't need to get no bigger," Teagan teased as she sexily approached me and gently fondled my reproductive sex organ. "That monster already pumps up nice, long, and plump, baby."

"See, why you wanna start something like that?" I asked as I slyly moved back.

"Why are you acting so shy right now?" she questioned with a raised brow.

"Why you ask that?"

"Because last night, you were pretty bold to ask for exactly what you wanted."

"I was, huh?" I cracked when I thought back to when I asked if she was down to eat the groceries, something I would've never asked Oaklyn because I knew she didn't play that shit. "I only asked you that because I always hear the comedians on TV clowning about it. I just wanted to see if chicks really did that shit."

"Welp, now you know," she bragged as she came back into my face, blowing her minty fresh breath.

Why the fuck couldn't I find something wrong with this Teagan chick? I mean, anything! She could've at least had some jacked-up feet or some fake body parts, but no. All of her shit was real and on point.

"Yes, you definitely showed me," I answered jokingly as I grabbed my keys before she talked me into another round of sex.

Just like clockwork, Teagan slid the keyring from my grip and tried her best to convince me to stay. I probably would have, too, but I couldn't stop worrying about Oaklyn.

"What's wrong, babe?" Teagan probed as she entered into my personal space. "Your thoughts seem to be miles away."

"It's just that I can't think straight right now. I got so much on my plate."

"Like what?"

"Well, I'm tryna concentrate on this new track that has to be done by the end of the month, and I can't even find a decent studio since the one I used to record at shut down."

"What can I do to make things easier for you?" Teagan interrupted as she assumed the position.

She was really trying to keep a nigga on that damn yacht. Sure, the head was good, but that pleasure was only a temporary feeling. Shit! As Teagan worked her oral magic, I silently plotted to pry away and get up and run. It didn't work, though. Nothing could, because all my greedy ass could think about were the possible benefits that came along with fucking this chick—all the money I could get from her and all the good I could do with it.

Then there was the downside of it, the side where I lost my family—if I hadn't already.

"I gotta go," I whispered as pulled back from her oral hold while I cautiously lifted her to her feet.

"Huh?" Teagan smirked as she stood in front of me and wiped her lips with the back of her hand. "What's wrong?"

"I can't even concentrate."

"Why?"

"I got too much on my mind right now, Teagan."

"Like what?"

"Like, I need to get home and get these gigs booked. I told you, baby. I'm tryna get me a studio, and as good as it sounds and as much as I want to, I can't stay here all day and kick it with you. I gotta go chase this bread."

"What if I help you get you a studio?" Teagan looked at me as she got her phone from the bed and started fiddling with it. "Will that lessen your load?

"Why would you do that shit? You barely know me."

"Simple. You're a smart Black man with a hell of a lot of talent. Well, quite a few great talents. And I want to see you succeed," she purred and hugged me.

When she let go of me, my CashApp alert went off. "What's that?"

"I just sent you the money for the songs you sang for me last night, and I'll give you enough dough to get started on your studio this week. Is that cool?"

"Ah, I guess so. I just wasn't expecting all this. Like I said, you barely know me."

Before Teagan could get a word out, my phone was ringing. I almost didn't answer it, but then I saw it wasn't Oaklyn. It was my boy Chachi, a lifesaver for real.

"Let me get this," I told Teagan as I answered my cell and told Chachi to hold on while I pecked her cheek. "I'll call you in a little while."

"Okay, make sure you do," she answered and watched me walk out on the deck and exit the yacht.

As I hurried down the ramp leading to the parking lot, I got back to my call. "Hey, bruh."

"Braxton, what's up, boi?"

"I can't call it," I panted as got in my Charger and told Chachi what was going on.

"Nigga, I thought you were tryna stay in Oaklyn's good graces, and you out there in them streets doing that crazy shit?"

"Chachi, I made some serious dough last night, though," I told him, eagerly waiting to brag.

"Is that so?" He laughed and listened while I vaguely explained that I got paid for the show, then told him about the tip from Teagan's parents, and finished it up by explaining how Teagan broke me off for the private show on the boat. I left nothing out but the specific amounts.

"You are fuckin' lying, bruh."

"Shit, you think I would risk staying out all night if it wasn't worth it?"

"Would it still be worth it if Oaklyn got you back by staying out all night or fuckin' another nigga? Or if she left you altogether?"

"You heard she was messing with another nigga? She have another nigga around my seed, bruh?"

"Calm the fuck down and worry about that one girl who prevented you from taking yo' black ass home last night. That's the bitch who seems like she'll be trouble."

"I hope not."

"Well, I'm just saying, Braxton. You may have gotten caught up cheating a majority of the ten years you've been with Oaklyn, but this is the first time you stayed out all night, man. I mean, if she's been blowing you up and you ain't answered her, she's gonna be heated and then do all that shit she threatened to do to you in those texts you said that she sent you. Man, honestly, the only way I see you making that shit up to her is to go home fucked up, and I'm not talking about drinking. I'm talking about being physically injured."

"Nigga, you watch way too much TV. I'm not going through all that." I laughed as I drove onto the freeway ramp. "You ain't got no better ideas, man?"

"It depends on how much you made last night."

"I know this shit sounds crazier than a muthafucka, nigga, but I got almost twenty thousand, bruh."

"Are you fuckin' kidding me?"

"Nope," I answered with a laugh.

"For one night?"

"For one night, Chachi."

"Well, then, shit!" he replied, sounding surprised. "This should be easy then because Oaklyn is on assistance, and some of that under-the-table dough will do her justice."

"You think so?" I asked him.

"Hell yeah. Nigga, remember when you gave her that two hundred dollars last year when she wasn't expecting it? Shit, just think how she'll act if you toss a couple grand in her lap."

"I didn't think about it like that," I confessed as I pulled over at the corner of the block where Oaklyn's apartment was. I wasn't quite ready to face the music just yet.

Instead of going to her place to hash things out empty-handed, I sped off toward the bank to get some cash out. By the time I got there, I had a plan, but Chachi came up with something better. It sounded real good. I just wasn't sure if I could afford it all. To buy Oaklyn a new car and move her into a new place so she could get off state housing was going to be costly.

"That's a lot of dough, Chachi."

"Yeah, but it would be an investment and good for you guys in the long run. Just think. You could finally live comfortably in peace, without worrying about nosy neighbors threatening to call housing to get y'all kicked out," he reminded. "Plus, from what you told me about Oaklyn's ride breaking down twice in the past few months, I'm sure she would appreciate something reliable to get her and Brazil around town."

"Well, damn, I probably can go flip her a whip right quick, but getting a place won't be that damn easy. Shit, I got mediocre credit, no record of steady employment, and no fucking rental history. Who is gon' rent to me?"

"Well, just start looking into a place and see if you can use your payout records from YouTube and social media for employment verification. That may take a minute, but you can go get Oaklyn a car now."

"Damn. Can't I just fix the one she already has? That'll probably be cheaper because it's paid for," I huffed, just thinking about how much another car would cost.

"You ain't gotta buy nothing new off the floor, nigga. Just go on over there to Eighty-second and find that girl a nice used ride. You can find her something real flyy for less than ten Gs. That ain't shit for you right now, Brax."

"Ten thousand ain't shit for me, Chachi? Nigga, that's more than half my damn money!" I replied in an elevated tone as I choked on my bottled water.

"And it's much more than you had before you did that fucking gig last night. You over there thinking the glass is half empty instead of that muthafucka being half full. Think about it like this, man. If it costs you all of the dough you made just to keep yo' girl happy, then I say it's worth it," Chachi said to enlighten me.

Sure, it made a lot of sense, but I was a Leo, and I hated to part with my money, especially when the total for another whip for my baby mama would be close to five figures. "Damn, I guess yo' ass is right this time, but fuck. Drop ten Gs all at once on a fucking ride that ain't even for me?"

"It just sounds like a lot because you ain't never got no dough like this in one whop," he went on. "Get used to this shit, though, bruh, because your talent is gonna get you to where you need to be."

"Teagan got me there quicker." I laughed. "In one night."

"Yeah, but it was your singing that wooed that chick, just like all the other females that you done fooled around with. Out there serenading the panties off these thirsty bitches and the money out of their wallets."

"But all those women always wanted something in return from me. It was different with Teagan."

"How? Didn't she take you back to her parents' yacht to do a private show for her?"

"Yeah, but—"

"Didn't you get paid for every song that you sang her?"

"Yeah, but—"

"But nothin', nigga. You got paid for that shit, so it was work. Well, at least that's what I call it . . . unless you just wanna admit yo' ass is a ho."

"Fuck you, Chachi!" I cracked, laughing loudly as I made my way to his house. "Just have yo' shoes on because I'm about to swoop you."

"For what?"

"Because I can't drive two cars at once. Now, come on and go with me to the car lot since this was all yo' damn idea."

"That's what's up, nigga, but lunch is on you today because I'm starving."

"Say less. I'll be there in ten."

When I hung up with my boy, a smile crept across my face. Damn, I was really able to go out and buy a car without payments for the first time in my twenty-eight years on earth. Even though it wasn't for me, I was still excited and couldn't complain because it was for someone special, Oaklyn, the only woman I truly loved with all my heart.

Chapter Five

Oaklyn Jones

My temper was already on ten behind Braxton being missing in action for nearly twenty-four hours. Then, to make matters worse, my car broke down in the middle of my search for him. Raggedy-ass shit.

"Don't you have AAA?" Koola questioned.

"No, my policy expired a couple of months back, and I ain't had the money to renew it," I complained as I popped the hood of my Hyundai Sonata and got out. As a thick cloud of smoke fled from the engine and filled the air, I stood back and waited for it to clear before checking to see what the problem was. That was something I had gotten pretty good at. Having a bucket and living on a budget would force you to learn a lot of shit just to save a few bucks.

"What's wrong now, boo?" Koola got out and asked as a black Lincoln Navigator crept up on us.

"Y'all need some help?" the driver offered as he veered to the side of the road without waiting for a reply.

Initially, I couldn't see his face, but when he got out and came toward me, I began to gasp for air. Boy, was this man handsome. Standing well over six feet tall, with pretty brown skin, properly groomed, and well-mannered, this cutie had it all. The red, white, and black Portland Trailblazers short outfit with the Jordans he was sporting looked damn good on him, too.

"You play basketball or some shit?" Koola interrogated as he stepped to my car and checked it out.

"I used to play, but now I'm the varsity coach at my old high school, Wilson," he explained as he wiggled around some wires under my hood. "My name is Gunner West."

"Oh, shit! I knew you looked familiar," Koola screamed. "You got drafted to the Boston Celtics, but then you got injured. You tore your ACL or something like that, right?"

"Yeah, and I see you follow sports, huh?"

"Just basketball and football. My brother was Jeremiah Jacobs."

"No fuckin' way! I played summer league with him a few years back. So sorry for your loss," Gunner apologized as he became quiet and got on his cell. When he finished, he told us that he had called the tow company, and they would arrive soon because they had a driver nearby. I definitely appreciated him.

"Thanks a bunch, but I really don't have the money to pay for a tow," I stated.

"No worries. I always pay it forward."

"Well, I'll try to keep it going best I can." I laughed and looked up at Gunner only to catch him staring at me in a lustful manner.

"You can start right now by allowing me to take you out sometime," he suggested while handing me a business card. "You can reach me at both these numbers."

"Well, as good as that may sound, I have a man at home."

"Oh, that nigga came back?" Koola whispered loudly and added an elbow to my arm. Fucking clown.

"I'm in a relationship."

"A very complicated relationship." Koola continued to embarrass me.

"Anyhow, if you change your mind, you have my number." Gunner laughed as the tow truck arrived. What quick service.

"Tow it wherever they like," he told the driver before climbing back into his vehicle.

As badly as I tried not to look at Gunner before he left, I found myself locking eyes with him one last time. Damn.

"Girl! That nigga is fine and paid. You had better call him. You can even use Brazil as an excuse because you know she loves basketball. Maybe y'all could hook up, and you can get her an autographed ball or something."

"Please, Koola. I got a whole man."

"Please don't say at home because we don't know where yo' baby daddy is." She cut me off as the tow truck driver hooked up my car and gave us a ride back to my place. The entire time we were in the truck, Koola kept asking the driver's opinion. Had him all up in my damn business.

"Why you do that shit?" I asked her when we made it back to the housing projects that I lived in and went inside my place. "You can never let up."

"Why didn't you give that man your number, Oaklyn? That's the least you could've done."

"Shit, he wouldn't have even known my name if you wouldn't have blabbed it. Besides, I don't wanna start nothing new until I end the situation with Braxton, and that's not so easy when we have a daughter together, Koola. All I know is when I see that nigga, it's on. He don't do me like this and think it's okay. He got me so heated I'm ready to find him and fuck him up. Ugh!"

"Well, you need to calm down before Braxton shows back up. I don't want no fighting up in here."

"Why you think I sent Brazil over to my mama's house?"

"Fuck that, Oaklyn. Y'all better not be over there doing no wild shit. Just have a simple conversation with that nigga, and if he ain't on the up and up, just tell his ass to bounce. No need for fighting."

"Oh, I ain't about to fight a man that I know I can't whoop," I told her as I retrieved the small handgun that my mother gave me and wiped it off. "That nigga is out of line for pulling this fucking disappearing act. He ain't never done that shit, Koola. That's why I know he had to be with a bitch. My gut is telling me that shit, and it ain't never wrong."

"While you over here with that fucking gun like you in the Wild, Wild West and about to blow a nigga's head off, did you even think that something could seriously be wrong, Oaklyn? Braxton could be hurt, or—"

I cut her ass off. "Bitch, please!" I clowned. "You don't think I called all the local hospitals and checked the jails? That nigga ain't locked up nor hurt bad enough to be hospitalized, so when he walks through this damn door, I'm gonna make sure both of those things happen."

"No, you might fuck him up, but you're the one who'll get locked up. You ain't even thinking about your daughter. Brazil would be devastated if anything happened to either of her parents. Now, put that shit away and at least wait to hear an explanation before popping off," Koola strongly suggested as she got up from my round blue swivel chair. "Literally, Oaklyn."

As she paced the living room of the nice, two-bedroom, low-income apartment that I was renting for $28 a month, I thought about my relationship with Braxton. I did love him and the family we created. We may not have had much, but it was more than enough for me. The question was, was it enough for Braxton? Was he not happy? If he wasn't, and that was the reason he left, why couldn't he just tell me that instead of disappearing? Ain't nobody have the patience or understanding for all that worrying and wondering. At least, not me.

"Don't be over there plotting, Oaklyn. You already got me nervous enough with that damn gun. Got me pacing the floor and everything."

"I'm not plotting, girl. This shit ain't even loaded." I smirked. "I wasn't even thinking about harming that nigga. Believe it or not, I was thinking about everything you said, and you're right. I need to at least listen to what he has to say when and if he ever calls or comes home."

"Hush with that nonsense, girl. You know that nigga ain't got nowhere else to go."

"He already got most of his stuff at Uncle Pete's."

"Yeah, but after that bitch next door called housing on you and they threatened to kick you off the program, it was a good idea to have him move his shit over there. Just know that Braxton ain't about to stay over there with it, though. He already told you a million times he can't stay in a place where they smoke inside, and Uncle Pete is puffing every chance he gets, all up and through there."

"Braxton can always stay with Chachi," I reminded Koola.

"He sho' don't wanna stay over there. That fool only got one bedroom, and he got bitches running in and out of there. A revolving fucking door, and I still don't get why, though. He's scrawny as hell, chest ain't got a bit of definition, and he got the nerve to let his hair grow so he could rock some braids. That hair probably weighs more than he does. Nah, Braxton definitely won't stay over there. He'll come running home anytime now. Just wait and see, girl," Koola teased with a forced grin.

As the tears began to roll down my cheeks, she rushed over to me to give me a hug. For me to cry hard enough to bring out the gun, it had to be serious. That was something that I never did. But then again, staying out all night was something that Braxton never did. That made this entire situation different, and now I felt out of my element and didn't know quite how to deal with it.

"It'll be okay."

Right as Koola began to speak, we heard a bunch of honking outside my door. By the way the parking lot of our one-level complex was designed, I knew that the car that was blowing had to be nearby.

"Who the fuck would be there laying on the horn like that? It's so rude. All that fucking beeping!" Koola complained as she walked over to the window and partially opened my blinds. "Oh, hell nah!"

"What is it?" I asked anxiously as I hopped up and ran over to see what she was gasping about.

When I spotted Braxton and Chachi standing outside beside a nice white Nissan crossover with a big red bow sitting on top, I gulped and covered my mouth. Right away, I assumed it was for me, but I couldn't show how excited I felt on the inside. Nope. Not until I got to the bottom of where my baby daddy was all night.

"You ain't going out there, girl?" Koola questioned as she clenched my arm and tried to drag me to the door. "Come on."

"You think a car will make up for him not coming home last night?"

"Shit, it would be enough for me," she replied with a serious expression. "The most expensive thing a nigga ever bought me was an outfit, a bag, and got my hair done. That didn't even total a thousand dollars, and I thought I hit the jackpot."

"Well, I ain't hit no jackpot, and Braxton is out of line."

Before Koola could start up again, here comes this nigga and his sidekick, Chachi, coming through the door. "Didn't you hear me honking outside, baby?" Braxton questioned as he came toward me with his lips puckered up.

Using the palm of my hand, I mushed his mouth as soon as he came within reach. Oh, he didn't like that shit.

"Damn, baby! I brought you a gift, and—"

"What you should've brought was yo' black ass home last night!" I shouted and went to pick up the empty gun off the table like I was big and bad, knowing I wasn't. "Now, where the hell were you?"

When I cocked the hammer, both Braxton and Chachi held their hands up. I almost burst out laughing when I saw the way their eyes bucked.

"Where is Brazil?" Braxton asked.

"With my mama, and she's fine, so don't you worry about that shit."

"You really try to shoot a nigga over nothing?"

"Where you been, Braxton?"

"I was working. You know I had a gig. It was a private party, so it lasted all night. I ain't have no phone charger, and I couldn't leave when I was getting paid by the hour to stay. Chachi was with me," he explained as he nudged his partner to vouch for him, but I didn't want to hear it.

"Blah, blah, blah is all I hear coming out of your mouth." I placed the gun down and cut my eyes, then folded my arms across my chest while he consistently chanted bullshit my way.

"It's no lie, though, baby. How do you think I was able to buy you that fly ride with *cash?* No fucking payments! Come on. Come see the shit!"

"Yeah, let's go see, Oaklyn," Koola butted in. "Lord knows you need a new whip after yours just broke down on us again."

"See, baby? Right on time."

"What the hell you know about right on time, Braxton?"

"Look, Oaklyn. I know you're upset and shit, baby, but I'm sorry."

Braxton apologized repeatedly, but that wasn't enough. I needed an explanation that made some damn sense.

"Why didn't you call me from a landline? You should have my damn number memorized. It's been the same for years."

"When I got my phone charged up, I was gonna call you."

"Then why the hell didn't you?"

"Because I was busy getting your surprise. If I would've called you, then I would've blabbed that shit out. You know a nigga can't hold water when I'm excited. Maybe it was the wrong way to go about things, and I see that shit now, but it's nothing else to it, baby. All this I did was straight from my heart." Braxton tried to sway me. "You know you're the only one for me. I love you, girl."

"I love you too," I confessed as I allowed my man to hug and kiss all over me.

"See!" Koola clowned as she snatched me up and pulled me outside to see the car Braxton bought me. "And you thought that nigga would show up with another song to sing."

"Well, that was how he got me in the first place." I laughed as he snuck up behind me and dangled the car keys in my face.

As I got inside the crossover, I reminisced about the first time I met Braxton. He was singing over there on Ainsworth for money with his uncle. His voice was so heavenly that it made me see something special in him, even through the tacky haircut and dingy clothing.

"This is certainly a level up," I acknowledged as I heard the passenger door open.

Braxton climbed in without an invitation, then reached over to squeeze my hand a few times before releasing it. He was doing everything in his power to make up with me.

"You know you deserve this shit and more, baby," he said. "Remember the first car we got when we moved in together ten years ago?"

"That Dodge Aries?" I giggled as I checked out the inside of my new car. The tan leather interior and wood paneling were beautiful. "How could I forget that damn Dodge? That muthafucka putted every time we pulled off."

The small talk that Braxton was making was cool and all, but he wasn't as slick as he thought. He was only doing that shit in order to avoid the subject at hand. Where the fuck had he been? That's all I wanted to know.

"So, you wanna tell me where you really were last night? And please don't lie and say you were still at the Grand Ballroom because you know our phone lines are on the same account. I pulled up your last location, and it was somewhere on the damn water. Where were you?"

"Ah, I told you, Oaklyn, I was performing at a party. The main event was at the Grand Ballroom, and the after party was on a yacht in the marina, over there by Jantzen Beach. That's it. Nothing more. I swear," he explained enough to convince me to believe him, at least for the moment.

Just as my guard slowly lowered and I was ready to forgive Braxton, his cell started ringing. Instead of answering it, he glanced at the screen and ignored the call. Although I appreciated the courtesy, I wondered who it was, especially when it rang back twice more.

"You can get it," I urged.

"Nah, ah, it ain't nobody." When he stuttered and turned away from me like he always did when he lied, I snatched his cell and answered it for him. Oh, he didn't like that shit and even tried to tussle with me to get it back, but I was too quick.

"Hello?" I answered as I hopped out of the car and stepped back before Braxton could get out and try to take his phone from me.

"Ah, hello?"

"Yes?"

"This is Teagan. I'm looking for Braxton."

"How can I help you, *Teagan*?" I pressed as I watched Koola and Chachi stop him from coming toward me to get his phone.

"Is he available?"

"Not at this moment, *Teagan*. Can I take a message?" I asked, dying to know who this bitch was that was calling him.

"Just let him know that he left his watch on my parents' yacht last night. I didn't want him to think it was lost."

"The only thing that's lost is this nigga's mind!" I yelled and looked straight at Braxton as I held his cell in the air. "You fuck this bitch?"

"What?" he said as I eyed the beaded sweat forming on his forehead.

"Did you fuck this Teagan bitch? The one who's on your phone right now?" I yelled as I fought back the tears that were threatening to fall. This shit was crazy! Right when I wanted to forgive that man, the truth was revealed. That was nobody but God!

"You are seriously trippin', Oaklyn."

"Okay, if you don't wanna answer me—" I started, then put the phone back to my ear. "Teagan, you and Braxton fuck?"

"Well, if that's what you wanna call it." She giggled.

The sound of her laughter would forever haunt me because that shit right there was all the clarification that I needed. Braxton cheated on me. Once again!

"Give me my damn house keys, nigga! I can't keep going through this shit, Brax! I need you out of my life," I hollered as I threw the keys to the car at him while I continued to hold onto his phone.

"Stop trippin', Oaklyn. We have a daughter, and I'll always be in your life."

"Look, Teagan, you got a place for this nigga to stay? Because he can't stay here. He gotta go."

"I sure do," she answered anxiously.

That shit burned me up even more, and just as I was about to flip out again, Koola came and got the phone from me and gave it back to Braxton. "You are such a disappointment," she told him.

"I got her a car!" he countered.

"And you fucked another bitch! Now, give me my house keys," I hollered.

"I ain't giving you these keys."

"You ain't on my lease. You don't live here—"

"Some of my shit is in here."

Now this asshole was really trying to get me kicked out. He knew damn well that housing already gave me two warnings about him staying with me, and there he was, shouting it to the entire complex that he had some of his things there. I was too done. So done that I walked back into my apartment without fighting Braxton for my keys again. Why do that when Koola could change my locks herself in under ten minutes?

"Damn, boo. You gave him back the car he just got you. You must be really done with him, Oaklyn," she said, panting as she followed behind me.

"Let me show you how done I am." I sniffled as I got Gunner's card out and sent him a text message. "Now I may not fuck that nigga anytime soon, but I'm ready to go out on a date to get my mind off Braxton's sorry ass."

"Oh, bitch! You are serious!" Koola cheered as I told her what I said in the text.

I just wonder how Gunner's going to respond.

Chapter Six

Gunner West

When Oaklyn sent me a text saying that she wanted me to call her so that we could possibly go out and get something to eat, I couldn't help but smile. I didn't think she would use my number after insisting that she had a man. Now, I was interested to know what had happened in that short amount of time to make things change. Anxious to find out, I sat back at the desk inside my home office and dialed her up.

"Hey," she greeted me.

"Hey, Oaklyn. What's good with you?" I asked as I fiddled with my personalized ink pen and swiveled my seat from side to side. "Did you get your car taken care of?"

"Yeah, I got it towed, and thanks again," she replied. "Bad thing is, it's not worth fixing. I'm just gonna have to save some money and buy another one when I can."

"Well, I know we don't really know each other, but maybe I can help you out."

"Thanks, but I couldn't accept anything from you. We just met today. I wouldn't feel right," Oaklyn sniffled.

The change in the tone of her voice alerted me that something was off, and I wasted no time asking. "What happened?"

"Nothing. I'm okay."

"Are you sure? It sounds like you've been crying."

Oaklyn didn't want to tell me, but after five minutes of me harassing her, she finally gave in and told me all about how her baby daddy did her. Although it was typical male shit, I felt bad to hear the pain in her words.

"So, he cheated on you, then bought you a car to make up for it?" I double-checked to ensure I had the story right.

"Oh, he tried, but I gave him the keys back as soon as that chick called his phone and told it all. How the hell could I accept that car after he did me like that? If I did, it would be just like me saying that I accepted his apology for fucking off on me."

"Was this his first time?"

"His first time what?" Oaklyn asked.

"Was this his first time cheating on you?"

"No, it wasn't, but best believe it was his last," she cleared up. "That's why I'm walking away."

"But y'all got a kid, right?"

"Yeah, but I'm not staying with a man just because we share a child. I want more for me and my daughter. I don't want her to have two parents that do nothing but argue and fight. That's not healthy for any of us."

"No, it's not," I agreed and listened to how Oaklyn articulated her words. Sure, she spoke hood as hell, but I could still tell that she was well educated. That was confirmed as our conversation continued for hours. We talked about everything from pole dancing to politics. There wasn't a subject that I brought up that she didn't have some type of knowledge on.

"You know about a lot of shit," I teased Oaklyn.

"I watch CNN along with the local news so that I can keep up with current issues, and I also spend time scrolling social networks, which keeps me updated on everything else. I want to know what's going on in the world around me," she explained.

"I feel ya," I replied with a yawn. When she heard that, she rushed to say that she would let me get off the phone. Thing was, I wasn't ready to. I wanted to know more about Oaklyn.

"Nah, I'm good. I wanna hear more about you and how you grew up. You got sisters, brothers?"

"Nope, just me and my mama, Draya, who raised me. You would really like her. She *loves* basketball and has my daughter hooked, too." She laughed, then went on to explain about how she grew up with hardly any money, but never really felt poor.

"What do you mean?" I questioned.

"I'm saying that we may not have had everything we wanted, but we definitely had everything we needed. Besides, some things can't be bought."

"Like what?"

"Well, for starters, money can't buy love, and it certainly can't buy loyalty," Oaklyn said.

"You are so fucking right about that. You can have all the money in the world and still feel lonely, too."

"I can't believe you've ever felt that way," she spoke softly. "I'm sure you've had plenty of women throwing themselves at you. You're handsome, wealthy, and seem to be pretty cool."

"In my line of work, I mainly meet the bougie type of women, and I don't see myself being in a serious relationship with nobody like that. I'm from the hood, and I saw how strong and humble the struggle made my mother and father. They always found a way to make things happen, to make sure we had the necessities growing up, like a roof over our head, clothes on our backs, and food to eat."

"So, you didn't grow up rich?"

"Hell nah. My pops had big money for a little minute, meaning he blew it soon as he got it. Shit, I didn't know what real money was until I was drafted to the Celtics. Even though I got injured in the second season, they still had to honor my contract, so I was good in the financial department. To stay that way, I made sure not to blow my dough on women and hanging out. Instead, I invested, and the return has been very good to me. This coaching job is just something I love to do. It makes me feel like I'm giving back to the community. You know, helping the kids."

"Oh, you like kids?" Oaklyn giggled.

"Yeah, and I would love to meet your daughter when the time is right."

"Okay, I like that answer," she replied with a slight giggle.

The more we spoke over the phone, the more intrigued I became with her. She was so easy to talk to and so down to earth, not like the other chicks I was used to kicking it with. All they wanted to talk about was the newest fashion, or they were asking for something. That wasn't the case with Oaklyn, and I was digging that shit. I mean, really digging it.

"So, now that I told you all my dark secrets, Gunner, tell me about some of your crazy exes. Start with the most recent one."

"Oh, boy." I chuckled as I got up from my chair, retrieved my earbuds off the counter, and put them in, then finally retreated to my bedroom.

"Come on, now."

"Look, I'm just gonna say this. I have a protective order against my last girlfriend. She was a clout chaser who lied and sold bogus stories to the press to make a quick buck. Shit, I had to sue a few publication companies and her ass, too."

"Are you for real?"

"Yes, and that's why I haven't dated for the past six months. I had to wait to get through with all that legal shit first."

"So, you good now?" Oaklyn clowned in a deep voice.

"You got jokes?"

"Nah, I'm clowning, but she does sound a little dangerous."

"I ain't worried about that chick. Besides, she moved back to California with her sister. The farther away, the better."

Just as those words came out of my mouth, Camille was sending me an email from an unknown source. This shit was getting ridiculous, but I wasn't about to say anything to Oaklyn about it, not when she could use it as a reason not to fuck with me. I didn't want that.

"Okay, I'm about to let you go for real this time, Gunner," Oaklyn said. "My mom is bringing my daughter, Brazil, home early in the morning, and I wanna try to get some sleep."

"I thought your homegirl was over there."

"When I came in my room to talk on the phone, she left without saying a word, but she always does that type of odd shit."

"So, you good? You don't need anything?"

"I might want a few things, but I don't *need* anything at this moment. Thanks, though."

"Oaklyn, if you don't mind me asking, what are some of your wants?" I inquired, hoping she would say something that would get me over there. It wasn't that I wanted to sex her this soon. I just wanted to see her again.

"Hold on," she whispered as I heard her fumble with the phone. When she got back on the line, she was cussing and fussing about the car being gone. "This nigga really came and took the car, then sent me a text and told me that I can have it back when I let him in."

"Well?" I pressed.

"Well, he can keep that muthafucka and shove it up his ass. I will walk a country mile with Brazil on my back before I let him bribe me with a car just for me to let him in my place. Nope, not gonna happen."

"You can just use one of my cars. No strings attached. I can get online and add your name to my insurance right now. All you gotta do is send me a copy of your driver's license."

"Now you got jokes."

"No, I'm serious. Dead-ass serious, Oaklyn."

"Are you sure, Gunner?"

"A car ain't nothing but a material thang that can be replaced. Don't even worry about it."

"It seems like an awful lot to accept from a stranger."

"Oaklyn, send me a copy of your license, and I'm about to send you a link to my bio. Or better yet, check Wikipedia. All my business is on there, too," I said.

"You famous like that?" She gasped.

"I don't look at myself like that," I said clearly. "Now, send me your info and your address, and I'm about to drive the car over to you. You want to drive the Benz or the Navigator?"

"Are you serious, Gunner?"

"Oaklyn, which one, shawty?"

"Shit, I don't know. Surprise me." She giggled and sent me her information.

Within the hour, I was pulling out of my garage in the black drop-top E350. The Navigator may have been too much for her to handle. "Am I trippin', or am I really loaning one of my vehicles to a total stranger?" I laughed to myself as I turned onto MLK and headed north. As soon as I made a left on Columbia Boulevard, my pops was calling me to check on me. After the shit Camille had put me through, he and my mother had been worried about me.

"Hey, Pops," I greeted him when I connected the call.

"Hey. What you up to, son?" he questioned me right off the top.

Without thinking first, I told my father all about my meeting with Oaklyn and how I was feeling about her. Hell, I even confessed to him that I was about to let her use one of my whips. Instead of reacting negatively, as I expected, my pops told me that he was proud of me for not only moving on, but also for being kind enough to help a person in need.

"Just be careful, son. You said that girl's baby daddy was still in the picture."

"Oh, I ain't worried about all that, Pops."

"Well, you should be," he grumbled. "Apparently, you haven't been watching the news. All these shootings over senseless shit is crazy, and it's mainly happening in the neighborhood you're on your way to."

Maybe my father had a point, but I was a grown man who knew how to use the registered gun that I carried. Not that I was worried, because I wasn't.

"A'ight, son. I'm gonna let you go, but do me a favor."

"What's that?"

"Please don't tell your mother nothing about his new girl just yet. I don't want her worrying all over again," my father urged. "Oh, and make sure you watch your back while you're out in the north like that."

"Gotcha," I replied as I finally arrived at my destination.

After I parked and got out, I walked up to Oaklyn's door and hit the alarm, then lifted my fist to knock. Before I could complete the task, she was swinging it open, wearing this tight-fitting jumpsuit. It hugged every curve on her body and had my ass standing there stuttering.

"Ah, ah, ah—"

Chapter Seven

Braxton Carter

A few days later . . .

"Oaklyn ain't answering my calls or calling me back or nothing. She can't be that fucking mad," I complained to Chachi as we sat at the bar over on Killingsworth, just east of Fifteenth Street.

"Man, yo' baby mama has every right to be hot as fish grease right now. You took that car back from her after she found out about you fucking off on her then didn't wanna let you in. You're dead wrong for that shit, and you had to know how it would turn out after Teagan called like that," Chachi clowned. "You can flip the shit in your mind all you want, but right is right and wrong is wrong. You ain't thinking clearly. You couldn't be. Taking that whip when it wasn't just for Oaklyn, but for yo' shorty, too. Yo' ass is straight trippin'."

"Fuck that shit. I ain't trippin'. Oaklyn is. She wanna play games and not let me in the apartment, then so be it. She's the one who'll suffer. Hell, I got a car and money."

"Nigga, seriously? You can't be that damn heartless towards the one person who believed in you when nobody else did. The one person who loved you when you didn't have shit. Come on, Brax. What happened to the humble man you used to be? You really let some fame and money go to your head like this?" Chachi persisted.

"I'm still humble."

"No, the hell you ain't. If you were, you wouldn't be taking your blessings for granted."

"What the fuck you mean by that?" I questioned Chachi.

"Look how God has been blessing you."

"Why the hell you preaching to me when you ain't been to church in I don't know how many years, Chachi?"

"You don't have to go to a sanctuary every Sunday to know the Word, or know right from wrong, Brax, and I'm definitely not tryna go biblical on you. I'm just telling you what my mama would've told me if I was in your situation."

What my homeboy said made a lot of sense, but I wasn't trying to hear it. All I wanted was for Oaklyn to let me in the fucking apartment so we could work out our issues and be the best parents that we could be for our daughter. Was that too much to ask?

"I'm about to go over there—" I started before my boy cut me off.

"Not without that car you ain't."

"Nah, I'm about to take it back, apologize again, then promise to do better."

"The same shit you always do. Nigga, that shit is getting old. It ain't no use in promising to stay faithful when you're still dealing with the Teagan chick. I done told you. All money ain't good money."

"I'll just get my studio up and going, then break ties with her altogether."

"So, you think it'll be that easy? You think she's doing all that shit just because? No, nigga! She's doing that shit because she likes you, and you don't wanna play with a chick's heart. Some females don't take that shit too well."

"You really gotta stop watching *Snapped* and all those other bullshit shows. That bitch ain't gonna do nothing but be mad for a few weeks and then get over it. Just like all the other females."

"Okay, when that girl act a stone-cold fool on you, don't say I didn't warn you, Braxton."

"Just come on and ride with me to take Oaklyn this damn car."

"Whatever."

Chachi waved me off, then we both downed our drinks. After I paid the tab, we got up out of there and went over to my uncle's to pick up the car.

"I sure hope you have a good plan, Brax, because for some reason, I see this shit going all wrong."

"It's gonna be cool."

"Nah, I don't even wanna be in the middle of yo' shit, so when we drop the car off, you run me home before you go back and deal with Oaklyn. You're on your own on that one, buddy."

Even though I knew Chachi was overreacting, I agreed before handing him the keys to the other vehicle. When he snatched them and shook his head, I couldn't help but think about all the unwanted advice he gave me. The more I pondered Chachi's words of wisdom, the worse I felt. Like he said, I couldn't keep apologizing then doing the same shit over and over. There were only so many times that Oaklyn would forgive me, and I prayed that this would be one of them. Slowly but surely, my insecurities began to get the best of me. Just the thought of my girl calling it quits really hurt a nigga's heart. *Damn.*

"I hope she ain't on no bullshit," I whispered to myself as I drove into the parking lot of the apartments that Oaklyn stayed in. After I parked next to Chachi and waited for him to get in so I could run him to his crib right quick, this nice-ass Benz drove up and parked on the other side of me. The windows were so darkly tinted that I couldn't see who was inside, but with me being curious, I couldn't stop staring until the door opened.

"What the fuck?" I gasped as I saw Oaklyn climbing out of the fly ride wearing some sexy denim dress. "Who the fuck car is that, and where the fuck is she coming from?"

"You see that shit?" Chachi clowned with a laugh as he hopped into my passenger seat.

As he jumped in, I leaped out. I needed some answers. "Who the fuck car you driving?" I hissed and ran up on her.

"That's none of your business, Braxton. You got a whole lot of nerve even asking me that shit after you gave me a car and took it right back in the same day," Oaklyn snapped and shoved me out of her way.

"I brought that shit back." I ran behind her, trying to explain.

"Well, you can take it right back with you because I'm good."

"Who the fuck car is that? And don't try to lie and say it's a rental because I see it ain't."

"It ain't none of your business, and if you don't get the fuck off this property, security will come and escort yo' ass off."

"Why the fuck would they do that shit?" I asked curiously as I gently clenched her arm to stop her from entering her apartment.

"Because I had yo' ass trespassed off."

"What about Brazil? I gotta see my daughter."

"You can see her when she gets back. My mama took her to Seaside for a few days to enjoy the beach. I'll call you when she's home."

"What the fuck, Oaklyn? Don't she have school on Monday?" I yelled loud enough to make her tattletale neighbor come running out of her front door.

"You get your hands off that girl before I call the law on yo' ass!" she threatened as she held her cell up in the air.

"You want me to leave, baby?"

"Didn't she say that she had yo' ass trespassed off the property, or are you deaf and dumb, nigga?" the neighbor clowned.

"Who the hell was even talking to you? Mind your own fucking business, bitch," I responded as I smirked and released Oaklyn's arm before the cops showed up. "You miserable muthafuckas can rot in this roach-infested complex together."

As I walked away, my baby mama cussed me out for talking about the home that she shared with *our* daughter, and how sorry I was for not providing more. It got me heated, but not as mad as it did when she started screaming that child support shit.

"That woman done lost her damn mind!" I huffed as I got back in my car and slammed the door.

"Well, you about to lose yours as well, my nigga." Chachi laughed and shoved his cell in my face.

This computer whiz had already gotten online and ran the plates of the black Benz my baby mama was driving. He must've been just as curious as I was.

"Gunner West?" I gasped in disbelief. "How the hell she know that nigga?"

"All I got to say is, I told you so."

"Not now, Chachi. Not now."

"Well, what you wanna do? Because we can't sit here. You heard Oaklyn and her messy-ass neighbor. You're trespassed off the property, dude."

"Then get my fucking car. I ain't about to leave it here when she rolling that nigga's whip."

Never in the ten years knowing Oaklyn had I even thought about her fucking around on me. This was definitely an eye-opener, and my chest felt like it was about to burst open.

"You a'ight, man?" Chachi checked, making me repeat myself.

"Yeah, but can you just go get the fucking car? I ain't about to leave it here when she obviously has other means of transportation."

"Yeah, she got a ride."

Chachi cracked up and really thought that shit was funny, but I wasn't laughing. Especially when I pictured Oaklyn with that nigga Gunner.

"You really think she's messing with dude?" I asked as I heard the sirens in the distance.

"I don't know, but you're gonna have to worry about that shit later, Brax. Let's get the hell up outta here. We can come get that shit tomorrow."

"What if they tow it?" I asked as I pulled out of the parking spot and shot out of the lot before the cops arrived.

"Let that shit get towed. You rather them take that car away than to take you."

That was what I didn't want to happen. "You ain't lyin'," I replied.

This whole situation wasn't sitting well with me at all, and I began to feel confused. I needed to know what was up with my girl and that Gunner dude.

The more I thought about Oaklyn driving his car, the more I wondered about how long they had been acquainted. I mean, they had to be pretty damn close for her to be driving his whip.

"Damn, I really fucked up this time." I sighed heavily as we made it to Chachi's house.

"Come on in and have a drink, man. It looks like you could use one."

"You got jokes, bruh, and I can't even think about laughing. My head is all fucked up."

"Why? You had to see this coming sooner or later, Brax. How long did you think that Oaklyn was gonna stand by and let you keep cheating on her?" he asked as we got out and went inside his place.

As he poured us both a shot of Jack on the rocks, we went into his living room and sat down. From there, it was one drink after another, and before I knew it, I was too fucked up to drive, and I was feeling more emotional than before. I had to literally fight back my tears so that I wouldn't lose it in front of my homeboy. If I did that shit, I would never hear the end of it.

"Toughen up, B, and just wait until tomorrow to try to talk to Oaklyn. It might not be as bad as you think. They're probably just friends."

"He has to be a close fucking friend to let her drive that nice-ass whip, Chachi. Niggas don't just do shit like that around here."

"Not unless they're—" He paused, then looked at me. "Nah, it probably ain't nothing, man."

My boy didn't have to finish what he was saying because I knew just where he was going with it. Just like me, Chachi thought Oaklyn was messing around with Gunner.

"Fuck it. It is what it is."

"You good?" Chachi checked as my cell rang. "Is that Oaklyn?"

"Nah, this is Teagan." I sighed and ignored the first call. When she called back a second time, I decided to answer it. With Oaklyn already being through with me, what did I have to lose now?

"What's up?" I greeted her after connecting the call.

"You, babe. I thought you were coming by today. I had a surprise for you," Teagan announced happily.

"Right now, a nigga can't drive nowhere. I done had too damn much to drink."

When she offered to come and get me, I didn't think about being stuck with her for the rest of the night. Not until the next morning.

Chapter Eight

Teagan Hoffman

With Braxton continually pulling ghost moves these past few days, I figured that he had to be running behind his baby mama, trying to get her back. After that phone call, she had to be upset to find out that her so- called man had a new boo. I could hear it all in her voice when she asked if we were fucking. As much as I wanted to tell Oaklyn all about how incredible sex with Braxton was, I didn't want to completely mess things up before they even got started good. That was the only reason why I kept my cool and laughed right into that phone. That shit was funny when they hung up on me, but I didn't let that stop me. Nope, I called Braxton endlessly for two days straight until he finally answered.

When he did, I could tell that he was a little pissed that I didn't deny Oaklyn's accusations, but why would I? I mean, he was the one who told me that they weren't even together anymore. With him all in his feelings, he didn't answer my calls until last night. That was when he agreed to go out to dinner with me, then stood me up.

Determined to find him, I went to hunt his ass down and didn't stop until I found him drunk off his ass over at his boy Chachi's. I was just going to leave him there, but when he started talking dirty, I couldn't help but take him home with me. Braxton was so intoxicated that he talked for ten minutes straight, then just broke out snoring. He was so out of it when we made it to my house that I practically had to drag him inside. Instead of trying to help him sober up so I could tell him about the surprise I had for him, I took him up to my room, stripped him down, and put him in the bed. Afterward, I climbed in with him, then wrapped my arms around his waist and fell asleep with him. Truthfully, I hadn't slept in a man's hold in quite some time. It felt so good.

Too bad it didn't feel that way when Braxton woke up in a panic and jumped up like the bed was on fire. "Where the fuck am I?" he gasped and gazed at me as if I were the damn devil himself.

Why, though? I wasn't the enemy.

"What the fuck is going on, and how did I get here?" he went on as he hopped around, trying to find his clothes.

The entire time he scrambled, I kept my eye on his morning woody. It was so long and plump that all I could do was think about easing down on it.

"Calm down, babe. You're at my place," I explained, beginning with how I had picked him up from Chachi's.

"Damn, I don't remember nothing after getting fucked up at my boy's house. I definitely don't recall you picking me up and bringing me here. Wherever 'here' is," he went on as he slipped into his boxers, then went to check out the rest of my place.

"This is my house, Braxton."

"Damn, I didn't think you were living like this. This is like a fucking palace, and you live here by yourself?"

"Yes. My parents gave me this house after they had another estate built out in Clackamas," I explained as I wrapped up the tour and led him back to the bedroom, where I handed him the paperwork and keys to the studio that I had purchased for him. "I put everything in your name, but I kept myself on there as a private investor."

"So, it ain't really all mine then." He shrugged and gave me the documents right back.

Nobody had ever returned a gift I gave them, and that shit really hurt. Crushed my feelings to the core.

"Honestly, I didn't think it was a big deal putting my name on it, seeing that I emptied a nice chunk of my savings to pay it off in cash," I clarified.

"I appreciate it, Teagan, but I think I'll struggle to get it on my own. On my own terms."

"Well, if you're feeling that way, I can just take my name off of it, Braxton. I don't want to allow something so minor to get in the way of you taking your career to the next level."

"I appreciate it, and I'm sorry for being this way, Teagan. It's just that I don't wanna go into business with nobody."

"So, you're saying that you don't want the studio?" I asked as I hopped up to get dressed.

"Hell yeah, I want the studio, and I'll pay you the money back. We can even do a side contract or something. I just don't wanna go into this as a joint venture," he explained.

All of Braxton's responses left me feeling fucked up, and I did my best to shake it off as I strolled to the closet to get something to wear. "It's cool, and I totally understand. Let's just go and finalize the paperwork first, so you can go ahead and check the studio out."

"Cool." Braxton smiled as he hopped up and got himself together.

While I went to rush through the shower, I heard the doorbell ring downstairs. Instead of worrying about getting it, I asked him to answer it.

"Venezuela ain't here right now. Can you get it, please?"

"Who's Venezuela?"

"My housekeeper. She's gone, so can you go get the door, Braxton? Please?"

"You sure?" he questioned as I checked the app on my phone to see who it was.

"Yeah, it's just my friend Eva. Tell her that I'll be down in a minute."

As he disappeared, I hurried to wash up, get out, and throw on some clothes. My hair was wrapped, so all I had to do was pull my scarf off and comb through it.

Within five minutes, I was downstairs, wondering why Eva was all up in Braxton's face, looking star-struck. "You good, Boo?"

"Yes, I was just telling your friend here how I followed him on social network." She giggled. "So, I wanted to know, did you and your baby mama, Oaklyn, really break up?" Eva quizzed.

That girl was so fucking nosy, but I didn't say shit. Hell, I wanted to hear his answer too.

"Yeah, we broke up." He sighed and rubbed his well-groomed facial hair.

"Ah, man. I love the pics you used to post with your li'l girl, Brazil. She's so freaking cute, and she always has that basketball with her. Does she play?"

"She loves the game, and she can dribble pretty good, but that's about it," Braxton explained.

"I bet she would be good if she got on a team. Ain't she about to be seven?" Eva questioned.

Okay, that was quite enough of Eva commenting on Braxton's life. I didn't want to hear anything about what he had going on if it didn't include me.

"We were just about to leave to see Braxton's new studio," I interjected.

"Oh, can I come?" she begged and jumped up and down like a big-ass kid. Ugh! I couldn't stand the way she cut up sometimes. So damn embarrassing!

"Let her come. It's cool," Braxton said.

As much as I was against it, there were two against one. I had no choice but to agree and let my friend tag along. While frustration grew within me, I huffed all the way out to my car. When we got in, I warned Eva about talking too damn much and asking too many questions. You think she listened? Hell no!

That girl must've quizzed him about everything from the story of his life that he posted online to how he lost his parents. Luckily, Braxton's cell chimed before she could interrogate him about his uncle.

"What the hell?" he gasped as he opened his messages and viewed a picture.

From the driver's seat, I couldn't tell what or who it was, but judging by the expression on Braxton's face, it was something that bothered him something fierce. He was so angry that he excused himself as soon as we arrived at the new studio. He didn't even want to go inside until he made some calls first.

Well, damn.

Chapter Nine

Oaklyn Jones

The past few days with Gunner reminded me of how a lady was supposed to be treated—opening up doors for me, bringing me food and flowers, and just calling to check on me. Braxton hadn't spoiled me in so long that I had completely forgotten how it felt. Tonight, Gunner treated me to dinner, and it was amazing. The delicious food, the incredible scenery, and the intriguing company made it the perfect evening.

"That chopped salmon salad was delicious," I acknowledged just as I rose from the window-side table at the Chart House. After easing around the chair, I positioned myself in front of the glass and took in the nighttime view of Portland. Gunner quickly joined me. Without speaking a word, he placed his arm around me and gently drew me near. As I leaned my head on his chest and inhaled his familiar cologne, I thanked him again.

"My pleasure, Oaklyn."

Before we broke the hold, there was a series of flashes coming from both sides of us. When I looked up, I saw several people around us snapping photos.

"Gunner, is this your new love interest?" one woman asked as she held a mic in his face.

"Do you still have a protective order against Camille Rollins?" another one questioned. "Is it true that she threatened you with a gun?"

"Whoa?" I gasped and glanced at Gunner for answers.

"Y'all are blowing things up," he huffed and cut his eyes, then grabbed my hand to leave. Once we made it outside to the lot, we hopped in his truck and drove off. We only made it a block down the road before I began to hit him with a bunch of questions.

"You wanna tell me what that was all about? Was what that guy said true? What else aren't you telling me, Gunner?"

"That shit was just a rumor. That girl ain't pulled no gun on me, but she threatened to. Her and her sister Janille, they ain't wrapped too tight upstairs, but it's all behind me, and—" As he rubbed his face and explained, my cell began to chime.

When I checked it and saw that it was nobody but Braxton messaging me, I slid the red phone icon over, then shoved my phone down in my bag. He was the last person that I felt like talking to. Right then, I was trying to find out what the deal was between Gunner and the Camille chick.

"So, do you still talk to this girl or her sister?"

"Honestly, Camille has reached out to me several times using any and every means possible, but I haven't spoken to her or her sister," he said, trying to convince me. "I have no intention of talking to either of them or any other of their family members."

"Are you over her?"

Gunner laughed and veered over to the side of the road so he could look me in the face. "I'm completely over her, if that's what you're asking me, Oaklyn. I would've never stepped to you like I did if I still had feelings for her or anyone else."

"Look, I'm not harassing you about her because I know we're not in a relationship or anything, but—"

"But that's where I'm hoping this goes, Oaklyn. I'm really feeling you." Gunner smiled. "So, I guess, I need to be the one asking you. Are you still messing with your baby daddy?"

"No!" I laughed and shook my head. "After many years of being cheated on and taken advantage of, I'm ready to move on. I don't wanna waste another day being stuck in a relationship based on lies and deception."

"Okay, then."

When Gunner pulled back onto the road and merged with traffic, he began telling me about how glad he was that I had come into his life. "You've been the friend I've needed. You're easy to talk to and so beautiful that I don't wanna take my eyes off you."

"Stop it!" I blushed.

"No, I'm serious," he confessed shamelessly. "I promised myself that I would be patient and take my time once I met someone who captured my interest, not just jump into something headfirst strictly off their looks."

"So, what are you saying, Gunner?"

"I'm saying that you're beautiful, both inside and out, and I really want to see where this goes. Is that cool with you? Are we on the same page?" he pressed.

"Totally cool with me, and I agree with you. I think we should take it slow. I don't wanna get my hopes up thinking that you're gonna be the man of my dreams who comes and sweeps me off my feet."

"Why? That's just the man I wanna be." He laughed and reached over to rub my thigh. "One who sweeps you off your feet and makes all of your dreams come true."

"Well, that's kind of hard to believe when you've heard it all before, and those same promises did nothing but turn from sugar to shit."

"Know I'm not him, Oaklyn. I'm nothing like your daughter's father. When I'm in a relationship, I'm with that one person. Trust me, infidelity on my part was never a reason for any of my breakups."

That was good to know, but Gunner's words didn't make me trust him any more than I did. That would have to come with time.

"Well, Oaklyn, just know that however this turns out, I'm glad we met."

"Me too, Gunner," I shyly admitted as he turned into the parking lot of my apartment.

Once he parked his truck and came around to open my door, my mother was pulling up beside me with Brazil in the back seat. She was so excited to see me that she poked her head out the window and flashed that beautiful smile.

"Who's that?" Gunner questioned as my mother got out and approached us with a grin.

"I'm Oaklyn's mother, Draya, and you're Gunner West, right?" she probed and elbowed me while Brazil let herself out of the car.

"Yes, and nice to meet you," he replied with an extended hand and a surprised expression.

As they shook, Brazil got between them. "You are so tall! Do you play basketball?" She looked at Gunner from head to toe in amazement.

"He used to play for the Celtics before he got hurt," my mother explained.

"Wow! Can you teach me how to play better, Gunner? My dribble is pretty good, but I think I gotta work on my shot a little more," Brazil responded, then anxiously waited for an answer.

"Is that right?" Gunner laughed, then asked how old Brazil was.

"I'm six, but I'm about to be seven next month," she blurted out proudly.

"Okay, then, Brazil. I have a basketball camp starting in a few weeks. It's Monday through Friday during spring break. You wanna come?"

"Can I, Mom?" she pleaded.

"That camp probably cost an arm and a leg," my mother clowned and shook her head. "But it would be good for her. She loves basketball just like her nana."

"If she really wants to go, I got her. No cost," Gunner assured us. "You ladies ain't gotta worry about nothing."

"Well, I hope you got your car fixed by then, Oaklyn, because I don't know about all that back and forth every day for a week."

"Mom got a new car, Nana," Brazil blabbed. I wanted to cover her mouth and take her inside, but I knew my mother wouldn't allow that, so I refrained and sucked it up.

"I don't have a new car, Brazil. That's Gunner's car. He's letting me use it until I can get another one."

Why am I even explaining myself? Shit, I'm grown!

While my mother gasped, then went overboard thanking Gunner for helping me out, she made it seem like I was a charity case. That really bugged me.

"Okay, Mom. Thanks for bringing Brazil. I'll see you next weekend."

Finally getting the hint, she said her goodbyes and gave Brazil one last hug before she got in her car and exited the lot.

"Sorry about that," I apologized.

"No worries," Gunner responded as he walked me and Brazil to the entrance of my apartment.

"Thanks for inviting me to the basketball camp," my daughter said as I opened the door to let her inside. Since she had already had bathed at my mother's house and was in her pajamas, I told her to pick out a book for her to read to me.

Once she disappeared, my attention went back to Gunner. "I guess you met her sooner than I expected." I giggled. "That girl is a handful."

"She's very intelligent for her age, and I can't wait to see her on the court, especially after she told me that she could hoop."

"And she can," I clowned. "My mother bought her a basketball when she was two, and she hasn't put it down since. The only reason she didn't have it tonight is because my mom took it from her over the weekend after she broke another one of her vases."

"Damn." Gunner laughed. "I can't wait to see shorty's skills."

"I can't wait for you to see her play either," I confessed as he gently grabbed my hand, then peeked over my shoulder.

"What is it?" I asked and turned around to see what he was looking at. When I saw nothing or nobody, I repeated my question.

"I had to make sure your daughter wasn't coming." He smiled, then leaned into me before placing his hand around my shoulder.

My heart rate increased rapidly as his soft, juicy lips covered mine. The sensual contact caused fluttering in my belly, while the faint scent of his cologne made me moist between my thighs.

"Mmmmm!" He hummed and smacked his lips, then released the lip lock he had on me. "You taste so good that I didn't even wanna let you go. I just didn't want your daughter to bust me kissing all over her mama. I couldn't help myself, though. Mmmmm."

When I didn't say a word, Gunner used his hand to tilt my chin upward, and our eyes met. Now, I was really speechless.

"Nothing to say?" he teased and pecked my lips.

"Wow!" I gasped and touched my mouth with two fingers. "That's all I can say."

"You got jokes." Gunner laughed loudly. "Call me when you get your daughter to bed."

"I will." I giggled and closed the door.

Before I could go tuck Brazil in, I had to analyze what had just happened. "Did I really just let him kiss me?" I whispered to myself.

Gunner was the first man I had kissed since Braxton and I had gotten together ten years prior. It was not only unbelievable; I couldn't stop thinking about it.

"Let me go put this girl to sleep," I chanted and rushed down the hallway to Brazil's room, only to find that she wasn't in her bed. She was fast asleep in mine. Removing the book from under her arm, I gently tucked her in and kissed her cheek.

Once I got her taken care of, I went into the living room to call Koola. I had to tell her about my night. Before I could click onto my call list and find her name, my mother rang my line.

"Yes, Mom."

"Oaklyn, I know you seen I been calling you. Why ain't you answered me?"

"What's wrong, Mom?"

"Oaklyn, you wanna tell me what's going on between you and Gunner West?" she pried. She asked one question after another and barely gave me time in between to answer. Her interrogation had my head spinning.

"Mom, we're just friends."

"What about Braxton?" she probed. "I hope y'all are done this time because as much as I love that boy, he can't get right. I don't like how he does you, and I definitely don't like how he hasn't been there for Brazil like he should be. It's not like he has a full-time job or anything."

"Tell me something I don't know, Mom." I sighed heavily. "I don't even wanna think about all that. Right now, I wanna get myself together. You know? Use my degree to get a good job, move up outta here and start loving *Oaklyn* again."

"That's what I'm talking about, girl. I'm so proud of you, and you are a great mother. I love it, and I love you."

"Awwwww, I love you more, Mom," I whined. "Thank you, and I had a great role model. Thanks for always being here for me and Brazil."

"Always and forever," she promised as she always did.

"Always and forever."

When we hung up, I smiled and shook my head. God had truly blessed me with a wonderful family. My mother and my daughter were everything to me. Braxton used to be in the equation, but not anymore. Not anymore, and I wasn't mad about it. One door shut, and another one opened. That's the way I looked at it. Especially when the person who came through the open door was Gunner West. How intriguing.

Chapter Ten

Gunner West

A few weeks later . . .

For the past three weeks, I had been busy with business stuff, but I still managed to take Oaklyn on a date every other day. Whether we went out to eat, caught a movie, or just enjoyed a stroll through the neighborhood, I always made the time to let her know how important she was to me.

"Gunner, you sitting over there with your head in the clouds when I need you to be focused right now. I know you have that camp going on right now, but you know we got that charity game next Sunday over at Portland State University. We need to make sure we have enough players. If you remember, each quarter goes by age groups, and the older folks like me are gonna play first," my pops explained. "The kids ages seven to ten will play last quarter."

"I got it, Pops," I assured him as I took a stack of flyers from him. "You know people don't pass these things out anymore? They usually promote online and on all the social media platforms."

"Well, since you know so much, did you do it?"

"I sure did. I have a guy I pay to take care of things like that. We already have all the slots filled, and all the tickets are nearly sold out."

"Are you serious?" my father asked, looking surprised.

"I am, Pops."

"You had time to get your camp together and handle the charity basketball game planning, too? I gotta give it to you, son. You can multitask better than anyone I know."

"Thanks. I try." I laughed as I grabbed my keys, then reached for a hug.

After we embraced, I headed to the door so I could get to the first day of basketball camp early. "See you later, Pops," I yelled out.

"Wait a minute, son. Let me tell you something right quick."

"What is it, Pops?" The seriousness of his voice made me back up and go back to the kitchen, where he was sitting at the counter. I needed to see his face when he broke the news.

"What is it, Pops?" I repeated.

"Camille—"

"What about her?" I mumbled as I felt myself becoming anxious.

"She came by here earlier asking for your new address. I showed her a copy of the restraining order to remind her that she was to come nowhere near you."

"Did you call the cops?"

"Yeah, but by the time they got here, she was long gone. She and another gal who was waiting for her in a car, but I couldn't see her face or the plates. It was just an ordinary black sedan." He sighed heavily. "You know that girl crazy, right?" My father knew damn well that Camille was certified coo-coo, and he should've gotten her ass arrested. Shit, I wasn't ready to deal with any of it.

"Just call me if she comes back by here, even though I doubt she will."

"She said that she was just passing through."

"Well, Pops, let's just hope she's telling the truth for once."

With Camille lurking out there somewhere, I was cautious when leaving my parents' house. Now, if my mama wasn't away on her yearly rejuvenating cruise, I wouldn't be worried because she wouldn't hesitate to pop a cap in that bitch; but my father, he wasn't about to hurt a damn fly.

"Let me call Oaklyn back," I whispered as I jumped on the highway and tapped the phone icon on the dash screen. Just as her info popped up, she was dialing me back.

"Good morning, Gunner."

"Good morning, beautiful. I know you said you were bringing Brazil a little early, and I'm almost there."

"Okay, I'm not rushing you. Brazil is." Oaklyn giggled. "This girl had me buy her a new basketball and every-thing."

"And she dribbles with the NBA official size, too?"

"Yes, she does," Oaklyn bragged with a laugh.

A girl her age with the basketball skills they claimed she had was rare. To believe that shit, I would have to see it for myself.

"I'm pulling up right now," I informed her as I entered the lot and parked next to my Benz, where Oaklyn and her daughter were standing. As I climbed out of my truck, my eyes stayed on Brazil, who was dressed in a red Nike gym shorts set, red-and-white Jordans, and a sweatband around her head to match. Under her arm, she clutched a red-and-blue Spalding Varsity basketball.

"Okay, now. I see you, girl." I laughed and rubbed the top of Brazil's head. Today, she had all of her long braids pulled back into a ponytail like she was ready to ball.

"That b-ball just about big as her," Leslie, one of the workers and a close friend, teased as we walked into the Matt Dishman Center with the group of people waiting.

"I can't wait!" Brazil cheered. "This is gonna be so exciting, but I'm nervous."

"Don't be. You just go in here and have some fun. Don't worry about the bigger kids that are able to do things you haven't learned yet. We all learn at our own pace," I reminded her as we entered the gymnasium.

Without acknowledging what I said, Brazil stepped onto the court and immediately began dribbling. One person's cheering created a domino effect, and within seconds, she had all of our attention.

"Look at shorty!" Leslie hollered as she got out her phone and started filming.

With all eyes on Brazil, I could see a couple of the little boys becoming jealous. I wasn't going to say anything until they started talking mess.

"You can do better?" I challenged.

"That girl too little. I don't wanna embarrass her," James Barker, a ten-year-old returning kid, clowned, making the others laugh. Meanwhile, Brazil remained on the floor, taking the ball through her legs and around her back.

"Okay, James. You think you're so good, go out there and take the ball without touching her. If you foul her in the slightest, you apologize and refrain from sarcastic remarks for the rest of the week."

"And what do I get if I take it from her?"

"If you get it in under thirty seconds, I'll give you an autographed basketball and a hundred-dollar Nike gift card." That was nothing for me because I had plenty of both at home, but for a kid, it meant everything.

"For real? You'll give me a ball and a hundred-dollar Nike gift card?" James checked as he walked out on the court, cool, calm, and confident.

"Yep, but you gotta do it within thirty seconds," I reminded him, then told Brazil what was going on.

"Oh, he ain't about to take my new ball, Gunner," she said as she squatted a bit more with her dribble and focused on James, who was walking toward her.

"Consider that ball mine!" he yelled and tried to reach for it.

Brazil switched hands on him and backed up, causing the crowd to react in shock. Even my mouth was hanging open. This little girl's determination was crazy.

"Nope, my ball," Brazil taunted as she bounced the ball through her little legs the next time James went for it.

"Fifteen seconds!" I called out.

"Don't even worry. I'm about to get it right now," he assured me as he went to her left. Right when he came near, she crossed him over and went around him.

"Five seconds!" I yelled.

"Ugh!" James grunted as he went for the ball one last time, but Brazil was too quick and took it behind her back before he could even touch it.

"Time's up!"

"Oh, snap! Everybody see that?" Leslie hollered and cheered, holding up her phone. "I got all that on video, and I'm uploading it to the camp website right now and our YouTube channel. Oh, and on my Instagram page, too."

While everyone was tripping off the little basketball wonder, I wanted to ask her mother why she was hiding her daughter's talent. That was a gift worth sharing with the world. "Oaklyn! Why you ain't tell me that girl got hands like that?" I gasped and went to give Brazil a high-five.

"Because my mom don't think I'm serious about it," she answered for her mother.

"No, I just know you never stick to anything, li'l girl."
Oaklyn smirked. "Like the drum set and the rollerblades
and the—"

"Okay, Mom! You're right, but I've always liked basketball. You and Daddy never take me to play, and ever since
we moved into our apartment, you won't let me play on
the playground because you said the kids were too bad,"
Brazil whined.

To avoid Oaklyn and Brazil getting into a debate, I intervened and suggested that we start checking everyone
in so that we could break up into groups afterward.

While they did that, Leslie and I set up the stations.
"So, you know that little girl?" she asked.

"I just met her mother a month or so ago. I didn't know
her daughter could dribble like that, though. Now we just
gotta get her arms strong enough to get that ball up to the
hoop—" Before I could finish, I was interrupted by loud
cheering. It was Brazil down on the other side of the gym,
doing layups. Damn! That little girl amazed me all over
again, and it continued throughout the morning.

By noon, the first day of camp was officially over, and
all I wanted to do was go out to eat and relax. "Who
wanna go to the Portland Ice Cream Parlor?" I offered a
few of the returning kids.

Brazil was the first one hollering that she wanted to go.
She obviously loved ice cream.

"I don't know, Brazil. Your dad is supposed to be picking you up at your grandmother's in a couple of hours,"
Oaklyn told her.

"Can't he just pick me up at the ice cream parlor, Mom?"
Brazil pouted.

"I don't want to interfere. We can do it some other
time," I suggested to avoid an awkward situation.

"I really wanna go, Mom. Can you just call Daddy?"
Brazil pleaded as she tugged on Oaklyn's jacket. "Please!"

"Come on now, Brazil."

"Mom, just try to call him one time, and if he doesn't answer or tells you no, I won't bug you again," she promised with her crossed fingers held high.

"Okay, Brazil. You win this time. Let's go. I'll call your father and tell him to get you from there." Oaklyn gave in. "So, Gunner, I guess we'll just meet you there."

"See you there." I smiled and hopped in my truck to head over to the restaurant. During the ride, I couldn't help but wonder how Braxton would act when he picked Brazil up. Seeing me with his baby mama would for sure strike a nerve or two. I hoped and prayed that he would be on his best behavior. If he wasn't, I knew just how to deal with him without making a scene. I already had it planned out.

Chapter Eleven

Braxton Carter

Going through hell and high water just to see my daughter these past few weeks had me fucked up. I couldn't believe that because of a funky-ass trespass order, Oaklyn wouldn't let me come to her apartment to pick Brazil up. Instead, she expected me to drive all the way to the other side of town to her mother's every time I wanted to visit with my child. Straight bullshit.

"What's on your mind, man?" Chachi asked, interrupting my thoughts as we drove down Alberta Street to get a haircut and get his car that was parked in front of Bernard's barbershop, where he had left it.

As I veered into a vacant spot on the block of the shop, I explained what was going on between me and my baby mama. I kept it brief because I didn't want to walk into Bernard's speaking on my business. Those niggas gossiped like bitches, and I didn't want to be their next messy topic.

While I tried to drop the subject with a hand motion across my throat, Chachi wanted to go on about it as soon as we got inside. He couldn't catch the hint to shut up. "This is the longest you and Oaklyn been separated. She must be really feeling that nigga Gunner," Chachi said soon as we sat to get cut and lined up.

To try to hush him, I changed the subject and asked about this new chick, Rhonda, he fooled with. Oh, he didn't want to speak on that, so he went right back to questioning me about Oaklyn out loud.

"If she's fuckin' with dude, she must be really done with you, Brax. I mean, you said she ain't been taking your calls and shit."

"Why you always gotta start talking my business soon as we get up in here?" I huffed as my cell chirped. "While you clownin', this is Oaklyn messaging me right now. She wants to meet me over by the Lloyd Center to get Brazil."

While I read the text over a couple of times, Tyrelle, one of the barbers hollered at me. "Hey, Braxton, ain't this yo' shorty? It gotta be 'cause I see Oaklyn's thick ass all up in the video."

"What video?" Chachi and I asked in unison.

"Go to YouTube and type in 'little basketball wonder shows out at Gunner West's camp,'" Tyrelle instructed.

Just to hear that name burned me up, and within seconds of watching the video, my eyes were bucked out of my head. I didn't even know my daughter could play that well.

"Why you ain't tell me Brazil be hoopin' like this, dude?" Chachi gasped. "That girl is good."

"She loves her basketball, and she always used to play with that Nerf hoop I got her, but I didn't know she was nice like that." I stared as a realization hit me. Performing at different gigs and tending to my own personal business outside of my family had overpowered my home life. It was a sad thing and actually made me feel like a bum-ass daddy for downplaying Brazil's love for the game. It reminded me of her nana, Draya's, obsession. Oaklyn's mother was the main one who continually encouraged Brazil to play sports, and the one who stayed buying her different equipment and the latest athletic wear, including every new sneaker that Nike came out with.

"Wait! Yo' baby mama fuck with Gunner West?" Tyrelle gasped loudly, suspending my thoughts.

Now all the attention was on me, and I didn't know how to respond to the question without making me look weak or feel more clueless than I already felt. To play it safe, I kept my answer short. "Tyrelle, man, they know each other. Why?"

"Well, the way that nigga was all in her face on that second video."

"What second video?" Chachi asked before I could.

While Tyrelle sent us both the link, I shot my baby mama a text asking how soon I could get Brazil. Although I anxiously wanted to see my baby girl, I was now more interested in talking to Oaklyn so that I could find out what the hell she was up to with this Gunner cat. Having other men around our child during a temporary split was a no-no. So, until we officially determined that we were going to stay apart, I wasn't about to play that shit. Something had to give, and as soon as I spoke with her, I planned on letting her know.

"I guess they are fucking around," Chachi whispered after he got up out of the chair and paid his barber. "This video tells it all, and this shit don't lie."

"Whatever. She's a grown-ass woman, and we don't stay together. That means that she's free to do what she wants, just like I am free to do what the hell I want," I responded seconds later when Bernard finished my cut.

Ready to get enough privacy to call Oaklyn back, I rose from the chair, settled my tab, then headed out the door. Chachi trailed behind, still asking questions.

"So, where you about to go?" he probed as we stood in front of the barber shop, chopping it up for a few seconds.

When I began to tell him where I was about to go, my cell rang. I checked the screen and took a deep breath. "I wanted to go get Brazil, but this is Teagan calling me, bugging me about meeting her to discuss other ways of generating money until I drop my first single. She thinks selling some studio time is a good way to make some quick cash, but I don't know about letting no hardheads up in there fighting, smoking weed, and being disrespect-ful. I done seen it all, and a lot of it ain't good, Chachi."

"That's a good idea, and what you need to do is screen niggas before you sell studio time. If they still tear up, you got insurance, right?"

"Yeah."

"Well, that covers shit like that." Chachi laughed and hit the alarm to unlock his Chevy Blazer. He kept his ride clean. I had to give it to my boy. Rims, paint, and trim were on point.

"True that," I replied. "I'll catch you later. I gotta get goin'."

"A'ight, Brax. Later."

As Chachi drove off, I hopped in my ride, pushed the start button, and let my vehicle idle while I viewed the videos of Brazil again. I had to watch her clowning that little boy again, as well as check out how my baby mama interacted with Gunner. Was she really messing around with this goofy guy?

"Fuck it! I'll just ask her when I get to the restaurant," I chanted under my breath as I shot to the northeast and parked in the side lot of Portland Ice Cream Parlor.

Just as I got out and hit my locks, I glanced over and noticed the same Benz that Oaklyn was driving parked a few stalls away. That shit rubbed me the wrong way and made me want to just leave, but I couldn't because I had to get my daughter. *Damn.*

"Please don't let my family be up in here with that nigga," I mumbled quietly as I stood at the door and sent Oaklyn a text to let her know I was there. After a few minutes passed and I didn't get a response, I became impatient and went all the way inside the parlor. Right away, I began searching for Oaklyn and Brazil. First, I went to the main room. When I didn't find them in there, I went into the party room. Closely scanning each area as I made my way through the double glass doors, I instantly spotted Gunner holding Brazil in the air to hit a pinata. Talk about wanting to beat a nigga's ass! This muthafucka had his hands on my baby girl.

"Oh, hell nah!" I gritted and stomped two steps before Oaklyn popped up in front of me to block my path.

"Let me get Brazil for you." She smiled all up in my face.

If she wasn't so damn beautiful and I wasn't so madly in love with her, I would've politely moved her out of my way and gone to check Gunner. I didn't like the way he was playing with Brazil, and I made it very clear to Oaklyn before I let her walk off to get her.

"Whatever," she scoffed and kept right on going.

As soon as she stepped away, some of the kids were whispering while they pointed at me. I already knew what was next.

"Hey, aren't you Braxton the singer?" a young boy asked anxiously as he jumped up and down. "My mama watches your videos on the computer all the time. I think she likes you."

"Well, tell your mother that I appreciate her support," I replied with a grin.

As the young lad snapped a few pics, then ran off to tell his friends, Oaklyn came toward me. She had a grip on Brazil's shirt while she tried to tug away.

"What's wrong, baby girl?" I asked my daughter, extending my arms out to pick her up like I usually did. She pouted and refused, saying that she wanted to stay with Gunner and the rest of the kids. I couldn't believe it.

"Daddy, I'm not ready to go. Mom can go if she wants to, but I wanna stay. Can you stay with me? Daddy, please?"

Brazil's pleas were hard to deny, but this one I couldn't roll with. There was no way on God's green earth that I was about to stay there and kick it around a muthafucka that was pushing up on my woman while we were on a temporary break.

"How about I take you to Oaks Park?"

"Daddy, that's so boring," Brazil huffed dramatically, then put her hand on her hip and asked if I saw her video. Was she really feeling herself?

When I called her out on how funny she acted, Oaklyn cut me off and gave me the side eye. "Wonder where she gets it from?"

"A'ight, you got me." I laughed and shook my head in shame. Arrogance and greed had managed to put me in a lonely position, and I couldn't watch my child go down that same ugly road. Not on my watch.

Brazil was already acting cocky behind her basketball video that had over a million views in less than twenty-four hours, so I could just imagine what she would do once she got on television. At nearly seven years old, though . . .

"Look, Brazil. Daddy has some special plans for us."

"Like what?" she questioned without budging.

"I rented a house through Airbnb, and it has a heated pool and hot tub."

"Yes! Bye, Mom!" Brazil quickly grabbed her backpack from her mother. After slinging it onto her back, she held my hand tightly, then tugged me toward the exit.

"You have camp in the morning!" Oaklyn hollered out.

"I'll drop her off on time," I assured her as I glanced over her shoulder at Gunner, who was now staring me down, not in a threatening way, but as if he were trying to read me. Disregarding him with a confident smirk, I turned around and left the building with my daughter. She was talking so much that I couldn't keep up with what she was saying.

"Buckle up, Brazil," I reminded her as she hopped in the back seat and continued to question me.

"Is the house far, Daddy?"

"About a half hour away. It's only three, so we have plenty of time to go swimming."

"Okay. I can't wait."

"I know you can't." I laughed, then asked if she had fun at the camp.

"Daddy, you didn't even know I could play basketball like that, did you?"

"No."

"That's because when you lived with me and Mom, you were always gone. You were gone when I got home from school and on weekends, Daddy. That's why I go to Nana's. She's the one who helps me play basketball."

Wow! This little girl was too much for me. Too damn much.

"Sorry I haven't been there for you, baby, but—"

"But you and Mom been arguing like always."

"You are too damn grown, Brazil," I snapped, ready to let her have it. That mouth of hers was something else.

"I'm just a little girl. Almost seven, but I know what's going on around me, Daddy."

"Well, if you know so much, what's up between yo' mama and Gunner?"

"All I know is he's a good guy, he likes Mom, and he's nice to both of us. He's even gonna let me play in the charity basketball game next Sunday, too, Daddy. It'll be on TV and everything."

Brazil was cheering about this dude like he was a damn superhero, and it dented my ego. Complaining about it wasn't going to reinflate it, so my only other choice was to support her.

"You want Daddy to come and watch you?"

"I'll see if I can get you some tickets. Miss Leslie said they cost a lot of money, but after it's over, it all goes to kids that are less fortunate."

"What you know about being less fortunate, girl?" I teased.

"Those are people that are struggling to make it in this world, Daddy. Gunner told me that today," she said. "I'm getting smarter by the day, huh, Daddy?"

"Your mouth is," I whispered to myself as I put my thumb in the air and nodded my head.

While Brazil continued to be a little chatterbox in the back seat, I checked my cell, which had been going off the whole ride. It was Teagan.

Damn.

Chapter Twelve

Teagan Hoffman

Nearly three weeks went by, and I had barely spent any quality time with Braxton. He had been too busy searching for a place to move. To help him out, I had offered to let him stay with me until he got things together, but he gracefully declined. Figuring it was a pride thing, I took it upon myself to hook him up with one of the nice Airbnb homes my parents owned. Once he got settled in, he made sure I understood that he wouldn't be there longer than a month. In that same breath, he made sure I knew that he wasn't about to jump into another relationship until he knew the one that he had with Oaklyn was over for sure.

Braxton must've been the only person confused because from where I sat, Oaklyn had gotten on with her life. How clear did she have to make it for him to get the message? She kicked him out, got him trespassed off the property, and barely spoke to him. *I would say that shit was over.*

It blew my mind how Braxton could even consider going back to Oaklyn after all that shit. Child together or not, she didn't deserve him, and she damn sure didn't have anything to offer him. I was the one financing him and his career. Me.

"Okay, I'm gonna try one last time." After another heavy sigh, I dialed him again. This time, he answered.

"What's good, Teagan?"

Before I could reply, I heard a small voice speak in the background. "Can we get some food?"

What sounded like a child talking instantly captured my attention. It caused me to bypass Braxton's dry greeting. As nosy as I wanted to be, I bit my tongue and kept the conversation general.

"Hey, Braxton. I'm not up to too much. I'm at the house. I was just calling to see what was up with you. I wanted to drop by and bring you those extra towels and the green tea that you wanted for the Keurig."

"You ain't gotta do that. I already stopped by the store with my daughter. She's staying with me until tomorrow. We're headed to the house now to go swimming, order some food, then chill and watch movies," Braxton explained.

"So, you have her all night?"

"Yeah, I'm tryna enjoy some time with her because I gotta drop her off at basketball camp in the morning."

Braxton didn't even give me a chance to respond before hanging up. It was like he couldn't talk to me in front of his six-year-old kid. What did he have to hide from his daughter when he no longer lived with her and her mother? Didn't that mean that he was free to date other women?

While I was in deep thought, I heard the doorbell ring. Assuming that my housekeeper would eventually get it, I didn't move a muscle.

"Ma'am, your mother is here," Venezuela called out.

"You don't have to announce me, sheesh!" my mother complained as she straightened her sleeveless white cashmere sweater and cut her eyes. "Tell me again why you hired that woman?"

"Mom, please. Venezuela is the homegirl. I love her vibe," I teased as we strolled into the formal living room.

"Sit, Teagan."

"Why? What's wrong?" I pressed and became anxious. "Is everything okay? Is Papa all right?"

"Girl, I'm coming over here to see if you're okay, Teagan. I haven't spoken to you in a couple of weeks, and that's not like you."

As we sat there, I finally exposed the feelings that I had for Braxton and confessed to everything that had happened between us. I began with the night of the surprise party that she and my father threw me, then continued to how I bought Braxton a studio, and ended with how he had a baby mama and a little girl. All my mother could do was shake her head.

"So, you must be in love with this man. Is that what you're telling me?"

"Before you start, Braxton is nothing like Walter, Mom."

"Ah—" When her expression shifted and she pinched her lips, I knew something was fishy.

"What? Why did you just look at me like that?"

"All I'm gonna say is, please don't mention anything about Braxton to your father."

"Why not, Mom?"

My mother went on to explain how it bothered her whenever my father became involved in my personal life. I was their only child, and he was really overprotective of me.

"You know he would act a fool if anyone broke your heart or did you wrong. He is crazy when it comes to you, Teagan."

"Why would you say that?"

"Walter—" she began, then shut completely down.

"What does all of this have to do with Walter? He never did anything to me," I questioned curiously.

"Let me tell you this, and I need you to keep it between us," she started.

My chest pounded, and my palms were sweating profusely as my mother's eyes became teary. What was she about to tell me? Would she just spit it out before she gave me a damn heart attack?

"After the shit he pulled—"

"Who?" I gasped.

My mother's lips trembled along with her hands as she sat there and admitted that my father had an investigator watching Walter. She said that he wanted to make sure that he didn't have any skeletons in his closet before he gave us his blessing to marry.

"Walter and I didn't have any infidelity issues, Mom."

At least there were none that I knew of, until she broke the news that Walter had a whole family in Seattle, Washington. Apparently, he had used the money I gave him for a real estate deal that he claimed had fallen through, and he gave it to his *wife* and kids. How blind could I be?

"You buying Braxton that studio is going to send a red flag to your father."

"Wait, what happened to Walter? Did Daddy scare him off? Did he make him leave me, Mom?" I cried, ready to break down.

"Worse, Teagan." She sniffled. "You father had him killed."

"*He what*?" I yelled. "Just because he had another family?"

"No, because he had taken out a large life insurance policy on you."

"Oh, my God! Walter was planning to kill me?" I gasped and started panting as the memories of all the incidents that had happened months ago came rushing back. That man really tried to have me killed!

"I didn't mean to come and get you upset, Teagan. I came to warn you about how you're moving. As you know, our family is very private, and we don't need any attention drawn to us. Discretion is a must, and if your father feels as if anyone is threatening it, they have to be eliminated. Do you understand?"

"Yes, I understand, Mom," I mumbled as I sat back on the sofa and remembered everything that my father taught me as a kid. To sum it up: I should've known better, and I damn sure shouldn't have been surprised. Oh, but I was. I was very surprised.

"I thought Dad completely got out of the family business, Mom. He said he wasn't involved in any of that Mafia crap, Mom."

"That's exactly why I want this to stay between me and you, mija."

My mother walked over to me and drew me upward so she could hug me before she left. Her visits were never longer than half an hour.

"Call me tomorrow, Teagan. I love you."

"Okay, love you too, Mom."

As soon as I walked her to the door and closed it behind her, I ran to the bathroom and let it all out. Walter was dead. The only thing giving me comfort was knowing that if he weren't deceased, I would've been.

Thank you, Lord, for sparing me.

"I gotta pull it together," I whispered and washed my face. Once I dried it and applied a little moisturizer, I went into the den to pour myself a glass of wine. I needed to relax.

"Ma'am, Eva is here," Venezuela announced seconds later.

So much for my peace. This chick couldn't even walk into my house like she had good sense. No, she had to come running inside like someone was chasing her. She nearly knocked Venezuela to the floor.

"Look at this shit right here!" Eva shouted as she shoved her cell in my face. "Can you believe this?" Eva wasted no time showing me videos shot and posted earlier in the day, starting with the one with Braxton's daughter that went viral. I was impressed with Brazil's performance, but what did that have to do with me?

"Okay, that little girl got skills," I complimented, then looked at Eva for an explanation. "That should bother me?"

"No, but this might," she added as she showed me the video that someone posted when Braxton showed up at the Portland Ice Cream Parlor, where Gunner was treating some of the kids from his camp.

"What's wrong with that?" I questioned Eva. "Everyone was civil, and he wasn't all up on his baby mama or nothing like that."

"Put two and two together, Teagan. With Braxton's daughter being an overnight basketball success, under the wing of Gunner West, I may add, you think he's gonna play on the sidelines? Girl, that nigga ain't about to let another man be up and around Brazil like that. That's his only child."

"Just because you follow the man on social media don't mean you know what he will or will not do, Eva. I'm sure he doesn't get on there and tell all of his business. At least not the personal shit."

"Shit! They used to share everything up until the past year or so. Ever since Braxton has been in the spotlight, he hasn't been posting Oaklyn."

"Probably because he's over her." I laughed. "You can't take everyone everywhere you go. Maybe Oaklyn wasn't meant to come on this part of Braxton's journey."

"Girl, do you know how they met? Didn't I tell you?"

"Yeah, he was homeless and then got himself together."

"*No*! It wasn't that simple, Teagan. Braxton lost his parents in a house fire, leaving his young uncle to raise him on the streets. They used to squat in vacant homes and sing on corners for money."

"Okay, he already told me all that. And?" I challenged.

"*And* Oaklyn and her mother got them off the streets and into nice housing. It was she who had been there for him since day one, Teagan. They had to have created a great bond, and having a daughter together only makes it stronger. I just can't see him leaving his family like that. Not after they seemed so happy online."

Eva was looking too far into the matter. She couldn't pay attention to the present because she was so focused on Braxton's past.

"All that is over, and he's moved on to—"

"Please don't say bigger and better things," Eva hissed.

"I wasn't about to say that, but that bitch is bigger than me."

"Oaklyn may have some extra weight on her, but it's well proportioned."

"She's cute, but she's still fat, and Braxton is probably tired of her big ass. That's why he ain't with her. He's too busy sniffing over here."

"So, what are you saying, Teagan? Are you saying that Braxton is your man?" Eva pressed with her hands resting on her hips. She hadn't taken a seat since she busted through my door twenty minutes prior. Over here taking up for the fat girl when I was supposed to be her best friend. Ugh!

"Yes, we're kicking it, Eva."

"Have you two made it official? Like, has he asked you to be his girl?"

"Who the fuck does that anymore, Eva? That's like expecting him to write me a note asking me to be his girlfriend with those little boxes to check. Girl, bye!" I scoffed and cut my eyes. Why did she want it to rain on my parade? What had I done to her? "Are you seriously tripping about me messing with Braxton?"

"No, I just want you to be aware of what you're getting into. I don't want you to get your hopes up all high only for that nigga to let you down and stomp on your feelings. After Walter, I thought you would be a bit more cautious."

"Please don't start about Walter, Eva." I released a big breath of air, then panicked. With my mother's confession on my mind, it was difficult to hide my expressions or hold my secrets. If Eva only knew, and if I could only tell her. Blood ties were important to my family, and I would never cross those lines. If we weren't related, then you could not be included on private issues. Period.

"Please don't tell me that Walter is still a sensitive subject, Teagan."

"No, I just don't wanna talk about him. All my attention goes to Braxton, if you haven't noticed."

"Well, I warned you about him and the situation, Teagan. I'm telling you. I don't think it's over between Braxton and Oaklyn."

Just because Eva knew about everything he posted online didn't mean she knew everything about his life like she claimed to. The things he wanted the public to know, he put out there. The things he wanted to keep a secret, he didn't, including me and the studio I bought him. That was okay, though. All in time.

"You are so judgmental, Eva."

"Why? Because I used the information that I knew to help open your eyes? Is that why, Teagan?"

"You know the shit because you've been following him and his family like a little fucking stalker, Eva. Now, don't downplay what I've built with him."

"Like what, Teagan? What have you built *with* him? Because as far as I know, *you* are the one who bought a fucking studio for a man you've barely known a month. What Braxton and Oaklyn built in ten years can't be erased or bought, boo."

What the hell was Eva on, and what made her think that she could handle me like that? She was tripping.

"You are out of line tryna check me about how I spend my dough. I don't hear you complaining when I'm spending it on you."

Eva's face turned beet red before she answered me. She was really upset by my comment, and she had every right to be. It was uncalled for and evil, but she pushed me there, and I wasn't about to apologize. Not right then.

"Like I said, Teagan, you're trippin', and I'm not about to entertain that shit because I've never asked you for anything. Oh, and even though my money can't touch yours, it's earned and not given. Remember that shit!" Without allowing me to generate a response, Eva stormed out of my house and had the nerve to slam my door so hard that my windows shook. Yes, she had lost her damn mind.

"Is everything okay, ma'am?" Venezuela questioned as she rushed into the living room to check on me.

"I'm fine, thanks," I said, waving her off. All I needed was some peace and quiet so I could think straight. I couldn't do that with Walter's murder on my mind. I needed to focus on the living—Braxton.

I seriously have questions!

Was he really still in love with Oaklyn? Did he have her over at my parents' Airbnb? Was he that bold?

I pray not.

To make sure he didn't, I did what I did best. I went to see for myself, and I didn't go empty-handed. Nope, I had a plan, which called for a quick trip to the mall on the way.

Chapter Thirteen

Oaklyn Jones

After Braxton took Brazil for the night, I used that time to go with Gunner to pick up our custom order at Stackin' Kickz inside the Lloyd Center. Once we finished, we went back to the gym to get things set up for the next day of camp. Leslie and a couple of volunteers were there already in action. We barely had to do a thing.

"Wait. Before you guys leave, did either of you see the footage taken at the Portland Ice Cream Parlor? You two are streaming like the new power couple of Portland or some shit!" Leslie boasted as she ran behind us and caught us at the door. "Why didn't you tell me that Brazil's dad was Braxton Carter? That man can sing!"

"We're not together anymore, so I don't think he's relevant enough to bring him up in general conversation," I acknowledged. "But yeah, he can sing."

"I can't believe I didn't recognize you or Brazil from his YouTube channel. He used to post y'all all the time."

"Yeah, *used to*," I clarified.

"You are too funny," Leslie replied, reminding us about the reporters from Fox News who were coming to the camp in the morning.

"I don't know why they wanna talk to me," I huffed as Gunner and I exited the Dishman Center.

"Because you're Brazil's mother and you're practically raising her alone. They're always interested in a good, wholesome story."

That was what I was worried about. I mean, what if they were to ask me some uncomfortable questions? What if they made me and my daughter look bad or like a charity case? Better yet, what if they asked me about Braxton? Lord knows that I wasn't ready for that. I was used to staying in the background. For me, that was a much safer place.

"What are you about to do?" Gunner inquired as we walked to the lot.

"I'm about to write down some goals. This job you gave me woke something in me that had been sleeping for quite some time," I confessed. "I may even wanna go back to school to get my bachelor's."

"Look at you! I like it. That confidence looks good on you, Oaklyn." Gunner smiled and leaned in to hug me.

"Thanks. It feels good, too."

As we said our goodbyes, I headed to the car and rushed home. I needed to send Braxton a couple of messages to make sure that Brazil would be presentable when he dropped her off at camp in the morning.

Like always, he replied: I got this. That man really worked my nerves at times. Instead of going back and forth with Braxton, I left it alone and went to bed.

I slept so hard that night that I missed two calls from Gunner and didn't see them until the next morning. Before I returned his call, I showered and took care of my personal hygiene. Once I was fully dressed in the red Stackin' Kickz sweatsuit and the red-and-white Jordans that Gunner got for all of the workers and volunteers to match, I dialed him up.

"This is so cute," I whispered to myself as I snapped a few pics while I waited for him to answer.

"Good morning!" I sang happily before he could get a word out.

"Oh, okay. I see somebody slept good. You greeted me with some of that good energy. I like that shit," Gunner teased and let me know that he was already at the gym, laying out the kids' red camp shirts he had personalized for each of them.

"I'm right behind you," I assured him and hopped into the Benz.

Arriving there in the next fifteen minutes, I parked and went inside to help set up the new stations for the kids to warm up. The rest of the equipment we needed had just come in.

When we finished, I walked back outside just as the news team arrived and unloaded their vans. Dipping around them with my head down to conceal my identity, I went toward the parking lot to wait for Braxton. My hope was to stop him before he got out of the car, but I was too late.

Surprisingly, he had arrived early. Before I got to him, he'd had time to park and get out with Brazil. Luckily, I ran up on him and was able intercept them. I didn't want no funk between Gunner and my baby daddy, especially since the media was already inside the gym, waiting to interview me and my daughter.

"What are you doing here, Oaklyn?" Braxton had the nerve to question me with a frown. He turned up one side of his lip and everything. Looked right at me like I was covered in shit. "You don't trust me enough to drop our daughter off on time?" he spat. "And what are you doing with that sweatsuit on? Showing all yo' damn curves."

"You're funny, Daddy. Mom works here with Gunner and Leslie. She knows all the drills, too."

"Girl, stop tryna clown yo' mom!" I teased Brazil and gently clenched her arm to try to rush her.

"What's the hurry?" Braxton asked.

"The media is inside, and they want to interview me and Brazil. I just came out to meet you to make sure her face was washed and her braids were good."

"Daddy hooked me up, Mom, and his friend did too. She came to the house yesterday and brought me a swimsuit because I didn't pack one. Plus, she got me this new outfit and sneakers, too. You like it?" Brazil did a full circle spin, then posed with one hand on her hip and the other held high with a peace sign. That little girl was something else.

"Look at you! You better not get in there and start showing out, Brazil. Act like a respectful young lady."

"She's only six," Braxton fussed.

"Seven next week, Daddy," Brazil reminded him.

"Either way, she's just a kid, Oaklyn. Don't make her grow up too fast." Braxton smirked, then decided to invite himself inside the gym. "They know I'm her father?"

"That right there is irrelevant right now, so step back. Like you told me: I got this. Everything is not always about you, Braxton."

While we stood there in a minor debate, Gunner came out looking for us. He interrupted our conversation to let us know that the reporters were set up and ready.

"Y'all ready?" Gunner checked with me and Brazil without even acknowledging Braxton, who stood there appearing too shocked to say a word. His actions said it all. The evil way he glanced back and forth between me and Gunner made me think that he was salty about us being dressed alike. Whatever it was, we didn't have time for it. We had to get inside. Without entertaining him further, we turned and walked away, and Braxton didn't follow. I guess he finally got the message.

"Gunner, will they let me dribble for them? I practiced this new move last night," Brazil cheered loudly as she ran ahead of us, then skipped side to side all the way inside the Dishman Center.

Leslie met us when we entered and escorted us to the spot they had set up for the interview. "You ready?"

"I guess so." I sighed nervously.

"While you talk to the reporter, Leslie and I will help Brazil warm up with the rest of the kids," Gunner clarified, then left me there alone to deal with the lights and camera. He knew how shy I was when it came to stuff like that, and he still left me.

Why, though?

In the middle of my mental rant, a young Black female reporter came and greeted me, then showed me the spot where we were to stand. "Hello, Ms. Jones. I'm Jasmine Devine, and I'll be asking you a few questions, but before we start, and off the record, Braxton Carter is your daughter's father, right?"

"Yes, and I hope we ain't about to discuss that on camera." I sulked.

"No, I wouldn't do that in a kid-friendly environment. That's why I'm asking you now." Jasmine giggled, then stepped a little closer to me. "Why ain't he here supporting?"

"I'm right here," Braxton called out anxiously. He couldn't wait to be seen and heard. That egotistical asshole. To show up like that after being informed that his presence wasn't needed was wild to me, but I wasn't about to make a scene. Shit, I didn't have to. Jasmine handled him just fine.

"Good to meet you, Braxton. You can stand right over there while I interview Oaklyn. It shouldn't take long." She smiled, then turned to me and gave me a wink.

It felt damn good to have someone stand up for me because Braxton would have surely taken over the show. Probably would've had me looking like a damn fool in the process. Thankfully, he didn't get the chance to do a thing because after Brazil got on the mic and bragged on Gunner's achievements and generosity, he left. He didn't even wait for the interview to end before he went storming out. I was sure someone had captured that on video too. No need to worry about it. Braxton left peacefully, and we had a wonderful day at camp. Those kids were awesome.

"You did a great job, and you're a great help here at the camp, too. The kids are lucky to have you. We all are," Gunner flirted as everyone grabbed a sack lunch and Gatorade that we provided for them.

By the time the kids ate and cleaned the tables, it was noon. The camp was over for the day. A half hour later, my mother showed up to get Brazil. During spring break, they usually traveled out of the state to do something special. This year, my daughter chose basketball instead, so they had to resort to doing a shopping spree instead. Right up Brazil's alley.

"I saw you guys on the news," my mother hollered happily as she ran to her only grandchild and scooped her off her feet. "I'm so proud of you."

"Thanks, Nana. It was so much fun. All of it is. I'm so happy Mom let me come here."

"Me too," I replied loudly.

Brazil skipped ahead of us, and my mother hurried to take advantage of a semi-private moment. "Girl, you sounded so good on that TV, and I couldn't be prouder of you. It was refreshing watching you take your life back after living in the shadow of Braxton. I love it, Oaklyn, but I can't help but worry about what he'll say when he hears you claiming to be a single parent."

"He can't say a thing, Mom."

"You're right, Oaklyn. He can't argue facts. He can only claim to be the man of the house if he's been the provider.

Oh, and buying you and Brazil those trinkets he's been giving you the past ten years don't count. I'm talking about stability. That's what you and Brazil both need."

"Don't forget loyalty and respect, Mama," I added, then tried to catch myself.

"Please don't tell me—" she started, giving me that look, but I cut her off.

"Then don't ask. I just wanna go on with my life. Maybe somewhere down the road our paths may cross again, but right now, I'm cool on Braxton. He's caused me too much pain, and I seem to have lost myself somewhere in the midst of it all. I just wanna find joy again."

"Well, I see some type of joy jumping between you and Gunner. What's up with you and him?" she pressed as we approached her car. "It seems like you two done got a little closer."

As I helped Brazil into the back seat, my mother and I wrapped up our conversation. "There's not enough to tell yet, but do me a favor," I requested.

"What's that?"

"Find out what's up with this Teagan chick that Braxton has been dating. She's been buying Brazil things and telling her stuff. I'm not sure exactly what it is, but I have a feeling that she's up to something. I just wanna know what it is before it gets out of hand."

"Say less." My mother laughed at her own lingo. "You know I'm all for it when it comes to my girls. Y'all all I got."

"Awwwww, Mama. We love you."

"Yes, we *love* you, Nana," Brazil chimed in.

That made me wonder how much of our conversation that little girl had really heard. She was always ear hustling. Just like her damn daddy.

Chapter Fourteen

Braxton Carter

"Man, do you believe that shit Oaklyn said on TV? She acted like I didn't even exist. Like I didn't even have a hand in raising Brazil. Like she was the one who taught her everything she knows," I complained to Chachi as we lifted weights at the Roy Pittman gym. After listening to how Oaklyn erased me out of their lives on the air, I had to work off some steam. That shit crushed me.

"Did you teach her to dribble?" Chachi clowned.

"Well, no, but Oaklyn didn't either. Her mother did."

"And she said that in the interview. You are over there worrying about the wrong shit, as usual. Focus on yo' shorty, Brazil. She's destined for great things. I'm not the only one who sees that shit, either."

"Yeah, she's become a local celebrity overnight," I bragged.

"Nah, she's gonna be a worldwide celebrity. Her video has played all over the country and is trending like crazy. Be proud of that, Brax, not upset with Oaklyn for being a great mom."

"What is up with y'all? First, Brazil acting like that nigga Gunner is a superhero, now you acting like Oaklyn is a supermom," I huffed and slammed the dumbbells onto the mat.

"You need to get a fucking grip, dude. You can't be in the spotlight all the time. It's time for the rest of your family to shine. Be happy for them."

How the hell could I cheer for them when they weren't including me in their happiness? It was as if Oaklyn had forgotten what we had, how happy we were.

"Whatever. Who said I wasn't happy for them?"

"You ain't gotta say it, Brax. Your salty vibes are leaking with your every word. You won't get shit straight movin' like that. Not while you're still fooling with Teagan for your own personal reasons."

I heard everything that Chachi said, but at the end of the day, Oaklyn still wasn't talking to me, and all Teagan's money and gifts couldn't take the pain away. I needed my family back.

"What am I gonna do now? Just sit back and watch that nigga take my girl and my daughter away from me?" I whined and held my emotions in check.

"Step your game up. Keep apologizing until she accepts it, but while you're doing that, get yourself together. Use some of that money you made to get your own spot instead of staying in Teagan's parents' Airbnb. I know it saves you money, but that ain't important right now. Getting things right with Oaklyn and Brazil is all that should matter. Keep telling yourself, and you'll be good."

"So, you're telling me to give Teagan the studio back?"

"It's in your name, but I can't tell you what to do."

"What would you do?" I pressed Chachi.

"I would sell it and use the money to get another studio. That way, there won't be a tie there. If she gave it to you out the kindness of her heart, then there shouldn't be a problem."

"And if she didn't?"

"Then she will play the hand she was dealt, and y'all may have to handle it in court. That, or just give it back.

Either way, someone is gonna lose. Remember, this cold game of life teaches us lessons constantly. This is just one of them."

"What's the lesson I was supposed to learn?" I probed.

"Honestly, there's a bunch of them, but I'll start with the most obvious. Do unto others as you would have them do unto you. That's what you should've learned."

"What's that supposed to mean?"

"Brax, it means that if you're in a relationship, respect it. You should always treat your woman how you would want her to treat you. For example, how would you feel if you found out today that Oaklyn was sleeping with Gunner? What would make it any different than you sleeping with Teagan and all the other women? You can't expect her to be faithful when you're not."

My chest tightened with just the thought of Gunner making love to my girl. Damn, I had really fucked up this time, and it was killing me inside. "You're right, man, and that shit would mess me up," I admitted as I sucked up the tears threatening to fall. "I don't even wanna think about Oaklyn sleeping with nobody else besides me."

"Well, how you think Oaklyn felt when Teagan told her that you guys slept together?" Chachi was getting in his therapist mode, and I didn't want to hear it. All I wanted to know was how I could fix it.

"Fuck all that shit you saying, Chachi. Just tell me how to get my girl back. That's all I want you to do."

"I just told you. Weren't you listening?" He laughed as we walked to the locker room to shower and change.

Once we finished, we met back out in the lobby of the gym, then walked out together. That was when Oaklyn called me. Since this was my chance to talk to her and apologize again, I cut the conversation short with my boy. I didn't want to talk in front of him.

"I'll catch you later, Chachi." I waved as I jogged to my ride and climbed in, so that I could take the call in private.

"What's good?" I answered.

"Just calling to give you the information on the charity game this weekend. It's gonna be a big event, and I'm sure Brazil will want you there," she explained.

"Yeah, she told me about it. I'll be there if she wants me to."

"Why would you say it like that, Braxton? It's not like she's pushing you out of her life."

"But you are." I sighed and sat fidgeting in my idling car. "I love you, Oaklyn, and I wanna make things right between us. I'm ready to stop all this nonsense, and I'm looking for a house now. Just give me a few more weeks and *please . . . please* tell me that you ain't gave up on me, baby."

"I wish I could tell you that, Braxton, but right now, I can't. I need time to work on me instead of living in the shadows of your fame."

"Don't you love me?" I questioned. My stomach tightened as I waited for an answer. It seemed like it took forever.

"I will always love you, Braxton, but I'm not *in love* with you."

A sudden case of nausea came over me, and I could feel the hot liquid rising in my throat. To suppress it, I grabbed my water bottle from the middle drink holder and guzzled down half of it.

"Is it because of Teagan? Because if it is, I can leave her alone today. I will never see or talk to her again," I promised.

"If that were the case, you wouldn't still be fooling with her, Braxton. I can't even lie. Your cheating ways had become so normal that I grew numb to it. I used to be so in love with you and would do anything for you, but you took my love for granted too many times."

"I'm sorry, Oaklyn. I can't say it enough. I learned my lesson, and I want my family back," I pleaded.

"I'm sorry too, Braxton, but I'm over it. I'm over you," Oaklyn replied, then ended the call.

With no more fight left in me, I released the floodgates. Never did I think that I could hurt this badly. The anxiety that came over me was indescribable, and it scared me. Was I really about to lose Oaklyn?

No longer in control of my tears, I used the back of my hand to swipe them away as I drove from the gym and headed to the Airbnb property. All the way there, I beat myself up about fucking around with all the females that I had. The numerous brief encounters gave me nothing more than a few minutes of pleasure. It definitely wasn't worth breaking my bond with Oaklyn. How could I be so stupid? Why would I go out and cheat on a good woman who had everything that I needed at home and more?

Damn, as soon as I thought about how my baby mama got down in the bedroom, I wanted to break down again. I would be damned if I let her go to another nigga. Not after ten years and a daughter. Nope, I wasn't about to let that shit happen. Ready to do whatever it took to get Oaklyn back, I decided to break it off with Teagan, and if I had to give her that studio back, so be it. That's how serious I was.

"Let me get this chick on the line," I mumbled to myself as I arrived at the Airbnb and packed all my stuff.

When my last suitcase was stuffed to the max and I still couldn't get Teagan on the phone, I simply left the key in the box outside and then went and got a hotel room. I would've stayed with Uncle Pete until I found a permanent spot, but he had this young chick shacking up with him. No, thank you.

"Residence Inn by the Lloyd Center is gonna have to do," I whispered as I sat in my car and paid for a week to get one of their two-bedroom suites through my Hotel Tonight app. It was the go-to when I wanted a room at the last minute, and this time it included breakfast.

After I backed out of the garage, I closed it, then stopped to put the opener in the lockbox before I got up out of there. I didn't want to have to go back there for anything.

"Here this chick go now," I mumbled when I saw that Teagan finally hit me back. "What's good?"

"I just called to tell you that I have a lot going on with my family right now. Can I call you back in about an hour or so?"

"That's cool." After I replied, I hung up and set my cell down. With Teagan too tied up to listen to my truths, I put dealing with her on the back burner and began to focus on Oaklyn again. I needed to talk to her.

"Maybe I should just go over there and beg her to take me back." I laughed as I drove toward her house. "I can remind her about how we first met and how much in love we were."

As badly as I wanted to go over there and do just that, I opted for something more sensible: dropping her flowers, her favorite chocolates, and a few gifts. Sure, it was probably a lame-ass thing to do, but I was desperate, and I needed to get her attention. I just prayed that it would work.

Placing my pride aside, I ran around town and gathered up a bunch of gifts, then drove over to Oaklyn's. When I was on her block, I decided to park on the street instead of in the lot, since she had me trespassed off the property. With my hands full, I strolled over to the complex, trying to talk myself out of knocking on her door.

Another rejection would really fuck me up, especially if she did that shit to my face.

"What the fuck is this?" I whispered as I spotted Gunner walking Oaklyn to her door.

When I noticed that he left his truck running, I assumed that he wasn't going in with her. That was a good thing.

"Today was a good day," I heard Oaklyn speak as I stayed behind the tall row of bushes at the end of the walkway. I looked like a damn fool holding flowers and gift bags for a chick who stood there checking for another man. I couldn't believe this shit. The more Gunner grinned in Oaklyn's face, the more I wanted to go knock his ass out. It took everything in me to stand there hidden and listen to those two flirting without reacting.

"Every day that I get to spend with you is a great day, beautiful," Gunner replied with a little more bass.

My fists balled so tight that a few of the stems on the roses were crushed. Feeling like such a fool, I quietly set down everything that I was holding and gently slid it all behind the last bush. When I glanced up as I rose, I became frozen in place. Oaklyn really let Gunner kiss her. Did she really have her left leg kicked back like that? What the hell was going on?

As I gritted my teeth, I planted my feet in the dirt to stop myself from walking over there to fight that muthafucka for putting his hands on my girl. If I did that, then I would surely go to jail. To play it safe, I held my position and waited for the perfect opportunity to check this nigga.

Chapter Fifteen

Gunner West

A smile always spread across my face after getting some lip service from Oaklyn. It was something about her kisses that made me hold her and not want to let her go.

"I guess I'll see you at camp tomorrow." She giggled as she backed into her apartment without losing eye contact.

"Unless you wanna see me later. You did say that Brazil decided to stay with your mother tonight, right?"

"She sure did. I'll call you after I shower and change to see what you're doing. Cool?"

"Cool," I replied and watched Oaklyn disappear behind the closed door.

With my head on cloud nine, I walked down the pathway, grinning so wide that I could feel my cheeks crack. As I contemplated going home, I thought about going to get something sweet to eat. Oaklyn loved those little cakes from She She's Bakery on MLK and Stafford. It wasn't too far, so I decided to run by there and pick up the variety box.

"Hey, can I speak to you for a minute?" I heard a voice come from the shadows before I reached my truck.

As the figure stepped out into the light, I saw that it was Braxton, Oaklyn's ex. The way he mean-mugged me, I assumed that he had seen the exchange of kisses and wanted to confront me about it. No biggie, because I stayed ready for whatever.

"What's up?" I asked as I folded my arms and sized him up. Even though I had him by three or four inches, dude was rocked up and may have had me by about twenty pounds or so. I wasn't worried, though. I was in the best shape of my life.

"Hey, man. I just wanted to make sure you know the history behind me and Oaklyn. The ten years that we've been together—"

"Let me stop you right there, partna. What do you think I should know? About how Oaklyn and her mother Draya met you and your uncle out on the streets? How you sang Oaklyn a song? How they helped you get a place? How you and her fell in love and had Brazil? Or how you've been continually breaking her heart for years by cheating on her?" I asked calmly. "Is that what you want me to know, Braxton?"

"Since you know so fucking much, you should know that you pushing up on my baby mama is interfering with us getting back together."

"Does Oaklyn know that?"

"Does she know what?" Braxton asked as he eased closer.

"Does she know that y'all are working on getting back together? Because I didn't get that memo, man." I laughed right in his face.

This cat had jokes, but as long as he didn't come within arm's reach, he would be safe. If he did, then I hoped the fool knew how to bob and weave because a punch was definitely coming his way.

To avoid all that shit, I just told Braxton that I wished him the best of luck. "I respect you because you're Brazil's father, but don't get this shit twisted. I'm never gonna let you disrespect me or Oaklyn behind your insecurities."

"Did this nigga just call me insecure?" Braxton mumbled under his breath as he took another step closer.

One more and I was ready to lay him on his back. "Look, I'm diggin' Oaklyn, and she's diggin' me. If you have a problem with that, I don't know what to tell you, bruh," I chuckled some more as I shook my head and strolled slowly to my ride without turning my back to him. Love was a crazy thing, and folks were known to do crazy things in the name of it. Hopefully, this was not the situation.

"After this camp is over, stay away from my family," Braxton warned loudly as I climbed into my truck.

While I sat behind the wheel with the engine running, I rolled down my passenger window and bent down so I could see his face. "As bad as I hate to break it to you, *bruh*, that ain't yo' call. It's Oaklyn's."

"And I've made my choice," she said as she appeared at the end of the walkway. "I don't even know why you're over here when you know you're trespassed off this property, Braxton. Brazil is with my mother, and there's no reason why you should be here. I told you on the phone what was up, so you shouldn't even have to question that shit."

"So, you sayin' you choose this nigga over me? The father of your child? The one who's been there through thick and thin?" Braxton replied aggressively enough to bring me back out of my ride.

"Just go, Braxton," Oaklyn urged.

Being a little overprotective, I rushed to her side and stood partially in front of her. "You heard the lady."

"You hear this, nigga! This is my girl, and—"

"We are not together, Braxton, so do like I said and leave before the neighbors start coming out and call the cops. Just go."

"You know what? I'm gonna go, but this shit ain't over by a long shot, Oaklyn. I love you, and I know you love me—"

"I already told you, Braxton!" She cut him off, then turned to go back to her apartment. When she clenched my hand, I followed her inside.

"I'm so sorry," she apologized just as we heard the doorbell ring.

Fearing it would be Braxton acting up, I accompanied her to the door.

"What the hell is this?" Oaklyn smirked as she picked up the flowers and gift bags that her baby daddy had left for her. It was all nice and everything, but she didn't seem to think so. She proved it by throwing all of it in the garbage without even opening it up. "I'm so sick of dealing with him. I swear."

"Is this the first time you and him broke up like this?" I probed.

"Nope, but it's definitely the longest, and to be honest, I don't miss it. All the worrying about who Braxton was with and what he was doing. I never really trusted him after the first time I caught him cheating. I just dealt with it because I loved him so much."

"Don't you still love him?"

"Gunner, let me tell you like I told him. I love him, but I'm not *in love* with him. There's a big difference."

"You're right about that, but you know you're gonna have to deal with him for the rest of your life. Y'all got a child together," I reminded Oaklyn.

"I plan on working out a better visitation plan. Other than that, why would I have to deal with him?"

"Did you see how he just showed up over here? You think he won't do that again?" I pressed.

"Hopefully, I won't have to worry about it too much longer. I have a job at the camp, and I applied for a position over at the Dishman Center. With a steady job and a little hard work, I can get off housing and move into a better place," she explained. "I wanna move somewhere where Brazil can play safely outside. Maybe even have a small yard or something."

All the things that Oaklyn desired were quite simple— just a place and a safe environment. I could help her with that, if only she were willing to let me.

"What if I told you that I could possibly get you into a house? My pops buys older properties and fixes them up for resale. Every year around this time, he chooses a family to donate a house to. I can put in a good word, which means it would be as good as done."

"Gunner! I couldn't accept nothing like that. You're talking about a whole house!" She gasped and shook her head. "I would never be able to repay you."

"Didn't you hear me say that my pops donates the house? That means that you don't have to worry about anything but the utilities and the property taxes. Just think of it as good Karma. You and your mother helped Braxton and his uncle get housing when they were homeless. This is just good luck coming full circle."

"Are you serious right now, Gunner?"

"Hold on." I got on my phone and dialed my pops up to explain Oaklyn's situation. Once I mentioned her daughter, he started with the interrogation. I couldn't answer one question well before he shot another one my way.

"I'm over here now, Pops. I just wanted you to know her housing situation and how it's affecting Brazil," I added before attempting to wrap up the call.

"Say no more. The house is as good as hers. Send me her information so I can get all the paperwork in order. We'll be announcing it after the charity game next weekend," he enlightened me.

"Thanks, Pops, and I'll talk to you later."

I let Oaklyn know what he had said, and she started crying right there. "I can't believe this, Gunner."

"I told you. That's that good Karma," I reminded her. "Embrace the blessings, love."

"How about I embrace you?" she teased as she came over to me and wrapped her arms around my waist.

As our bodies intertwined, her cell phone began to bounce across the table. Oaklyn ignored it and welcomed the big kiss I planted on her lips. This time, it turned into much more than that, and the next thing I knew, we were grinding on the sofa. Without a condom, I wasn't about to go all the way. Not this soon, and especially not with her baby daddy lurking somewhere nearby. Nope, I didn't feel comfortable.

"Why don't you come spend the night at my place? You've never been there, and this would be the perfect time. You could bring your swimsuit so we can get in the hot tub. It's a beautiful night," I said, trying to persuade her. "No pressure, of course."

"I'm going to my room to pack my bag right now. Give me three minutes." Oaklyn giggled excitedly.

Those were the three minutes I needed to get my dick to go down. It was so erect that it was ready to bust out of my pants.

"Calm down, boy." I laughed to myself as I got up, shoved my hand in my boxers briefs, and situated my manhood. To help it deflate quicker, I walked around the living room to check out the few family pictures she had hung on the wall. When I got to the bookshelf near the kitchen, I noticed an older photo of Oaklyn with Braxton. They looked so happy back then.

Why would he mess up a good thing?

Oaklyn was a great woman with a lot of potential to be something greater. He had to see that shit, and so did she.

"Okay, I'm ready!" Oaklyn shouted as she heaved a pink-flowered duffle over her shoulder. It was so heavy that she nearly tipped over. Moving quickly, I scooped it up and we laughed together as I took her load.

"What the hell you got in here?"

"My personal stuff, something to sleep in, a couple of swimsuits, and my sweatsuit to wear to camp in the morning. By the way, do you want me to drive the other car tonight, or you'll bring me back here to get it?"

"Why? You don't wanna arrive at the camp together?" I teased her with a kiss and grabbed her hand to leave.

"Oh, I was just tryna protect yo' image. I'm good," she assured me with a point of a finger and a twirl of the neck. She was so damn funny.

"Come on, Oaklyn. You're riding with me."

"Gotcha." She smiled and locked the door behind us.

Instead of looking out for Braxton, I kept my eye on Oaklyn. I wanted to see if she was nervous. "You good?"

"Like I said, I'm great." Oaklyn cheered and held her hands up high, then spun around with a smile. "I'm wonderful, Gunner."

The display of excitement got me amped, too, and it made the drive to my house pleasurable. The way she rubbed on my thigh and the way I rubbed on hers while talking about her hopes and dreams of being self-sufficient totally relaxed me.

"We're almost there," I informed her as I turned off the main road.

"You live in this neighborhood?" she blurted out as I entered the code on the keypad. "I haven't even been in a gated community before."

"It's not like it's the lifestyles of the rich and famous out here. It just means the folks living here pay more homeowner association fees to have extra security and amenities."

Now sitting straight up in her seat, Oaklyn gazed out the window at all the incredibly nice landscaping of the area. "The waterfall at the entrance was so beautiful, and the fancy streetlights make me feel like I'm somewhere special."

"You are." I grinned and pulled into my roundabout driveway. "Let me show you around."

As I used the app on my cell to open the door and cut off the alarm, we entered the foyer. Oaklyn gasped loudly, then covered her mouth to stop herself.

That was just the beginning.

Chapter Sixteen

Oaklyn Jones

After touring Gunner's estate, I was in total awe, so much so that I cut my ringer off without a care in the world. That way, I could spend a wonderful night with no distractions, starting with the wine in the hot tub.

Whoo-wee!

"You are making me feel so special right now," I whispered and looked into Gunner's eyes.

"You are special, and no matter where this thing between us goes, I'm gonna make sure you know that shit." He smiled and pecked my lips. "Oh, and while you're planning on getting another job and going back to school, you may wanna think about being Brazil's manager if she plans on pursuing a basketball career. Leslie sent me a text not that long ago stating that she already had a few companies call her about your daughter."

"Companies?" I asked, not quite understanding.

"Yes, companies that want to endorse her. Use her to promote their products. They pay quite a lot for contracts—"

"My baby will be seven next week. I don't even want to think about her growing up that fast," I replied honestly. "Right now, all I want to do is enjoy this moment with you."

"There could be many more, if you like, Oaklyn," Gunner said, making me blush. It had been so long since I felt that way, and I couldn't get enough of it. "I'm really feeling you."

"And I'm really feeling you," I repeated sexily as I scooted as close to him as I could.

Using his upper body strength, Gunner lifted me as if I were as light as a feather, then gently sat me on his lap. As his hands fondled my backside, the jets directly beneath me shot straight through my thin bikini bottoms and penetrated every sensitive spot between my thighs, from my asshole to my coochie, right on up to my clit.

"Shit." I giggled as I began grinding on him.

Gunner's dick plumped up instantly, and between the aggressive water irrigation and the thrusting of our hips, I squirted in my bikini bottoms. It had been too long.

"Damn, I want you," I whispered as I felt the next orgasm build up. "Shit, Gunner, ooh, ahh." As I squeezed my upper legs together tightly, I climaxed for the second time—with absolutely no penetration. Wow!

"I want you too, baby," he responded quietly, holding me long enough for my coochie to calm down, because to be honest, that muthafucka was still jumping.

"Come inside with me," Gunner mumbled between kisses as he climbed out, then helped me out so that he could wrap the oversized towel around my voluptuous body.

As he held me close, we entered the beautiful basement that was fully equipped with a bar and entertainment area. When he kept going, I stopped him and asked if we could stay down there. Everything was so comfortable and inviting. The nice, soft music playing on the speaker system, along with the oversized furniture, fireplace, and dim lighting, set the mood perfectly. While I walked in a daze over to the bar and poured another glass of wine, Gunner ran in the downstairs bathroom and came right back out with a small bag and a couple of dry towels. After laying one down, he gently drew me over to lie on it.

Unequipped with the proper words, I stretched out on my back and welcomed Gunner's kisses. They went from my lips to my neck, right down to my lower half, where he took his time removing my bottoms. The excitement got the best of me when his tongue touched my clit, but I held back my scream, clenched my jaw, and moaned instead. This shit was incredible! It was like he knew just where my special spot was and took his time to please it.

Shit!

The way Gunner swirled his tongue around my little man on the boat to tease it, then sucked it just enough to make me cum again, drove me crazy. By now, I was delirious and horny for the dick. I had to have it.

To get what I wanted, I had to speak up. "You have protection?" I whispered.

"Yeah." He smiled and kissed me once again before he retrieved the little bag that he had brought with him from the bathroom. As he stood there opening the package, my eyes focused on his manhood. I had to see it as soon as he brought that monster out.

"Damn!" I hissed playfully as Gunner capped his dick. It was so amazingly breathtaking that I almost wanted to return the head but couldn't because I was too anxious for the D. Taking control, I reversed positions, and now he was the one on his back. It was time for me to ride. Carefully climbing on top of him, I lifted my 220-pound frame. The length and width of Gunner's penis required me to ease up and down on it until I could finally take it all. I definitely wasn't used to all the dick he was dishing out.

"Damn, you feel so good, and I'm really feeling you, baby. . . . Fuck. I'm so glad we met and that we're here together. . . . Shit," he spoke while looking into my eyes.

His words penetrated my heart while his dick penetrated my pussy, and within seconds, I climaxed. Once
again. Denying me the chance to catch my breath, Gunner
flipped me over into missionary style. Now, it was his
turn to release his load, and it didn't take long.

"Sorry, baby," he whispered as he pulled off the condom and wiped himself off before cuddling with me.

"For what?"

"For bustin' so damn fast. I guess I was just that excited," he admitted with a laugh.

"Everything about that encounter was perfect. Nothing
like what I expected, but great nonetheless," I teased and
kissed his lips.

"It really was, but I was hesitant."

"Why?"

"Because, honestly, I was afraid to jump into the phys-
ical part of the relationship when things with you and
Braxton may not be over."

"Oh, it's over, boo," I cracked. "Trust me when I tell you,
Gunner. I would've never slept with you if I was still in
love with Braxton. That's the truth."

"Let me ask you this, Oaklyn. Am I the first guy you've
slept with?"

"I haven't slept with anyone else since I first started
dating Braxton ten years ago. There were so many times
that I wanted to, just so I could get back at him, but I
could never bring myself to do it. To me, sex is more than
just a good feeling. So much more. It's passionate and
personal, and I couldn't share that with anybody that I
didn't care about."

"So, you care about me?" Gunner pressed with a grin.

"Of course I do. How could I not, when you've been like
a knight in shining armor ever since I met you? That shit
feels good when you've been the one saving folks all your
life," I explained truthfully.

As we lay there talking and cuddling, I threw up a silent prayer to thank the Man above for all of His blessings. I was truly grateful.

"Someone's sleepy," Gunner spoke as he lifted me from the sofa and escorted me up to the master bedroom. It was more like a big bonus room with space for his full living room set and a king-sized bed.

"Do you want to sleep in here with me, or would you be more comfortable in the guestroom?"

"I'm good right here with you," I confessed as I followed him to the bed and climbed in.

Hugged up in a cozy position, I drifted off and didn't wake up until the next morning, when his alarm went off.

"Good morning, beautiful." Gunner greeted me with a grin and peck.

That was all he got until I rushed into his adjoining bathroom and freshened up. "You coming in here with me?" I asked playfully as I started the shower and watched the water shoot from several different heads.

"You ain't gotta ask me twice," Gunner replied as he quickly joined me.

With him there with me, the shower took way longer than we expected and almost made us late to camp. That caused us to drive up at the same time as my mother did with Brazil. It wasn't so bad when she busted me up as soon as I got out of the car with Gunner, but when she pulled off and Braxton pulled up unexpectedly, everything really got awkward.

"Can you walk Brazil inside, Gunner, please? I'll be in there shortly."

"You sure?" Gunner checked, making Braxton frown up.

"Yes," I assured him.

To save the day, Brazil made things easier when she grabbed Gunner's hand and rushed him away. That halted her daddy from acting a fool.

"What are you even doing here, Braxton?"

"Since you ain't answering my calls and you ain't been home all night . . ."

"What?" I gasped, realizing that my baby daddy had been spying on me. For what, though? What we once had was long gone, and that meant that I owed him no explanation about where I went or what I did.

"Did you think I would just let our relationship fade, Oaklyn? We have ten years and a child together."

"And I shouldn't have stayed that long, Braxton. I should've left yo' black ass after that China chick you messed with last year. I'm just thankful you ain't never gave me a disease or had a baby on me."

"I would never do that shit, Oaklyn," Braxton whined, and I almost let it get to me, but I held back because I realized that it was the same dramatic shit that he said every single time we broke up.

It wasn't like that this time. This time, I was done.

"None of that shit matters now, Braxton. It's over, and I'm not even upset. Actually, I'm relieved that I no longer have to worry about who you're with or what you're doing. That right there makes it easier for me to sleep at night."

"Are you really doing this to me, Oaklyn? You're not giving us another chance? Not even for Brazil? She deserves a mother and father."

"And she'll always have both of us. Just not at the same time, Braxton. You gotta just let me go," I urged. As I felt myself become a bit choked up, I knew I had to cut it short. He needed to leave, and I needed to get to the gym and help out. The other kids were already showing up.

"I'm not about to let you go without a fight, Oaklyn."

"Look, Braxton, I gotta go," I huffed and grew impatient. "There ain't much else I can tell you other than it's over. You're free to stay with Teagan, and there's absolutely no hard feelings." Maybe I shouldn't have added that last sentence because it began another argument, and I wasn't up for it. I had to get inside the Dishman Center.

"The shit with Teagan was strictly for financial gain."

"Is that supposed to make me feel better?" I smirked and cut my eyes. "It makes you sound like a damn whore."

As I walked off, Braxton ran up behind me. "Wait—"

"Get the hell outta here!" I spun around and snapped before he reached me. "If I have to tell you again, it's gonna be all bad." The warning came from my lips harshly, and I didn't have a bit of remorse behind it. I was tired of Braxton and his games. I wanted no part of them, or him either, for that matter.

"Can we at least talk this weekend?"

"Brazil is playing at that charity event this weekend, and I'll be tied up with—"

"You'll be tied up with that nigga?"

"Bye, Braxton!" I yelled out with my back turned to him as I stormed off to the entrance of the building. Thankfully, he didn't follow behind me. That gave me a chance to calm down and place a smile on my face before entering the gym.

Chapter Seventeen

Teagan Hoffman

After Braxton left the Airbnb with absolutely no warning, I knew something had to be wrong, so I went looking for him. Besides the studio, I had nowhere to search except for his homeboy Chachi's house. That night, I shot over there and staked the place out. By daybreak, with no luck, I decided to go home and continue calling Braxton. It wasn't until after eight the next morning that he finally answered.

"What's up?" He greeted me dryly.

"Are you okay?"

"No, I just left the Dishman Center trying to see Brazil, and Oaklyn don't wanna hear shit I gotta say. I swear, it seems like my whole world is crumbling beneath me," he sulked.

With Braxton being in distress, I rushed to get into savior mode. Whatever he needed. "Let's just meet up at the studio and talk about it. Or just go to sing and release some shit from your mind. It's your safe place, right?" I reminded him.

"Yeah, you may be right."

"I'll get you some breakfast delivered."

"And a bottle. I need a damn drink." Braxton sighed heavily.

"Don't worry about a thing, Brax. I gotcha." Determined to go and get all of his breakfast favorites and three bottles after we hung up, I got up and got on the ball. On the liquor store run, I picked up one pineapple Cîroc, one Apple Crown, and one Ace. Then I picked up the order I had placed at Mississippi Delta before I headed to the studio.

Praying that Braxton was okay, I shot right on over there and parked next to his ride, then went inside with my hands full. "Here you go."

Braxton spun around in the chair and drew his shades off, revealing his red, puffy eyes. It looked as if he'd been crying for days.

"What's wrong?" I gasped and went to hug him.

His arms squeezed me so tightly that I could feel his pain. It was strong enough to bring tears to my eyes. To allow Braxton his moment, I stayed quiet and let him hold me for as long as he needed to. I didn't want to disturb him, so I stayed quiet and waited for him to speak.

"I think I lost my family," he finally said. "I really fucked up this time."

"Brazil will always be your baby girl. No one can change that. And as far as Oaklyn goes, I thought y'all were done over a month ago."

"We've been split up, but I thought we would get back together like we always did. Not this time, though. She said she's done, and she means it. I can feel the shit," he confessed sadly.

As Braxton lowered his face into his cupped palms, my heart went out to him. What could I do to make him feel better without sounding bitter about him being broken up behind Oaklyn? Not wanting to overstep, I stayed on neutral ground and kept my comments to myself. I just wanted to make sure that he knew that I was there for him and would never betray him.

"Well, I know we're not together, Braxton, but I'm here as a friend, and if you need anything, I gotcha."

"Why are you being so fucking nice to me when I'm sitting here crying over another female? You must think I'm pathetic." He sniffled and dried his face.

"I think you're a beautiful person who got his heart broken. We all go through it, but you gotta know, life ain't over, Braxton. You have your health, you have your career, and you have me. I'll always be in your corner. I believe in you," I admitted shamelessly.

"You barely know me, and I don't know anything about you, Teagan. You live in some big mansion and got big money, and I came from the streets."

"See, that's the type of thinking you gotta change, Braxton. It ain't about where you came from. It's about where you're going and *baby, baby*! With a voice like that and all that charisma that you hold, you are definitely going straight to the top. You just gotta work hard and keep the faith. Start believing in yourself again."

"You make it seem so simple." Braxton laughed as he got up and hugged me again. "What did I do to deserve a friend like you?"

"You must've done something right because friends like me don't come around too often," I teased and pecked his lips.

It caught him off guard, but I think that was just what he needed. He needed to feel loved, and I had a whole lot of love to give him. Maybe it was wrong for me to take advantage of Braxton's weak moment, but I wanted him. All of him.

"Fuck!" he grunted as I dropped to my knees, drew out his semi-erect shaft, placed my warm mouth on it, and quickly brought it to life. Bobbing my head to the mellow R&B track that played in the background, I swirled my tongue and hummed as I gripped his hips. Enabled to control the rhythm of the thrusts, I slowed down and increased my suction.

Braxton lasted all of three minutes before he begged me to stop. "Let me feel you," he whispered as he lifted me to my feet and turned me around, then bent me over.

Using my hands to grip the sides of the digital audio workstation, I threw my ass back to match his powerful thrusts. It was as if he took out all his frustrations on my insides, and I welcomed it all. The dynamics of the encounter had me climaxing multiple times. It felt so good. So right.

"Shit," Braxton grunted as he released and immediately pulled out to apologize. "I'm sorry. I got caught up in the moment and didn't even think about strapping up. Fuck!"

"As long as you ain't got shit, I ain't worried." I laughed and went into the private bathroom to clean myself up before I brought him a soapy rag.

"Although that shit is very important, I wasn't talking about giving you an STD or an incurable disease. I'm more concerned with giving you a damn baby. Unless you're on the pill or some shit."

"No, I'm not on the pill or any other birth control. No, I don't have any STDs or incurable diseases either." I smirked and took the washrag from him, then walked into the bathroom, opened the hamper, and tossed it in. "As for the baby, I think it's a bit soon for anything like that."

Why did I stand there and tell that bold-faced lie? Shit, if I found out that I was pregnant by Braxton tomorrow, I would jump for joy. Little did he know I loved him—everything about him. The only thing that worried me was his loyalty. The last thing I wanted was for him to do me like he did Oaklyn because I wasn't so forgiving, and neither was my family. Getting involved with me came with stipulations. I had found that out the hard way, and so had Walter.

"How about let's not worry ourselves with all that right now? How about I go in the sound booth and blow this new song I wrote? Cason is on his way to work the boards."

"Here he comes now," I chanted, watching the security screen that displayed the front of the building as the alarm chirped.

Cason keyed the code in and entered into the lobby, then immediately joined us. "Hey, what's good?"

Once the greetings were out of the way, both Cason and Braxton took their places, and magic was made. Real magic.

"Wow." I gasped as I listened to the lyrics of the sad love song that he beautifully belted out. It was so touching that I couldn't fight the tears. Even though I knew Braxton was singing about his relationship with Oaklyn, it showed me how big his heart was, how loving he could be. Now, if he would just see what I saw in him, his career would take off. He just had to believe in himself and know that there was so much more to life. All Braxton knew was our hometown of Portland, Oregon. He needed to explore the world and see what it had to offer.

Don't get me wrong. I loved the City of Roses; I just loved to travel more.

Chapter Eighteen

Braxton Carter

Did I just fuck that girl raw again? Damn!

I seriously had to stop moving so carelessly without considering the consequences, especially with the bad luck that I had been having. If I weren't mistaken, I would say that Karma was on a nigga, and I couldn't seem to dodge the bitch. All the wrong that I had done to Oaklyn came back to me tenfold and slowly broke me down. If this was anything close to how bad she felt when she caught me cheating on her, she had to be torn up and tired.

They say when a woman gets fed up, there is nothing a man can do about it. Was that shit really true? Instead of worrying about it, I needed to do something to soothe my soul. I needed to sing. Everything that I wanted to tell Oaklyn was expressed through the new song that I wrote. It was about how sorry I was for breaking her heart, and how mine was broken too.

When I finished, I had a good feeling that Teagan understood the song was written for my ex, because tears were streaming down her cheeks. I was unsure whether the crying was due to hurt feelings or if she had been touched by what I sang, so I remained silent and waited for her to speak first.

"That was amazing, Braxton." She smiled and came to embrace me.

"You are always surprising me." I laughed as I drew back and gave her a quick peck on the lips.

"What?" Teagan giggled and dried her tears with her free hand. Once she wiped the wetness onto her skirt, she shyly looked my way.

"You never judge me, do you?" I questioned.

"What right do I have?"

"Okay, I see you," I said.

"I see you too," she repeated with a serious expression. "And I believe in you, boo."

"Thanks, Teagan. I really appreciate you."

Just as we broke apart, Cason got our attention by hollering about an offer that he had just received on one of his social media platforms. "Man, Braxton. Urban Records may wanna sign you, boi. They're already talking about you joining their West Coast tour since you're more popular in Washington, Oregon, and California. So, all the major cities."

"How they hear about me?"

"Oh, I forgot to tell you that I was live streaming when you just did that song."

"We ain't even record that shit yet.

"Yes, *we* did." Cason laughed. "I record everything. The tracks were already laid, and all it needed was the vocals. Nigga, you did that shit! We ain't gotta change a thing."

"Are you kidding me?" I gasped.

"I'm dead-ass."

"Nah, Cason."

"Yes, Braxton, and my fault on going live without telling you, but I had a feeling if I did, then you wouldn't let loose like you did. Man, I'm telling you. You did that shit. Feel my arm! I still got the goosebumps from the passion you put in that piece."

"Oh, wow, thanks, man," I replied as I felt my luck beginning to spin around for the better. This was the opportunity that I had been waiting on for years, and I wanted to be ecstatic, but something was missing. It was the one person who really needed to be celebrating with me. My one true love, Oaklyn.

"This video is gettin' mad play, Brax," Cason continued as he showed me and Teagan the number of hits on his cell. It was unbelievable.

"Oh, yes! You did do that shit, and I'm so happy for you," Teagan cheered and leaped into my arms.

Before I could object, we were in an intimate embrace. While I held her close, I realized that this chick was genuinely down for me. That was just what I needed right now, and I was glad to have her in my life—as a friend, though. Nothing more. Not until I knew for sure that Oaklyn was truly done with me for good.

"What do you want me to tell dude?" Cason blurted out loudly to regain my full attention.

"Shit, set up a meeting. Let's see what he's talking about."

While Cason handled that, I freed Teagan from my grip and held onto her hands, then stared down at her. Millions of things must've gone through my mind at that moment, but to avoid overthinking the matter, I chose to go with the first thing that fell from my mouth.

"You know, Teagan, I don't know where this is going . . . this thing between us." I smiled and withdrew one of my hands to point my finger from her to me. "But know I'm digging this friendship we're building."

"Me too, Braxton. Me too." Teagan's excessive blushing brought about a beautiful glow to her milk chocolate skin as she flashed her genuine smile, which lit up the room.

Shaking free from the momentary daze that overtook me, I led Teagan by the hand so that we could leave the studio and celebrate. I felt that if I allowed her to occupy my time for the remainder of the day, it could possibly keep my mind off Oaklyn. It may have been far from a solution to my problem, but it was a temporary fix. That, I could work with.

"Let's go eat and get some drinks to get this party started. I'll even drive. You can leave your car here," Teagan suggested as we walked outside to the lot.

It was a nice, warm spring day, and the sun shone brightly. There was no rain in the forecast, and that was rare for Portland, even in the springtime. Since the weather permitted, we chose a small, minority-owned diner on MLK and sat out on the patio facing the street. The view enabled us to watch the busy two-way traffic and the pedestrians visiting the many specialty shops.

Enjoying the food, drink, and company, I began to loosen up. Next thing I knew, Teagan and I were toasting to everything good that we could think of. During the celebration, we went through a fifth of Crown Royal and two bottles of champagne.

"Shit, I'm fucked up." I laughed and excused myself to go to the bathroom.

When I came out, the owner came over to me and asked if I could return that weekend to sing at a party that a customer had paid to host. Initially, I thought about declining, but something sparked in me to ask about the pay.

"Five Gs? For five songs?" I checked.

"Yeah. Can you do it?"

"I sure can." I smiled and took a moment to silently thank God.

"Did that guy ask you something about performing here?" Teagan questioned me as she got up to stand.

After I explained what the owner had offered, she hugged me and shook her head. "Braxton Carter, you are about to do great things. I keep telling you, but you ain't listening. You ain't believing. Just think about it. The studio, the song, the contract, the gigs. Everything is falling into place."

"You are so right."

Ever since I had met Teagan over a month ago, she had been speaking fame and fortune over my life, and slowly but surely, it was happening, just like she said.

"That's crazy, Teagan. You did say that shit, though." I laughed as we hopped in her ride. "Wait. I didn't even pay the tab."

"I tried to take care of it when you went to the bathroom, but the guy you were talking to told me it was on the house."

"Oh, okay, cool. I'm so lit that I forgot all about the shit until now."

"No worries."

As Teagan drove south down MLK, she asked if I wanted her to take me to get my car. Knowing damn well that I had too much to drink, I declined. Before she could question me about what hotel I stayed at, I suggested that we go to her place. That way, I could chill until I sobered up, and then decide on what to do after that.

"Whatcha wanna do now? It's your day. It's all about you," Teagan teased as we entered her house and removed our shoes. "We can go out to the pool, or we can—"

When she suddenly stopped what she was saying, I turned around to see her standing there naked. My dick stood straight up. "Or we can what?" As I stood there with a lustful expression, I fondled my hardness through my pants. I couldn't keep my big boy down. Once it plumped up, it had a mind of its own, and now it was leading me.

"Damn, baby," I moaned and got things started by hitting it from the back right where we were standing.

I must've screwed that girl from the living room to the pool and then in her bed, where we ended up. By then, I was sober and feeling stupid once again.

"Fuck!" I grunted and hopped up with my naked dick swinging, no condom in sight.

"What's wrong, babe?"

"Me! I'm wrong, and you ain't been making it any better," I complained and went into her adjoining bathroom to clean myself up.

"What did I do?" Teagan shrieked and walked up behind me with her face all tuned up.

"You just keep letting me go up in you raw. I can't keep doing that shit. I'm trippin'." I sighed heavily as I took it upon myself to start her shower and step in to wash up.

Teagan hurried to join me, but I was too quick. I washed up and got out before she had a chance to put her hands on me.

"You act like you're mad at me, Braxton. I'm sorry," she apologized.

As I got my clothes on, Teagan kept asking for forgiveness when she didn't need to. The problem wasn't with her. It was with me. I had to do better.

"Don't trip. I'm the one who fucked up, and I just took it out on you because sometimes it's easier for a person to place the blame elsewhere rather than accept their mistakes," I explained.

When I went over to hug her, she held onto me and cried her heart out, and that made me feel worse. That shit fucked with me.

"You know I didn't mean that shit, Teagan. I'm just under a lot of stress, and knocking you up would only put more on me. I don't wanna do that to you or myself."

"Let's not worry about all that shit right now, Braxton. Let's just enjoy these good times before you make it big and forget all about us small folks," she teased with a sniffle as she broke away and went into the bathroom to wipe her face. Afterward, she wandered to the closet to get fully dressed.

The doorbell rang several times. When I asked if she was going to get it, she pushed a few buttons on the device next to her bed. Right away, video from the front door was displayed on the screen.

"It's Eva, and Venezuela is getting it."

"Venezuela?"

"You know, Venezuela, my housekeeper," she said and slipped on her shoes before heading downstairs.

Not wanting to sit there and wait for her to kick it with her homegirl, I walked down behind her in hopes of her taking me to my ride. I definitely didn't want to stay there all day.

"Heyyyyy, y'all. Did I interrupt something?" Eva questioned us with a look of suspicion.

"It ain't like you ever call before you come anyhow," Teagan teased. "What's up, though?"

"I was coming to show you something online, but I see you got company."

"What you see now, girl?"

"Well, now that I see Braxton over, I'm thinking maybe I don't wanna say it."

"Speak yo' mind, Eva. Don't mind me." I laughed while wondering what the hell she was up to.

"Okay, well, the video trending now is one with your daughter, your baby mama, and Gunner West. They are all wearing white athletic gear from that new Portland-based sports company while doing a TikTok dance. It was done to announce a new possible sponsorship for Brazil. From what it said on the video caption, there's no signed contract yet. Did you know about that, Braxton?" Eva asked.

Did I know about it? Hell no, I didn't know about it!

My blood boiled in silence because I didn't want to make a scene. I had to play it cool. Real cool.

Chapter Nineteen

Gunner West

The following Sunday . . .

For the past ten days, things had been wild. Between spending time with Oaklyn, assisting with the tons of deals presented to Brazil after the camp, preparing for the charity game, creating TikTok videos, and coaching, I had barely slept. Honestly, I couldn't complain because it was rewarding and well worth it, especially if Oaklyn decided to sign one of the endorsement offers. She wasn't so sure about doing that. Out of seventeen legit proposals, Oaklyn had only considered one so far. She didn't want to overwhelm herself or her daughter, especially when she still had almost three months of school left before summer break.

Feeling a bit out of her league, Oaklyn came to me for advice, and that led me to introduce her to my mother. She knew more about the backside of the sports industry than I did because she used to be my manager. Once my mother got together with Oaklyn, a friendship immediately evolved. My mother said that Oaklyn was just like the daughter she never had.

"Y'all ain't outta here yet?" my mother asked as she joined me and my pops in the kitchen. "I just got off the phone with Oaklyn, and her and Brazil are already on their way over to the charity event. You would wanna be there before the crowd gets thick."

"It's sold out like it usually is, but traffic has never been an issue, Mom. They always have the roads blocked off for us to go through the side entrance."

"You don't think that this time it'll be a little different?" Pops added.

"Why? We still sold the same amount of seats."

"Gunner, are you forgetting all the attention Brazil's basketball has stirred up? Everyone is after her. They wanna interview her, sign her, and even want her to be a guest speaker at a few schools. This is not an ordinary child, son. She's special," my pops continued. "She not only has the skills. She has the smarts to go along with it."

To prove Pops' point, my mother got on her cell and showed me the current coverage at Portland State University. The crowd outside blew my mind. They carried signs and banners supporting Brazil. Some were even chanting her name. It was like she had her very own fan club, and I loved the attention she received. I just wasn't so sure about Oaklyn. Unlike Brazil, she still struggled to be in the public eye, but she couldn't hide. No matter how often Oaklyn ducked and dodged the media, it became impossible after she shared her life story in an intimate interview with news reporter Jasmine Devine. The public found Oaklyn's testimony inspirational and instantly took to her.

With the good came the bad because although the world embraced her and her daughter, the ugly facts of Braxton always seemed to surface. The people wanted to know why he wasn't in the picture. They wanted a reason for the breakup. That was something that Oaklyn didn't want to share.

"Get your head out of the clouds and get these bags in the truck so y'all can get out of here, Gunner." My mother hollered loud enough to shake my thoughts. "Oaklyn and Brazil are probably already there, and this crowd is getting wilder. Where in the hell is the damn security when you need them?"

"Oaklyn ain't about to let nothing happen to her baby," I assured my mom and grabbed the bags off the floor. "I'm more worried about Brazil when she gets in front of all those people. A small gym with under a hundred people and a large dome like Portland State University arena, which seats 3,400, is a big difference."

"Gunner, please." My mother laughed. "That little girl has so much spunk and confidence. She'll be just fine. Now, Oaklyn, she's the one to worry about. She's been so nervous about all this attention that she called me last night to vent."

"Seriously, Ma?"

"Yes, Gunner. She wanted to know how I dealt with all the fame when you made it big."

"I don't know how she did it, son," Pops said, then laughed. "You might not realize how your mother moved mountains behind the scenes, but Gladys did it all. Yep, that right there is Superwoman for real."

"Hush, Gerald." My mother giggled. "I had to do what I had to do, and that's what I told Oaklyn. She's much stronger than she thinks she is. I believe it's because of how she lived in Brazil's father's shadow for so long. She lost herself. She's gonna be good, though. She's just gotta believe it."

"You're right," I agreed.

"You darn skippy, I am. I'm right about that traffic, too. That's why I'm waiting for another hour before I leave here like I always do. I'll see y'all there. Now, get to going."

"That's what we're tryna do, Gladys," my father replied with a laugh.

It was hilarious how my mother had just tried to rush us out of the house a few minutes earlier, and now she was the one who wouldn't stop talking. Pops had to cut her off. If he didn't, we would've never gotten out of that house.

"Boy, I love yo' mama, but that woman can talk," my pops clowned as we double-checked the truck to make sure we had everything we needed.

After all was good, I went around to the driver's side to get in, but just as I opened the door, something caught my attention out of the corner of my eye. Shifting my head in the direction of the strange movement near the row of oak trees, I could've sworn I spotted Camille. As badly as I wanted to be mistaken, my gut told me differently. It had to be that bitch.

"What is it, son? Looks like you seen a ghost," Pops teased as I started the Navigator and checked the perimeter. "What is it?"

"Nothing, Pops," I lied. "I was just thinking about something."

After I drove off, I paid close attention to my surroundings. Camille wasn't about to catch me slipping. In order to stay safe, I had to get to her first and have her arrested. That would be the only way to keep her away from me because, obviously, that restraining order didn't mean a damn thing. However, as far as me depending on the cops to stop Camille, I could hang it up. Their hands were tied until I could prove to them that she had violated the order. With her sneaky ass, that had been impossible to do.

"Whoa!" I gasped, and my thoughts evaporated as soon as I spotted all the people outside the arena.

"Look at all these folks out here. They all wanna see that itty bitty Brazil." Pops laughed and shook his head as I flashed my ID badge at the security guard on duty, allowing me to pass through the barriers.

Once we cleared the crowd, we entered through the rear doors and headed to the gymnasium. Oaklyn, her best friend Koola, and Brazil were already there. When I noticed them standing there laughing, thoughts of Camille dissipated, and I was able to concentrate on the charity game.

Thankfully, it all went off without a flaw, but sadly, I couldn't say the same thing about afterward. As soon as my father left with my mother, there was drama at its finest.

"Hey, Brazil! Daddy is so proud of you, baby girl!" Braxton yelled as he ran up on us in the private section of the parking lot. "Are you coming with me?"

"No, she's coming with me," Brazil's grandmother, Draya, intervened. "I'm taking her to school tomorrow because we're going to dinner tonight to celebrate."

"Dang, Daddy can't get no love?" Braxton continued to try to get his way, but Oaklyn, Koola, or Draya would not let that happen.

"I love you, Daddy, and I'll see you next weekend, okay?" Brazil laughed and went to hug him.

While they shared a quick embrace, I wondered how Braxton had managed to get through security without the proper ID badge. If he got in, Camille could have too. That shit put me on edge, and I could barely pay attention to what Braxton was up to. With all the chaos around me, all I wanted to do was leave and make it to my own territory without being followed. To do that, I had to be able to watch my back.

"This nigga don't stop trying. Ugh. Loser," Koola grumbled.

Apparently, Braxton heard her because right after she said it, he began clowning again and getting all loud and shit. "Brazil, I'm coming to get you next weekend. Don't forget!" Braxton hollered out obnoxiously as his daughter walked off with her grandmother. As soon as they were out of sight, he turned to Oaklyn. The way he looked at her had me concerned, so I slid closer to her in a protective manner.

Obviously, Braxton didn't like it because now he eyed me down wickedly. When he failed to get a reaction out of me, he shifted his attention back to Oaklyn. "So, you signed an endorsement deal for Brazil without consulting me?" he questioned Oaklyn with a bit of a slur. "That has to be like a million-dollar contract or more."

Braxton eased closer and enabled me to smell the alcohol on his breath. Dude had to be intoxicated.

"While you're concerned with the money, I haven't signed shit yet. *And* . . . last time I checked, I had full custody of Brazil, so you don't have a say in this matter. You hear me? I don't have to consult you about a damn thing, Braxton."

"Legally, you may not have to, but morally, I would wanna think that you would, Oaklyn." Braxton's irritation grew as he stood there gritting his teeth. "I guess you just ain't got morals no more, huh?"

Before answering him, Oaklyn turned to me and let me know that she had the situation under control, urging me to go on and go home. Normally, I would've insisted on staying to have her back, but when Koola vouched for her security, I eased off.

"You sure?" I checked.

"Trust me. This nigga won't do shit. You can go, Gunner." Koola patted the handbag she had retrieved from the car when Braxton first walked up and assured me that everything would be all right.

"Call me when you make it home, Oaklyn," I told her as I leaned in even closer. Instead of pecking her lips like I usually did, I chose her left cheek to keep the drama down, but it didn't matter. Braxton still growled like a fucking dog again instead of using his words.

The smoke he blew without the presence of fire didn't mean shit to me. I took the win, then went and hopped in my truck and peeled out of the lot to make my way to my house. No time for fun and games with a lunatic on the loose. My full attention was required during the entire thirty-minute drive. I had to keep my eyes on everything. I couldn't even release the tension in my shoulders enough to make them drop until I made it through the security gate of my community with no other vehicles in sight.

Finally able to breathe and exhale a sigh of relief, I pulled into the garage and closed it behind me, then went inside. After I kicked off my sneakers in the laundry room, I went into the den and dialed Oaklyn up to check on her.

"Hey, Gunner. I'm good, and thanks for everything."

"My pleasure," I replied, then asked her what she was about to do.

When Oaklyn began to complain about her aching muscles, I asked if she wanted to come over and get in the heated pool, then soak in the jacuzzi tub.

She immediately replied, "That sounds so good."

Suddenly, I remembered about the paperwork and keys to the house that the charity game had paid for. With all the excitement and worry that day, I had totally forgotten all about giving it to her. Since she didn't want Pops to announce it at the event, I was supposed to present it to her in private.

"I have a surprise for you. Come and get it," I said, trying to persuade her.

"Let me go home and change right quick first. I'll be there in an hour or so."

Just enough time for me to set the towels and massage oil out, then get the tub ready—a simple, yet sexy setup.

Chapter Twenty

Oaklyn Jones

"That nigga done really lost it, Oaklyn. Why would Braxton just show up and show out like that in the parking lot? Better yet, how did he even get by security? Hell, we had to show our passes to get access," Koola complained as we dipped to get some grub from one of the food trucks right off Killingsworth.

My head pounded with frustration just thinking about how Braxton's drunk ass acted a fool after the charity game. If it weren't for Koola calming me down, I would've flashed on my baby daddy and really hurt his feelings. The nerve of him. To get mad at me for trying to get on with my life? Like it was my fault that we were no longer together. No, no, baby. All that blame belonged to his unfaithful, irresponsible ass, not mine.

"Koola, honestly, I'm just glad he didn't try to fight Gunner. I swear to you, girl. Every time we have a run-in, it gets uglier. I can't keep doing this with him. I just want some distance from Braxton so I can have some peace. You know—"

My sentence was cut short when Gunner called me and invited me over. Right on time! Don't get me wrong, now. I loved my girl Koola. I loved her to death, but I had to hurry up and drop her off so that I could go home and pack a little something and get over to Gunner's and soak in his huge Jacuzzi tub. My tired bones really needed it.

"I'm on my way." I giggled to myself as I left my apartment and headed over to Gunner's.

To deliver a heads up, I sent a text to tell him that I was en route. In response, I got a thumbs up and a heart followed by a request for me to use the garage door opener and park the Benz in there.

Once I read his full set of instructions, I set my cell on my lap, blasted the old school song that played on the radio, and sang along as I cruised down Lombard Street with the top down. The drive took more than half an hour, and I used every moment of it to enjoy the fresh air and good music.

"I won't love you anyway . . . even if you cannot stay." I sang loudly as I made it through the security gate right behind the car ahead of me. I didn't even have to key in the code.

"You're not mine," I continued to sing as I arrived on Gunner's block and veered into his fancy driveway. Fulfilling his request, I parked the car in the garage and went inside, calling his name and announcing my presence.

"Gunner? I'm here!"

Just as I stepped foot in the kitchen, he jumped out and lifted my large frame, then showered me with kisses.

"Whoa!" I hollered because he nearly startled the shit out of me.

"I'm sorry, baby. I didn't mean to scare you."

"It's okay," I said with a laugh. "You got me good, though."

Gunner placed me back onto my feet, and I immediately noticed the security screens lit up on the counter. They all displayed different views of the outside of the house.

"What's going on with the beefed up security?" I questioned.

"Just a new system I had installed. I was in here playing around with it to make sure it worked properly."

"Does it?"

"Well, it's recording, so I guess I did something right."

Accepting his explanation, I got right to the point and asked about the surprise he had for me. "What is it, Gunner?"

"Well, it ain't really a surprise because I already told you about it."

"The house?" I shouted happily and jumped for joy. "I really got it? I really got the house?"

"Yes, you did, and it's well deserved. It will give you and Brazil a fresh new start."

"Thank you so much, Gunner. You and your family."

"The profit from the charity game paid for it, so thanks go to the community for always supporting the event."

"Yeah, but you and your family chose me. For that, I'll be forever grateful," I cried as Gunner passed me the keys and the paperwork for the property. Although there were no photos to show what the house looked like, I saw that the address wasn't too far from Gunner's. That meant it had to be in a really nice neighborhood.

"I can't wait to see it. When can we move?"

"The workers completed the last-minute adjustments that I had them make yesterday, so you're good to go. You have the keys and paperwork. It's all yours. Congratulations, baby."

Tears flowed down my face as Gunner hugged me tightly. His vibes drew me in, and now all I wanted to do was celebrate, starting with the pool. "I brought my swimsuit," I hinted with a wink. "I have it on now."

"I'm a step ahead of you." Gunner laughed and led me out back. "I got us some snacks and some drinks."

"Okay, now," I cheered and began to indulge.

The soft music playing had me swaying, and the glass of wine he poured me had me dancing. I couldn't remember a happier moment in my life.

"Let's get in the water," I suggested as I removed my coverup, then eased in and splashed around.

"Coming!" Gunner assured me as he nearly tripped trying to get his pants off. His facial expression made me laugh. He was so comical. "Let me get this first, then silence this damn phone," Gunner explained as he picked up his ringing cell.

"Hey, Mom!"

The call lasted less than a minute, then he joined me in the pool and told me that his mother was on her way. I didn't know where she was coming from, so I didn't want to take the chance and start fooling around only to be busted.

"She's gonna drop the care packages that her club made up for you and Brazil," Braxton explained as he eased into the water and came to hold me.

"What kind of packages?"

"Housewarming gifts. They do it every year when we give away a home."

My heart, now overwhelmed with joy, beat quickly, and anxiety spread throughout my body. Why me? Did I really deserve all this? Out of the blue, I thought about the money from Brazil's endorsement deal. Once I signed those papers, I would have money to buy my own property. If I accepted the house knowing that I had dough coming, that would be greedy, and I didn't want that label. I would rather pass up on the house and figure out buying one for myself later. To share my concerns, I ran them by Gunner, who in turn laughed and asked if I knew how much houses ran these days. I had no idea, but I knew when I signed that contract, I would have at least enough for a down payment.

"Since it's a short-term trial contract, they offered me three hundred thousand upon signing, and then I would receive equal payments of around fifty-eight thousand monthly for a full year. That's when the contract would end," I explained.

"Okay, that's a good little hunk of change, but you will need most of that to pay on utilities, get homeowners insurance, and a warranty plan. You're gonna wanna furnish your house, get yourself a new car, and put money up for Brazil. Plus, you said you wanted to go back to school. Do that shit. *And,* if you still feel guilty for accepting the house, donate some of the dough you get to the family that gets chosen next year. That will help out more than you realize."

"Okay, I like that. Giving back. Yes!"

Once we settled that matter, I asked about getting in his Jacuzzi tub. That sounded damn good right then.

"Say less." Gunner smiled and helped me out of the pool, wrapped me in an oversized green beach towel, then led me into the house and up the stairs.

Upon entering his master bedroom, I felt like royalty. From the furnishings to the setup, it mimicked a scene from a magical tale. Unique and inviting. Each step I made toward the bathroom suite of his room felt as if I were walking on clouds. Was it the plush carpeting or the fantasy playing in my head? I wasn't sure.

"Let me get the water started for you," Gunner whispered as he went to the tub and twisted the large chrome handle to the left. "You can adjust the temperature before you get in and the pressure of the jets once you're in using these knobs on the side. Let me run to the closet down the hall and get some candles, and I'll be right back."

Before he left, he set his cell on the bathroom counter and started his playlist, which began with a smooth jazz song. After he disappeared, I hurried to strip out of my swimsuit and hopped in the tub. Thankfully, the temperature was just right.

"Yes," I whispered loudly as I wiggled downward in the bubbles to get comfortable.

Just as the water reached my chin, the house alarm went off, and the house went dark. Panic immediately set in.

"Gunner?" I yelled.

When he didn't answer, I hollered out twice more. The third time, I shouted out as loud as I could and held the note. In the midst of me screaming with my mouth wide open, someone palmed the top of my head from behind and shoved me under the water. Beginning to choke, I began fighting for my life. Doing everything within my power to come up for air, I clawed at the hand and arm restraining me. When that didn't work, I attempted to roll to the side so I could try to get up, but the jets shot the water right up my nose.

Please, Lord, help me! Please!

Who the hell had me like this? Who wanted to kill me? Whatever I had done to deserve this shit, I was sorry. Really sorry. I didn't want to lose my life. I had too much to live for. Brazil needed me.

Please, Lord! I can't breathe!

Just when I thought all hope was lost, two gunshots rang out, and then I was suddenly freed. Surfacing with fear, I struggled to catch my breath and wipe my eyes to see clearly.

"What happened?" I coughed as the beams of light from the cell phone blinded me.

"Wrap up and come here," I heard Gunner's mother instruct me as she handed me a towel, then ushered me carefully into the bedroom.

Darkness filled the room, and I couldn't see a thing. "What happened? Where's Gunner?"

"Stay right here and don't move," Mrs. West whispered.

When she ran off and left me all alone in the dark, I heard a whining over the music that was still playing on Gunner's phone. I didn't know what it was. Too afraid to move, I sat right there until the lights suddenly came back on. That was when I saw Gunner lying on the floor, holding his chest.

"Help me," he moaned.

Thinking the worst, I ran to him and applied pressure to his wound using the mat in front of the tub. "What happened?"

"Camille?" He groaned and nodded my way.

When I turned around, I saw a big, brown-skinned chick sprawled out on the floor with her head in a pool of blood. It grossed me out so badly that I had to turn away.

"The cops and ambulance are right down the street, son. Hold on, baby. They'll be here soon," Mrs. West cried as she kneeled down and clasped Gunner's hand.

"What happened?" I asked her.

"Camille. It was Camille," Mrs. West cried. "When I got here, I saw her going through the gate and around to the back yard. I tried to catch her before she got in, but I had to get my gun out of my glove box first. I'm so sorry."

"It's not your fault," I told her as I listened to the sirens getting louder. "Help is on the way."

With my focus on Gunner, I refused to look at the corpse lying on the golden-tiled flooring. Seeing a dead body definitely creeped me out.

"Gunner!" Mrs. West cried out loudly when his body went limp.

We couldn't wake him up. Both Gunner's mother and I panicked when the authorities came rushing into the bedroom with guns drawn. They didn't want to hear a thing we had to say. As far as they were concerned, we were the bad guys.

"I need to go with my son!" Mrs. West yelled as the medics hauled Gunner off on a stretcher.

"You can check on him after we get a statement from you downtown."

"You a damn lie! You can question us at the hospital. I need medical attention, and so does Oaklyn. That woman broke in, cut the lights, and tried to kill us."

"Who shot who?" one of the officers asked.

Mrs. West told the truth, and these muthafuckas hauled both of us to the station. We weren't even allowed to call her husband or my mother until we were finger-printed and booked. It took us at least six hours to get out of there, and we still didn't know how Gunner was doing. All we could do was pray until his father showed up to get us.

"How is he, Gerald?" Mrs. West sniffled. "Please tell me he's okay."

When Gunner's father got silent and the tears began to stream down her face, my heart sank to my stomach. It couldn't be true.

Not Gunner!

Chapter Twenty-one

Teagan Hoffman

Braxton and I were chilling at my house when he received a call from Oaklyn's mother. While she screamed and hollered into the phone so loud that I could hear her clearly, all he wanted to know was where his baby mama was. He practically broke out in tears trying to find out.

"Where's Oaklyn, and why the fuck would they lock her up if somebody tried to kill her? Is she okay?"

His concerned reaction both touched me and bothered me. Although I adored his loving nature, I hated that it was for another woman.

"Are they gonna let her out?" he questioned.

Anxious and worried, Braxton rushed to put on his shoes. He moved so quickly that I barely had a chance to ask where he was going and what had happened.

"I'm driving you. You don't need to be behind the wheel this upset," I offered, but I quickly got turned down. It crushed my feelings, but I didn't make a fuss about it. I just gave him his space and backed up.

In need of a level head, I dialed Eva up the minute Braxton flew up out of my house without so much as a simple goodbye. That shit burned me up.

"What's up, Teagan? I was just about to call and give you a royal announcement."

"And what's that, Eva?"

"I'm on my way over there," she announced with a laugh. "Roll out the carpet!"

Annoyed with her customary comical behavior, I began to question her, but the doorbell stopped me. "Is that you?"

"You know it," Eva clowned.

After I swung the door open with a frown, she instantly caught the hint. "What's wrong? Did I catch you at a bad time, boo?"

"Just in time to listen to me vent," I whined with my thoughts all over the place. The way Walter had left me and had me thinking that he ran off with another woman, only to find out that my father had him killed, had fucked my mind up. The ghosts of the past weren't the only thing that bothered me, either. The fear of the unknown was nerve-racking too. What was going on between me and Braxton? Did he dig me as much as I dug him? Those were just a couple of the questions that I had absolutely no answer for, and the only way to get them was to ask. How, though? Even if I found a way, was I mentally prepared to receive an answer I didn't like? I think not. Just the thought of rejection left me choked up. I couldn't even find the words to describe how I felt.

"What is it, Teagan?" Eva asked with a concerned voice.

"Where do I begin?" I whispered. The salty taste of tears in mouth caused me to swallow several times as I listened to Eva deliver comforting words.

With her arm wrapped around me, she sat me down on the edge of the sofa, then kneeled down on the floor beside me. "Begin at the beginning, Teagan."

"Let me start with Braxton."

After I sat there and told her all about how we had been getting down and his situation with Oaklyn, she got up and went over to the bar. "We gotta drink on this shit right here because that nigga is trippin'." With two shot glasses in her hand, she gave one to me and clinked her drink against mine.

"To better fucking days," I cheered, then swallowed down the alcohol with three gulps. On the last one, I felt a burning sensation, then it all came up, including the seafood meal that Braxton and I had shared earlier. The stench of it was so strong that it made me add to the pile of funk.

"Venezuela!" Eva hollered out.

Running into the living room in a panic, my house-keeper ran to my aid. She wiped my mouth with her apron, then rushed off to get me a couple of cold towels.

"Are you okay, boo?" Eva questioned with her head turned.

"I don't know where that came from." I coughed and thanked Venezuela for the wet cloths.

As she daubed my face and neck, Eva stood away from me, pecking away on her cell. She said that she ordered me some soda, soup, and meds to make me feel better.

"Let's go upstairs while Venezuela cleans this up. I don't wanna make you sick, too," I told Eva.

As she helped me to my feet, we went up to my room so that I could clean up and change my clothes. The whole time, she interrogated me.

"You think it was something you ate?"

"I don't think so. I was fine after I ate."

"You think it might be the flu?"

"No, I'm fine now. Maybe it was the liquor," I replied as my Alexa chimed, then the doorbell rang.

"Is that my delivery?" Eva asked.

"Yeah, they left it at the door. Venezuela is getting it now," I explained.

Eva hopped up and went downstairs to get the bag and came right back to my room with a strange look on her face. She was always up to something.

"What's up?"

"Take this test."

"What test?"

"This pregnancy test," she shouted and drew three boxes out of the bag.

"Where the fuck that come from? Just because I threw up?"

"No, because we get our period around the same time every month, and you ain't complained about cramps one time. I done came on and been off over a week."

"For real?" I gasped. I hadn't realized that I was late. For me, that wasn't normal. Curious to know if I could actually be pregnant, I snatched the boxes from Eva and ran into the bathroom. I didn't come out until I took all three of the tests.

"You will not fucking believe this shit, Eva," I whispered and became emotional.

"You are, huh? You're pregnant?"

"Yes! Can you believe it?"

Before Eva opened her mouth to answer, Alexa chimed.

"Who is that?" Eva asked as I rushed to check.

"That's my mother pulling up. Go downstairs and have Venezuela tell her that I'm not here."

"What? Why?"

"Eva, please!" I shouted.

The tone of my voice sent her running out of my room and down the stairs, but it was too late. My mother was already in the house.

"Teagan?" she called out seconds before she and Eva entered my room.

It all happened so quickly that I didn't even have a chance to get rid of the tests. I wound up shoving them under my leg. "Hey, Mom. What brings you over?"

"Well, I wanted to talk to you about family business, but I see you have company."

"Okay, I'll come over later."

"No, no, no. I'll come back this evening. I have a few runs to make. Give me a few hours."

After she bent down to hug me, she asked me to walk her out. How the hell could I get up when I had those test sticks hidden under my thigh? What excuse could I use?

"I'll walk you down," Eva offered. "Teagan hasn't been feeling good."

"I'm fine. It's just a little headache," I corrected her before I got fifty more questions.

As soon as my mother turned to leave, I held up one of the test sticks and shook my head at Eva. I didn't want her to blab my business. Not after what my father had pulled.

Grabbing the hint, Eva walked my mother out and ran back to my room. After looking me dead in my face, she asked for answers. This time, I couldn't hold back. I had to tell her what was going on, and once I swore her to secrecy, I let it all out, including the shit with Walter.

"If anyone finds out that you know about what I just told you, it could put your life in danger, Eva, so please!"

"Bitch, you think I wanna die?" She gasped. "Hell, I wish I could forget everything you just told me."

Little did my best friend know, I did too. I did too.

Chapter Twenty-two

Braxton Carter

Teagan handled it well when I denied her request to come downtown with me. Like a levelheaded female, she stayed at her crib and hadn't even called me. I really appreciated that shit. It gave me time to clear my head so that I could deal with Oaklyn's situation.

"I can't believe they locked my baby mama up after someone tried to kill her," I said, panting as I arrived at the Justice Center and ran inside to find out what had happened. Since her mother had Brazil and couldn't come, I had volunteered to go, hoping that Oaklyn needed me, or at least needed a ride.

Silly me.

When I got there and Oaklyn saw me, she cut her eyes and shook her head to silently make it clear that she didn't need or want me there. It hurt me, but I didn't give up. "Hey, Oaklyn?" I called out as I approached her while she spoke to an older couple at the counter. "You good?"

"What are you doing here?" she replied sharply as she and the other two began to take off toward the door.

"Your mother called me."

"I'm fine. Brazil's with her, and I'm fine."

"You sure?" I pressed, chasing behind them. I wanted to know what was going on.

"I gotta go, Braxton. Somebody just tried to kill us, and Gunner's in the hospital. They won't tell us anything over the phone, and we gotta get down there."

"Wait," I insisted, but Oaklyn kept right on going.

Running outside after her, I continued to question her until she hopped in a late-model Lincoln. Just as the engine revved, she rolled down the window. "I'm sure you'll hear about it on social media, or on the news."

"On the news?"

"Look, Braxton, thanks for checking on me, and I appreciate it, but I'm fine." Just like that, she rolled the window up on me and the car zoomed off.

What the fuck? This woman really left me standing in the middle of the street when all I wanted to do was check on her, to make sure she was good. Apparently, Oaklyn didn't want my help, and I wasn't about to keep offering it. If she was good, fuck it. Anger filled my body as I replayed what Oaklyn said to me about having to get up to the hospital to see about another nigga. Shit, she had a man right there who loved and cared about her. Why would she run to him? Oaklyn's actions continued to prove her feelings for Gunner, but how deep were they? Deep enough to stop fucking with me altogether? That was what I needed to know. The fact that I had to ask myself scared me. Why? Because the closer Oaklyn got to Gunner, the less chance I had to win her back.

Unsure of my next move, I went and got into my car and sat there thinking. I didn't even notice the tears falling until my vision became distorted.

"Did I really lose her?"

In need of a drink, I dialed Chachi up but couldn't get an answer. That left me with Uncle Pete.

"What's up with you, Unc?"

"My company just got here. I'm about to entertain. Let me get back to you later. Scratch that shit, nephew. You might wanna make it tomorrow," he clowned, then hung up on me.

Frustrated and lonely, I took my ass to the suite and stretched out on the sofa with the remote in one hand and a drink in the other. As I scanned through the channels, I came across the news.

"You gotta be fucking kidding me," I hissed as I listened to the reporter talk.

"Breaking news! There was a shooting this evening at former NBA player Gunner West's home. Sources say that West's ex-girlfriend, Camille Rollins, who West had an order of protection against, broke into his home and shot West and attempted to kill his current girlfriend, Oaklyn Jones. She is the ex-girlfriend and mother of singer Braxton Carter's daughter, Brazil. The young basketball star—"

"Girlfriend?" I gritted as the reporter's words trailed off. This shit was unbelievable. How could they announce that my baby mama was Gunner's girlfriend on national TV?

In the midst of my anger attack, Teagan called. I wasn't going to answer it until I thought about how she could take my mind off things. Just what I needed. *A pint and some pussy.*

"What's up?" I answered.

"Is everything okay?" Teagan asked.

All I had to do was say that I didn't want to talk about it, and she dropped it and asked if I needed to come over. I sure did. With two things on my mind, I went right over there and handled my business. When we finished fucking the first time and I sobered up, I repeated my actions until I passed out.

The next morning, I woke up with the worst headache. When I reached over to Teagan and found her gone from the bed, I got up and went into her bathroom in search of some Tylenol or ibuprofen.

"What are you doing in here?" a strange female voice asked.

Dressed in only my boxers, I quickly jumped and hopelessly covered up my morning woody, which had halfway popped out of the slit in the front. No control whatsoever.

"Down, boy!" The chick laughed with her eyes glued to my dick.

"Amari! What are you doing in here, girl?" Teagan smirked as she stood in front of the woman to block her view.

"This must be why your mother had me come over here to check on you, cousin." Amari giggled then smirked. "Does your father know about all this?"

"About all what?"

"About you dating a new guy?"

"Why would I need to tell him, Amari? I'm grown, girl."

"Age don't mean shit when it comes to family rules."

"What rules?" Teagan frowned and crossed her arms, then rested them on her chest.

"I know your side of the family has been out the game for a minute, but since Pop-Pop died last year, everyone has to do their part."

"I don't want no part of that life, Amari. I'm good."

The meaning behind the exchange of words caught my attention. Now I wanted to know why it was a big deal too. What was I missing?

"How the hell you get in my house anyhow?" Teagan huffed.

"Venezuela let me in and told me that you were upstairs."

"Remind me to fire that bitch," Teagan mumbled under her breath. "What brings you over, Amari?"

"Like I said, your mother wanted me to come and check on you. She said that your father thought that you were up to something, but I didn't expect this."

"Expect what?" Teagan asked with her hands now on her hips.

"I'm just saying. You know how your father is when you're dating new guys. He ain't to be played with when it comes to you. You ought to know that, cousin."

"Look, I don't wanna get into all that. I have company right now."

"So, you're kicking me out?"

The way she asked Teagan that shit made me think that it was about to be some static. I just didn't expect it to escalate so quickly.

"If you wanna take it like that. I mean, you came over here uninvited and unannounced . . . obviously to spy for my mother and my father, or yours. It doesn't matter. I'm not about to entertain any of it, so if you don't mind."

"Bitch, I can't believe you're tryna put me out behind some dick. Don't get me wrong. I saw that shit, and it's big and thick and all, but family comes first."

"Bye, Amari!" Teagan shouted.

As soon as she touched her cousin's arm, Amari swung on her, and there they went. Blow for blow, Teagan hung, but when she got Amari on the floor, she rolled her off and drew down her.

"You pull a gun out on me in my own house?"

"Be glad I ain't pull the trigger. Now, take this as a warning. Be careful of the company you keep because breaking family rules has consequences." Amari backed out of the room until she disappeared into the hallway and down the stairs. Teagan didn't go after her.

"I'm so sorry about that," she said.

"Don't be sorry. Just explain to me what type of family rules you got. By the sound of it and by the way that bitch drew down on you, it gotta be serious. Like some Mafia shit or something."

The mention of Mafia clammed Teagan right up, and she didn't want to talk about it or anything else, for that matter. All she wanted to do was take a warm bath and curl up in the bed. Feeling bad for her, I rubbed her back until she fell asleep. Then I got the hell out of there because I had a funny feeling that it wasn't safe for me to stay. Teagan's cousin didn't come over there on bullshit. She came over there to deliver a message, and I received that shit loud and clear, and until I found out otherwise, I would stay away. Far away.

Taking my ass right back to my suite, I showered, changed, and lay across the bed to rest, only I couldn't. Not with Oaklyn on my mind. To avoid bothering her, I called her mother, Draya, to see what was going on.

"Hey," I greeted.

"Brazil is sleeping, if that's why you're calling, Braxton."

"Give her a kiss for me."

"I will."

"Draya, is Oaklyn okay?"

"You didn't talk to her?"

After I explained how dirty her daughter had treated me at the Justice Center, she laid into me. She ripped me about how bad I had done her daughter, and I couldn't say shit. She was right.

"How long did you think she was going to stick around while you fucked off on her, Braxton?"

"I told her that I was sorry."

"What, then? You promised her the same thing you always promised her, but then just turn around and re-peated your foul actions?" Draya fussed. "Look, Braxton. I think you could be a real good person, but right now, you're not. You've hurt Oaklyn so much that she stopped loving herself. You got so wrapped up in your career that you neglected your responsibilities. You neglected Oaklyn, your daughter, your family."

"I wanna do better, Draya. I love my family, and I don't wanna lose them."

"It may be too late for all that, Braxton, but I'm gonna pray for you."

Pray for me? That's all she had? I needed more than a prayer. I needed her to go and talk some sense into her daughter, to make her see that she should give me another chance, to convince her that she needed to keep her family together. The overwhelming stress caused me to drink myself to sleep, and I actually slept pretty well. It was the reality that hit me the next morning that pissed me off.

Oaklyn was really fucking with Gunner.

Chapter Twenty-three

Gunner West

"What happened?" I whispered loudly to my mother as I looked around at the hospital room.

"You were shot, son."

"Oaklyn. Where's Oaklyn? Is she okay?"

"She's fine, son. She and your dad went downstairs to get something to eat. We've all been up here since last night."

"My shoulder," I grunted as I tried to sit up in the bed, but I didn't have enough strength to do so.

"Careful, Gunner."

"I'm okay, Mom. Please just tell me the cops caught that bitch."

The anesthesia had me loopy, and I could barely see straight, but I could hear. I needed to know where Camille was.

"When she shot you, I shot her. She didn't make it."

My mother sounded so sad and broke up when she told me, but I felt just the opposite. I felt relieved and thankful that she had eliminated the threat. "Thanks for saving us, Mom."

"Anything for you, son. I love you, and I'm just glad that I was there."

After she explained how things happened that night, my pops and Oaklyn came walking into the room. Her eyes lit up soon as they met with mine.

"I'm so glad you're all right, Gunner." She gasped and came to hug me on my right side. "I was so worried when you wouldn't wake up after your surgery."

"We all were," my pops added as he came and rubbed my head. "Glad you're okay, son."

"I'm just glad it's over." My mother sighed and wiped the sweat from her forehead.

"Thanks to you," my pops clowned. "Pistol-packing mama saves the day."

"Hush, Gerald." She smirked. "Ain't none of that shit a bit funny."

"I didn't make that name up, Gladys. The media named you that, and I just agreed with them while acknowledging your protective skills. *Baybeee,* they are on point! You saved our son and Oaklyn," Pops cheered and hugged my mother tightly, then rocked her body back and forth until she laughed with him.

While they stood there joking, my father told me that my old coach, Kevin Riley, had been up at the hospital, checking on me. "He's out in the waiting room."

"You just left him out there?" I asked.

"You ain't even supposed to have but two visitors now, and we're pushing it."

"Well, don't just leave him out there if he been here waiting," I urged my pops.

"Don't worry, Gunner. My mom is out there talking Coach Riley's ear off about basketball. She rushed up here as soon as she dropped Brazil at school." Oaklyn wore an embarrassed expression and used her hand to cover her face. When she looked up a couple of seconds later, she shook her head. "I told her that I was okay, but once she got to meet Coach Riley in person, she couldn't stop running her mouth. I'm so sorry."

"If you ask me, Kevin didn't seem too bothered by it. In fact, he looked like he was very well entertained."

"Lord!" Oaklyn grunted.

"It's cool," I replied as the nurse came in and shot some more meds into my IV. Drowsiness hit me almost immediately, and I found myself fighting to keep my eyes open. Needless to say, I lost pitifully and passed out while everyone stood around my hospital bed.

With no idea how much time had passed when I finally opened my eyes again, I saw everyone had gone except Oaklyn. "It's nighttime again already? What day is it?" Discombobulated and a bit groggy, I wiggled and pushed myself upward using my right hand until I could properly sit. My sore left shoulder throbbed, and the sling they had my arm in didn't make it any better.

"Yes, and the doctor said that they would discharge you tomorrow. Your parents offered to take you to their house until you recover a little more, but I know you probably wanna be in your own space."

"It's just my shoulder. I can walk and use my right hand. I'll be good."

"Are you sure? Because if you need me to stay with you for a few days to a week, Mom said that she didn't mind Brazil staying with her. She can take her to and from school. It's not a problem."

"You would do that for me?" I asked with a raised brow.

"Why wouldn't I?" She laughed and bent down to kiss my lips. "I care about you, and I ain't about to let you struggle by yourself. Besides, between me and you,

Gunner, I'm still traumatized by the whole ordeal. I couldn't even go home and shower—"

Cutting Oaklyn off, I told her that I didn't think it was a good idea to go back to my house. "My mother had the bathroom cleaned, but just being there might trigger some shit. Nah, I don't think we should do that."

"You wanna come to my place?"

"Your new house?" I asked with a grin.

"I haven't even seen it yet, Gunner. Stop playing." Oaklyn giggled. "That means that there aren't any utilities on or any furniture in the place."

"My mother already took care of that, and she has all the housewarming gifts waiting to be delivered."

"Gunner!"

"What?" I chuckled and stared at Oaklyn. Hypnotized by her raw beauty, I smiled and shook my head. This woman was the one for me. That, I was sure of.

"Gunner, you and your family have done so much for me and mine that I'm feeling overwhelmed and in debt."

"You don't owe nobody shit. Everything done for you, you deserve. You gotta believe what you bring to the table is valuable."

"What the hell I got that's worth a damn?" Oaklyn teared up and turned away, then eased over to the window. As she gazed out at the lights shining in the dark of the night, she remained quiet.

"Oaklyn, you have a bright future ahead of you."

"By being my daughter's manager? By making my money off her talents?" she replied, sounding annoyed. "That's her money, and I would feel guilty spending it."

"Are you serious?" I tried not to laugh.

"Yes, Gunner, and you probably don't understand. You make your own money."

Suddenly, I remembered about Oaklyn's desire to go back to school. If she used some of Brazil's endorsement money for the classes, then started her own business once she finished, she could pay her daughter back before she even knew she had used it.

"That's a good idea. I didn't even think about that." With a smile on her face, Oaklyn dried her face and came over to me with a hug and a kiss. I welcomed all the affection but got irritated when it was disrupted by police presence.

"Mr. West?"

"I already gave a statement."

"We're not here about a statement. We're here to let you know that the woman who was killed was not Camille Rollins, but her sister, Janille Rollins."

"What?" Oaklyn and I gasped in unison. "I saw her before she shot me. I heard her threaten me. It was her face . . . her voice. They do look alike, but damn!" I sighed in disbelief.

"I'm sorry, Mr. West. Her identity was confirmed by her sister, Camille Rollins, this morning."

Was I living in a nightmare that I couldn't wake up from? Was this cop serious? "Where is she now? You know I got a restraining order against her, right?" I explained. "And don't tell me she ain't dangerous because Camille went by my parents' house not that long ago, looking for me. She spoke to my pops, and I know she had something to do with all this. Y'all better get her for violating that fucking order."

"We don't have proof of that just yet."

"My pops said he called—"

"Until we have proof that it was indeed Camille Rollins who violated the order, we can do nothing but put a mental hold on her for threatening to kill herself and others in the presence of an officer. We already have her in custody. They're in the process of giving her a psych evaluation. We'll know more after that."

"What exactly did she say?" Oaklyn questioned with a scared look.

"I'm not at liberty to give specific details, but I can tell you that she is angry and dangerous."

"She threatened to kill herself *and others*, and you can't tell me what she said?" I questioned angrily. "Is my life in danger? Did Camille say she was going to kill me?"

"Actually, your entire family may be in danger, Mr. West, including your girlfriend—" The female officer paused and checked her phone. "Ah, Oaklyn Jones."

"That's me. She wants to kill me?" Oaklyn shrieked. "First, her sister tries to kill me, and now she wants me dead? I don't even know these folks, and I damn sho' ain't did shit to either of them."

"Wait, wait, wait!" I interrupted. "If she threatened to kill me, ain't that a violation of the restraining order?"

"Initially, but when she claimed insanity and threatened suicide, she was taken to the mental hospital. Things are out of our hands at the moment."

"Fuck that! She threatened my life. Am I safe? Are we safe?" Oaklyn yelled. "I'm fucking scared!"

"Ma'am, we realize that, and that's why we've assigned security to trail all of you."

"My parents too?" I inquired and immediately worried about them.

When I voiced my concern about their safety, Oaklyn suggested that we all stay at her new place. That way, we could all be together and look out for each other.

"No one knows where the house is, Gunner. I think it's the best solution until we find out what's going on with Camille."

"They're going to evaluate her mental state and go from there," the taller officer said. "We will keep you updated."

After the cops apologized again, they departed, leaving me and Oaklyn there to discuss things. I started out by asking her how she felt about all of this. My main concern was my family. That included Oaklyn, Brazil, and Draya too. That shit was mandatory.

Chapter Twenty-four

Oaklyn Jones

After I dialed up Koola to let her know that I was okay, she had a bunch of questions to ask. Seeing that I hadn't called my mother yet, I had to cut her short and tell her that I would hit her back later.

"I gotta call my mama and let her know what's going on." I panicked once I hung up with Koola, and I held tightly onto my phone.

"What are you gonna tell her?" Gunner probed.

Not wanting to repeat myself, I held my finger up to delay my response, then dialed my mother. Once it began to ring, I hit the speaker icon to make sure that I included him in the conversation.

"Hey, Oaklyn. How are you guys doing?" she greeted me.

"Hey, Mom. I won't hold you, but I just wanted to tell you about this weird visit we just had." When I had her attention, I repeated everything that the cops had told us, but she didn't respond. A man did!

"Mom, who is that?"

"That's Coach Riley," Gunner whispered with a laugh.

After shooting him a frown, I took my mother off speaker and questioned her about fooling with this guy. Hell, she had just met him that same damn day.

"Where's Brazil?"

"She's fine. She's in her room reading," my mother answered. "You don't have to worry about her, but I *am* worried about you, Oaklyn. What's going on, and what are you guys gonna do?"

"I don't know, Mom, but I'm scared," I confessed. "Me, Gunner, and his parents already discussed staying at my new house. I would feel more comfortable if you and Brazil come too."

"I don't think it's a good idea to worry Brazil about all this. It's already hard enough to keep her away from the news and the internet. You know that girl tries to read everything."

My mother was right, and I didn't know what else to do. How could I keep them safe?

"Look, I got a place up by Mount Hood. Draya, you, and Brazil can stay there," Coach Riley said.

"But she has school," I intervened.

"Oaklyn, you can call up there tomorrow and let them know you're taking her out for a week or so. If they question you, explain the situation to them."

"I don't want her to get behind," I said, worried.

"They can email you all of her work so she won't get behind, Oaklyn."

Although my mother had good points, I didn't like it. I didn't like it one bit, and when I hung up with her, I interrogated Gunner about this Coach Riley guy.

"He's as good as they come, Oaklyn. Your mother is safe."

"He ain't got no wife or crazy exes, does he?"

"Nope. His wife died a year ago, and he's been by himself ever since. I would say that I'm surprised that he took to your mother so fast, but I know exactly why he did," Gunner clowned.

"Why?"

"Her love for basketball and her knowledge of him and the game. Trust me, Oaklyn. I know that man," he said with a chuckle. "Besides, Brazil and your mother are about to have a ball at Coach Riley's six-bedroom house out by Mount Hood."

"Why?"

"He has an indoor basketball court, an indoor pool, hot tub and sauna, a home theater room, and a library full of books."

"Damn, I wanna go too," I joked, sounding like a big kid. "Nah, I'm playing. I'm too excited about seeing my new house to wanna be anywhere else."

"Well, go see it," Gunner urged.

"Not without you," I said, getting serious. "I'm not going anywhere by myself. That's why I brought my clothes to take a shower here in your room. I'm telling you, Gunner. I was scared at first, but now that the cops came and told us crazy Camille is still on the loose, I'm fucking terrified."

"Maybe she'll just go away."

"And maybe she'll come kill us all for killing her sister. You said it yourself that her sister was all she had left. Shit, what that girl got to lose?" I asked Gunner.

When he couldn't find the words to respond to my question, I grabbed my duffle and went into the adjoining private bathroom to shower and clear my head. With so much weird shit happening, I didn't know if I was coming or going.

"*Woooo!*" I gasped loudly and jumped forward when I felt a presence behind me.

Instantly pausing my movement, Gunner used his right hand to gently hold my shoulder, then eased my body backwards to kiss the rear of my neck. In between kisses, he whispered in my ear, "I'm sorry, baby. I didn't mean to scare you. I just thought I'd come in here and wash your back for you or something like that."

After he used his foot to close the door behind him, he slipped out of his hospital gown and exposed his hardened hunk of meat. Determined to get a better look, my eyes shot downward and zoomed in on it like a hawk. Amazed by the way he made his dick bob back and forth to entertain me, I became momentarily hypnotized. I didn't come back to reality until I heard Gunner speak.

"He's calling you," he teased. "He misses you."

Shit, I missed him too, and I wanted to hop right on that muthafucka, but I didn't want to hurt his shoulder. "Wait, your sling."

Hastily snatching the thick, clear plastic drawstring bag off the tall basket with the lid, Gunner handed it to me and asked me to help him put it on. I moved quickly to get the job done so that his erection wouldn't fade.

"I want you so bad," he mumbled in between kisses.

Not as bad as I want you.

To get Gunner in a good position, I backed him onto the built-in wooden bench and motioned for him to sit. Once his bare ass touched the seat, his hardness popped upward. Lifting one leg up, I straddled him, then eased down on it and released a loud moan. The powerful climax made my ears ring and made me want more.

"*Ooohhhh,*" I gasped and continued to bounce on his tool. With the hot water hitting my back and ass, along with Gunner's mouth that was full of my breasts, I couldn't stop myself. The sensation was amazing!

"Fuck, you feel so good," I chanted as he used his right hand to grip my ass and push deeper into me.

While his dick traveled to depths that had never been visited before, he hit a virgin spot. The unexpected thrill instantly sent my body into a sexual convulsion. "Oh, shit!" I hollered out.

"I'm cumming, baby!" Gunner shouted.

"Me too!"

It was like we were in our own little world and didn't care about anything except what was going on in that bathroom. That was exactly why we didn't hear the nurse calling out for Gunner to tell him that he had a visitor. We didn't have a clue until the bathroom door flew open just as we shared a very intimate moment.

"What the fuck?" Braxton gasped as I leaped off Gunner's dick. My baby daddy evilly stared down at my lower body as a thick clump of cum ran down my inner thigh. This man went off.

"Get the fuck out, Braxton! What are you even doing here?" I hollered and tried to grab a towel, but I couldn't because I got snatched out of the shower.

As soon as Braxton put his hands on me, Gunner got involved, and now it was a fight—titties, ass, and dick just swinging! To say I was embarrassed when the nurses and security came in was an understatement. There was nothing that I could do but grab a towel and wrap it around me.

"I'm sorry, but I'm going to have to ask both of you to leave." The female guard spoke rudely.

"Oaklyn ain't gotta go nowhere," Gunner hissed while still standing there with semi-hard shaft bobbing.

"Can you please cover up, sir?" the female guard requested. Her face reddened even more as she passed him a towel.

Gunner rudely snatched it from her, held it over his private part, and continued to go off. "Fuck that! Remove that nigga. He's the one who came in here without permission, and y'all had to be the ones who let him in."

"Sir, he told us he was family."

"I'm her baby daddy," Braxton panted and pointed to me.

"She's not the fucking patient," Gunner hissed. "I am, and the staff is wrong for letting this fool in here."

"You two are foul for fucking in here," Braxton argued. "Don't this go against hospital policy or some shit? Or do y'all condone shit like this? Either way, the press will have a field day with this—"

"Look, I don't want any problems," one of the doctors interrupted as he joined us. "I'm just going to ask that your visitors leave."

Without hesitating, Gunner went to the closet and got his bag of clothes. "You may as well draw up my discharge papers because if you kickin' my girl out, I'm leaving too."

"No, don't do that," I pleaded. "I'll just go to the house and—"

"Nope, I'm coming with you," Gunner insisted, then turned to the cops. "But you can escort that mark out who you let in without my permission. That's what you can do."

"I ain't do shit," Braxton snapped with rage present in his eyes.

"I see scratches on this young lady," the tall white cop acknowledged. "Are you okay?"

"I'm fine. I just want him gone," I replied honestly. "That's all I want."

Braxton tried to argue, but the officers ignored his pleas as they finally escorted him toward the door of Gunner's hospital room. Before he disappeared, he turned to me with tears in his eyes. "You really killed my heart with this one, Oaklyn. Damn, I can't believe it," he confessed.

When Braxton lowered his head and left the room, a strange lump formed inside my stomach. I actually felt bad for hurting him.

Damn.

Chapter Twenty-five

Braxton Carter

"What the fuck was that shit?" I gritted as I sat in my truck parked in the lot at the hospital. Damn the tears that fell; it was my heart that was crushed. Never had I felt that type of pain, not even when I was homeless, lonely, and hungry. Was this the type of anguish that Oaklyn experienced every time she found out that I cheated on her? If it was anywhere close to the pain that I felt at that moment, I knew that she had to be fed up.

"Fuck!" I yelled and pounded my steering wheel. As I bowed my head and closed my eyes to pray for clarity and peace, all I kept envisioning was Oaklyn riding that muthafucka like that in the shower. No matter how hard I tried, I couldn't erase those memories from my mind.

"Why the fuck did I come up here?" I sighed heavily as my cell rang. It was Chachi. Taking a deep breath, I wiped my face and connected the call.

"What's good?"

"I'm checking on you, nigga. I done heard what happened."

"You don't know half the shit." I sniffled and began to explain.

"Wait, I don't mean to stop you, Brax, but why did you even go up to the hospital?"

"Because Oaklyn almost got killed behind that dude."

"But you said you saw her at the Justice Center, and she shut you out," Chachi reminded me.

"She did, but I was still worried about her. All that shit I heard on the news. I just wanted to talk to her, and she wasn't answering," I explained.

"But what made you go to that nigga's room, though, Brax?"

"Instinct. Pure instinct," I answered truthfully. "It was a gut feeling. I guess it was just meant for me to see that shit."

"See what?" Chachi asked.

After I explained what I walked in on, this fool screamed and cracked up, like the shit was really funny. Fuck that! My feelings were hurt.

"See? I told you," Chachi clowned.

"Who the hell wanna hear that shit right now?" I snapped, ready to hang up on him. "I'm over here hurting, and you wanna joke."

"No, I don't mean nothing by it, but I've been telling you, man. It don't feel good to be on the receiving end of the bullshit, does it?"

"Hell no, nigga! This chick got me in tears."

"You crying?" Chachi gasped. "Please tell me you didn't break down inside the hospital."

"No, fool. I ain't that weak." I laughed. "But I did let all that shit out when I got in my truck."

"Where are you now, Brax?"

"Still in my truck, in the parking lot of the hospital."

When I replied to Chachi's question, I spotted Oaklyn going outside to get the Benz. Once she got it, she drove it around to pick Gunner up. He was waiting in a wheelchair just outside the main entrance. The nurse beside him helped him in, and they drove off. As badly as I wanted to follow them, I fell back and took the advice of Chachi, who was still on the phone, asking me a million questions about the fight. He couldn't get over the fact that I had fought with Gunner while he was naked.

"What was I supposed to do? Wait for that nigga to get dressed?" I gritted. "Shit, I should've taken his head smooth the fuck off. That's what I should've did."

"And then we wouldn't be having this conversation right now. You would be in jail waiting on that one free phone call, and I'm sure it wouldn't be to me."

"Chachi, man, you stay having jokes, and I need a laugh right now. Thanks." I chuckled.

"What you need is a drink and chill. Let's go to the Spare Room and shoot some pool," he suggested.

"I'll meet you there in thirty. Just let me go to the suite and change. This nigga done ripped my shirt and shit."

"Damn, you guys was scrappin' like that?" Chachi asked and laughed. "Let me find out that nigga whooped yo' ass."

"Shit, that's what you ain't gonna hear," I assured him before we got off the line.

Focused on finding a distraction, I shot to the hotel I stayed in so I could shower and change into something more casual. A drink with my name on it waited for me at the bar, and I was on my way.

"It's a little crowded in here tonight," I mumbled as I arrived at the Spare Room and entered the side door.

"Braxton, what's good?" a friend of mine, A.D., asked. "I heard about Oaklyn and that shooting over at Gunner West's house—"

"She's good." I cut him off and then waved in the air at Chachi, who stood behind him. "Good to see you, man."

If this was how the night was about to go, it was time to bounce up out of there. I wasn't about to stick around and be questioned about Oaklyn and Gunner all night, especially after I caught them fucking. Nope. No, thank you.

"What's got you uptight?" Chachi probed. "You ain't been in here but a split second and you already frowned up. What's going on, Brax?"

Once I explained what A.D. had asked me, Chachi shook his head and warned me that it was just the beginning. "What did you expect? You're a celebrity, Gunner West is an icon, and now Oaklyn and Brazil are well known in the city."

Fuck what he's saying. This was my life, and these questions were an invasion of privacy. What I did on my own time was my own business. As far as Oaklyn or Gunner went, I wasn't even going to speak on it. Nope, I wasn't going to do it.

To avoid another awkward situation, Chachi and I chose a table in the back and shot a couple of games while we drank. After that, I took my ass right on to the hotel.

"I can't believe her," I whispered to myself as I drove down Sixtieth Street heading south. "She really fucked that nigga. Raw, at that!"

What if she got knocked up? What if she had a baby by that dude?

My palms were sweaty as I arrived at the hotel and went into my suite. The thoughts of Oaklyn in that shower continued to flash through my head while I kicked off my shoes and poured a drink.

Beep, beep, beep. You have one reminder. You are scheduled for a performance tomorrow night at the Moda Center. Arrival time is 6 p.m., and stage time is 8 p.m. Beep . . . beep . . . beep.

The alarm that went off on my phone app continued to repeat itself until I finally cut it off. The way my life was going, singing in front of a bunch of folks was the last thing I wanted to do. The more I dreaded doing this gig, the more I was tempted to cancel, but if I did, I would have to repay the money they had already given me. I couldn't afford that shit.

Feeling defeated, I downed my drink and went to bed, praying that I would drift off without thinking about Oaklyn. To block the negative thoughts, I tried to reminisce about the good times, the times when we were madly in love. If only I could get those days back. If only I could get Oaklyn back.

Just to see where her head was, I wanted to call her so badly, but I couldn't risk appearing desperate—even though I was. Anxious enough to dial my baby mama up and beg her to leave that nigga Gunner alone, I picked my cell up, ready to lay all my cards on the table. Luckily, reason kicked in before it could happen.

"What am I gonna do?" I sighed heavily.

As I tossed and turned on the bed, I struggled to stop myself from calling Draya. The last time I did that, I had to hear all about my cheating ways. Maybe it would be different if she knew I had caught her daughter fucking Gunner in a public place.

Taking a chance, I called Oaklyn's mother and snitched on her, but it didn't go quite as I expected. Instead of going off and admitting that she was embarrassed about her daughter's behavior, she burst out laughing.

"Braxton, I'm sorry, babe. I love you like a son and all that, but maybe that's what you needed to see. No, no, no. Maybe that was what you needed to *feel*. That pain. It hurts, don't it?" Draya asked with a giggle. "I don't mean to poke fun at you, Braxton, but what else can I say?"

What else can she say? Did she really just ask me that dumb shit?

"My fault, Draya. I just thought that you would be embarrassed about your daughter having sex in the hospital right after she nearly got killed the night before."

"Hell, they were probably comforting each other," she teased with a laugh.

This time, I could hear a man laughing with her. Right away, I thought about Brazil and asked about her.

"She's sleeping."

"So, she's staying with you until when?" I pressed.

"Braxton, you gotta talk to Oaklyn about all that. I'm not about to be in the middle of y'all stuff."

"A'ight then. I'll call her," I said before hanging up.

Just as I scrolled to dial Oaklyn, Teagan called me and asked if I was prepared for the gig the following evening. How couldn't I be? There were only five songs to do, and I had my new black Versace suit hanging up and my new black leather kicks sitting beneath it, ready to go. My fresh cut and groomed facial hair were on point. What more did I need to do to prepare?

"What's up with you, baby?" I asked Teagan. "It sounds like you're in the car. Where you headed?"

"I just had this crazy idea to pop by Eva's house unannounced, since she's ignoring my calls."

Women could be so childish. All that ugly tit-for-tat shit was unnecessary.

"What if she don't let you in?" I questioned curiously.

"I have a key."

"Ain't that just for emergencies?"

"This is an emergency."

"What is the emergency, Teagan?"

"I need to talk to my friend."

Tired of going back and forth with her in a verbal never-ending war, I cut it short. "Look, just call me when you leave ol' girl's house. Maybe we can hook up."

"For sure." Teagan giggled. "Talk to you soon."

When we hung up, I lay there, thinking about sexing her from the back, then began stroking my dick. It felt so damn good when it stiffened up, but then a vision of Oaklyn riding Gunner popped into my head. *Fuck!* Somehow, I had to find a way to erase that shit out of my mind before it drove me crazy. Something had to give.

Chapter Twenty-six

Teagan Hoffman

Eleven o'clock at night, and there I was, driving around town, trying to find something to eat after I had let Venezuela off early without thinking first. Sure, I could've easily had food delivered to my house, but I needed some fresh air, and some chicken egg foo young with a side of fried rice sounded good at the moment. This Chinese food joint over on Eighty-second Avenue was nearby, so I stopped there and ordered a little of everything. It was all delicious. Leaving there full and happy, I hopped on the highway and headed home, but then changed my mind halfway through the trip. Being alone didn't sound like such a good plan now. This pregnancy thing scared me, and the one person that I could talk to about it was Eva, but she wasn't answering her phone. Seeing that it was unlike her to ignore my calls, I hopped off the freeway and decided to look for her. My first stop, her house.

"Where is she?" I chanted to myself as I entered Eva's gated community fifteen minutes later. Deciding to give it another try, I dialed her up again as I turned onto her block. Although she didn't answer, I spotted her car in the driveway, and all of her lights were on.

"Wow!" Beside Eva's new white BMW 5 series 540i sat a candy apple red sports car. It looked familiar, but I couldn't quite place where I had seen it before. Curious to find out who the expensive vehicle belonged to, I used my key to enter her house instead of knocking. Hell, she did it to me all the time.

"Eva?" I called out as I tucked my keys in my handbag and walked through the elegant, circular marble-tiled foyer. Over the loud clicking of my heels as I walked through the hallway, I could hear talking and laughing coming from the kitchen. Curious and anxious to put a face to the second voice, I altered my route and headed that way. The closer I got, the clearer the vocals became. One of them belonged to Eva, and the other one, my cousin Amari.

What the hell?

"What's good, y'all?" When I appeared and spoke, they both jumped defensively, as if I were an intruder. Imagine that.

"Teagan, you just walked in—"

"Yes . . . I did just walk into your house without knocking. Just like you do me all the time, Eva." I smirked, then looked at Amari, who wore a fake-ass smile.

"Whatever," Eva replied nervously. That threw me off. Like, what the hell was she hiding? It was already weird enough that Amari was over there. They barely knew each other. Or so I thought.

"What's up with you two?" I inquired. "I'm surprised to see you over here, Amari."

"Like I'm surprised you just busted up in my shit unannounced?" Eva interfered with a nasty attitude.

Why was she so irritated and upset, though? If she didn't have anything to hide and she wasn't up to shit, why did she behave that way? That was what I wanted to know.

"Whatever, Eva. I came by to vent, but since you have company . . ."

"I was just leaving." Amari smiled, then winked at Eva.

For just a split second, I wondered if they were fucking around. Now, Eva wasn't known for messing around with women, but my cousin, she would get down with another female in a heartbeat. That, I did know.

"You ain't gotta leave on account of me, cousin."

"I'm not." Amari laughed and shook her head. "I'll call you tomorrow, Eva."

"Let me walk you out."

My eyes stayed on them as they left the kitchen. Could they really be fooling around? Curious to know, I asked Eva as soon as I walked down the hallway and met her in the living room.

"What's up with you guys? When did y'all get so cool?"

"Whatcha mean?"

"I mean, she was over here. I ain't never known her to be over here, Eva. What's really going on?"

"Okay, damn!" She grunted and sat in the white rocker recliner opposite of where I was. "What are you asking me, Teagan?"

"I'm asking you what's up with you and Amari. When did you guys start hanging?" I repeated.

"We started talking at your surprise party."

"Talking how?"

"Don't judge me, Teagan."

"If you like pussy, just say that shit. I tell you everything, Eva. What's so hard about telling me what's going on with you and Amari?"

"See, that's why I can't talk to you about everything."

"What?" I frowned.

"I haven't even told you shit, and you're already looking at me crazy. Ready to judge me. I didn't judge you when you slept with Braxton the very first time you met him."

"Eva! You guys slept together?" I gasped loudly and covered my mouth. "You go both ways?"

After taking a deep breath, Eva shook her head and lowered it. When she lifted it several seconds later, she told me all about how she and Amari were drinking and how she took her back to her place. When Eva got to the part about how great my cousin ate her goodies, I was through. I couldn't listen to another word, probably because I was too worried about one thing: pillow talk.

"Please tell me you don't discuss any of my business with Amari."

"Whatcha mean, Teagan?"

This girl knew exactly what I meant, but I still broke it down to her. I regretted telling her about my father having Walter killed, and especially about my pregnancy. Could I even trust Eva now?

"Did you tell Amari about the test I took?"

"Why would I do that?" she asked without looking me in the eyes.

That meant that she was lying. That shit right there was a problem. The only way to deal with a problem was to get rid of it. I hated for it to come down to that. . . .

"So, Teagan, why did you decide to just *drop* by?" Eva questioned, bringing me from my thoughts.

No way that I could vent to her now, not after finding out that she was hanging with the opp. Cousin or not, Amari worked for the family business. Dangerous shit.

"What was it, Teagan?" Eva pressed with her hands on her hips.

"I wanted to talk to you about maybe not having this baby," I lied to see where her head was.

"What!" she shrieked. "Abortion is against your religion. Your family would flip."

How the hell could she know what my family would and wouldn't do? The only thing I told her about was Walter's murder, so whatever else she knew had to come from Amari.

"I didn't say I would do it. I said I thought about it, Eva."

"Well, just get that shit out of your mind, Teagan. You're going to have your baby, even if you have to lie about the father."

Why the hell would I have to do that? Braxton wasn't a bad guy. He wasn't married, and he definitely hadn't put life insurance on me. After I thought about it, telling the truth wasn't such a bad thing. It certainly was better than having Eva get me caught up by running her mouth to Amari.

"So, you are going to have it, right?" Eva checked.

"Yes, you don't have to worry about that. I think I was just scared."

"Be more afraid of your father if you get that abortion."

"How the hell would he even know? Nobody even knows I'm pregnant except for you, Eva. I ain't even told Braxton."

"You didn't have to tell nobody about Walter either, but they found out," she countered.

Her argument may have been good, but now I trusted her even less. This chick was up to something. Up to something no good.

Chapter Twenty-seven

Gunner West

Two weeks later . . .

As I sat on the built-in bench beneath the picture window in the living room of Oaklyn's new home, I stared out at the cherry tree blooming. They were ripe and ready to pick. Debating about going outside to collect a few, I went into the kitchen searching for Oaklyn.

"Pops, where's the ladies?"

"In the back yard picking blackberries. I told them to wait until next month when they get bigger and juicier, but they couldn't wait," he said with a laugh. "You really knew what you were doing when you hired the landscaping company at the last minute. I'm impressed with all the additions you made to this place."

My father referred to the spiral staircase with sliding banister that I had added. It went from Brazil's room down to the game room, where a ball pit waited to catch her. She hadn't seen it yet because Draya had her over at Coach Riley's vacation home. According to Brazil, she was having a ball—both her and her grandma.

"Hey, y'all!" Oaklyn laughed as she and my mother came through the back door with blackberries and plums too. "I love these fruit trees. The fruit is so fresh."

"Thank Gunner for that." Pops chuckled as he went and got the bucket of berries from my mother.

"Thanks goes to all of you and the women's foundation that organizes the yearly charity basketball games. You guys have changed my life, and I will forever be grateful." Oaklyn smiled, displaying her deep dimples.

"Oh, sweetheart." My mother reached out. "You and Brazil deserve everything given to you and more. Blessings on top of blessings."

"You will realize just how blessed you are when you sign that contract tomorrow and receive your first check," Pops replied with a slight chuckle.

"That money can't compare to how God has blessed me with an extended family," Oaklyn explained. "All my life it's been me and my mama, then Brazil came along, and my life grew with love. Now it's blossoming into something special . . . something real. Thank you. All of you."

The emotions overwhelmed me, especially when I watched Oaklyn begin to cry. The only thing that stopped me from getting drawn in was when my cell rang loudly and silenced us all.

"Hello?" I answered, then became quiet as I listened to the officer on the other line explain to me what they were doing with Camille's case. After the seventy-two-hour hold, they admitted her for further testing. As of now, they had diagnosed her with severe depression, bipolar disorder, and delusional disorder. That right there was enough to hold her longer.

"What's going on?" my mother questioned when I hung up and set my cell on the kitchen counter.

"Good news, for now," I started. "They're gonna hold Camille for the full thirty days. That'll give my attorney a chance to build a better case against her."

"Yes, I hope he does because ain't nobody trying to live in fear. I'm ready to go back to my house," my mother added.

After my pops agreed, my parents packed their things and went home for the remainder of the month. Since I had decided to take the rest of the season off and didn't have any prior commitments, that left me and Oaklyn there to enjoy ourselves.

"How about getting Brazil for the weekend? I miss my baby," Oaklyn whined. "I think it'll be safe since Camille is in mental lockup."

"Let's do it," I agreed. "We already have to go to Coach Riley's tomorrow and get her so she can go to the signing."

"Great. That works out perfectly," Oaklyn replied as her cell rang. When she drew it out of her pocket and checked the screen, she scrunched up her face. "It's Braxton."

"You haven't spoken to him yet?"

"Nope, not since the incident up at the hospital," she answered. "I've been avoiding him because of the disturbing messages he's been sending me."

"What messages?" I asked, surprised that Oaklyn had held a secret from me.

"I didn't wanna tell you this, Gunner, but Braxton has a lawyer, and he's trying to battle me for joint custody of Brazil. My attorney doesn't think he has a fighting chance because he doesn't have steady employment or his own spot. From what she says, he's still staying in a hotel. Brazil ain't about to go through that shit."

Oaklyn was overprotective of her daughter, and I loved that about her. She was one of the best mothers I knew. Humble and selfless.

"When and how did you get an attorney?" I questioned, then tried to figure out when she had time to find one.

"I called legal aid, and they appointed me one," she revealed.

"She may be good and all, Oaklyn, but I would feel better if I hired co-counsel for you."

"I can't accept that, Gunner."

"Accept it now, and if you feel like you gotta pay me back, which you don't, then we will revisit the topic. Deal?" I proposed.

Oaklyn hugged me, then thanked me several times. As we broke apart, her phone rang again.

"Let me get this over with." She sighed, then took in a deep breath before she connected the call. "Hello?"

"Oaklyn! Where the hell are you and Brazil? At the new house that you ain't gave me the address to? What happened to me coming to get her last weekend? She ain't even been in school, and—"

"And you wanna take me to custody court?" She cut him off.

Continuing to ear hustle, I listened while Braxton did everything that he could to rile Oaklyn up, including talking shit about me. Paying attention to the petty shit he said, I gritted my teeth and bit my tongue. Out of respect for Oaklyn, I chilled until Braxton crossed the line and spoke about the fight we had up at the hospital.

"Tell that nigga I ain't in a sling no more," I said.

"Hush!" Oaklyn giggled and playfully swung at me.

"That's where you are? With that nigga Gunner?"

"What business is it of yours, Braxton? Brazil's fine, and we have a police detail."

"What the fuck y'all need security for, and why you ain't been done told me some shit like that? Brazil is my daughter, too, and if she's in danger—"

"She's fine, Braxton, and I gotta go."

"Yeah, she gotta go," I added with a laugh. To irritate her baby daddy, I made loud smacking noises when I laid kisses all over her face and neck. "Oaklyn is busy right now."

"Stop it!" She laughed even louder as she tried to get away from me. "I gotta go, Braxton. I'll see you in court."

Boy, I know dude got highly upset when Oaklyn hung up on him because he called her nonstop. When she refused to pick up, he sent her a text with his new address and requested that she bring Brazil over there for the weekend.

"I think you should. You know, just to keep in good standing with the courts," I suggested, hoping that what I said didn't upset her.

"You're right. I'll just get her tomorrow and then take her to him Friday after the signing."

"You need me to come with you?" I offered.

"Nah, I better go by myself to keep the static down. You know how shit ended up the last time all three of us were together." Oaklyn smiled and hugged my waist.

As our lips touched, my manhood rose to the occasion. To satisfy his appetite and mine too, I took Oaklyn to her master bedroom and dove between her thighs—headfirst.

Chapter Twenty-eight

Oaklyn Jones

Two days later . . .

Gunner and I couldn't get enough of each other. The more time that we spent together, the harder I fell for him. Even Brazil could see the bond we created.

"Are you guys getting married?" she asked as I braided the last braid on her head.

"Brazil!" I gasped, wondering where the hell that question came from.

"No, it's okay, baby," Gunner assured her with a laugh. "Hopefully, one day I can get your mama to marry me."

"Don't get her started." I sighed with a giggle as I let Brazil up from the floor and had her turn to me so that I could see the style I did on her hair from the front. "Oh, girl! Look at you. Just beautiful."

"Let me see," Brazil yelled as she got up and ran to her personal bathroom down the hallway. "I love it, Mom."

"You knew just what you were doing," Gunner teased.

"What?"

"How you changed the subject when I talked about marrying you."

"Gunner, we haven't even officially said we were together. *And,* I definitely ain't heard you express your feelings for me."

"I show you all the time, baby." He smiled and kissed me.

"*Verbally*, Gunner!"

"Huh?"

"Yeah, it's okay. If you're not feeling me like that." I pouted playfully, then pulled away.

"Girl, you better come here," he whispered. "You know I love you."

Those three words left me speechless. As long as I had been waiting to hear them, I didn't know how to react.

"Wow." He smiled. "You ain't got nothing to say? You ain't gonna tell me how you're feeling . . . or *not* feeling?"

"I love you too, Gunner. I've loved you since the first day you showed me that I was special, and you haven't stopped since. I can't explain how you saved me when I was in a dark place. I honestly didn't think I could love again after my heart turned cold long ago. Me and Braxton may have only broken up a couple of months ago, but mentally, I've been checked out for quite some time."

While we shared another intimate kiss, Brazil burst back into the room, screaming and hollering. "*Ooooo-wee!* Y'all in love!"

"Hush, girl, and get ready to go with me to sign your contract, then I'll drop you at your dad's new house," I hissed then laughed.

"I just got here, and I wanna stay in my own room tonight. I just love my room. I love it here, Mom."

"What about Coach Riley's house?" Gunner asked.

"Yes, I love it there, too, but Grandma and Coach Riley are always wrestling and playing on the bed—"

"Whoa! Too much information." Gunner chuckled loudly.

While he was tickled to death over what Brazil tattled, I wondered what the hell was going on over there. Did my mama really get her groove back?

"I'm glad Coach is happy." Gunner smiled.

"I'm glad you guys are happy too," Brazil butted in. "Mom, I was tired of seeing you crying over Daddy. I love him, but not for you, Mom. Gunner is better for you. He's always here for us, and he never makes you cry. You love him?"

"Yes, Brazil. I love him."

"Good, Mom, because I love him too," she cheered and went to jump into Gunner's arms.

My mouth dropped to the floor. I was just astonished by her words. *When the hell did she grow up, and how did she know so much about relationships?* Apparently, she did pay attention to what was going on around her, more than I thought.

"Let's go, girl," I urged while grabbing her backpack off the floor.

"I'll drive my truck, so you can go drop Brazil off afterward. Is that cool?" Gunner checked.

Once I agreed, we left in separate vehicles and met at the company's business office downtown. Thankfully, the signing was private. Only select reporters were permitted inside. That made the process go quickly and smoothly, until it was time for questions. Brazil must have had a dozen of them.

"What am I getting paid for?" she asked innocently.

"For representing our brand. You'll be modeling and speaking to the public."

"Will I get to play basketball?" she inquired.

While she waited patiently for an answer, the small crowd laughed loudly and complimented her innocence. They were amazed by the little girl in front of them, and I couldn't be prouder.

"You sure will." The manager of the company smiled and went over to take pictures with Brazil.

Exhausted after an hour of photos, signing contracts, and answering questions, I was ready to leave. Gunner was too.

"That was intense," Brazil said, bucking her eyes. "A million dollars! Mom, what are you gonna do with all that money?"

"That's your money, baby."

"Nope! That's *our* money, Mom. We're a team. Always," Brazil cheered.

We didn't even notice the reporter behind us, recording the whole conversation until it was over. "That was so sweet. That is one beautiful little girl. Truly one of a kind," she gushed.

"Thank you." Brazil grinned and waved at the young redheaded woman, then blew her a kiss. "You're beautiful too." That was it. My daughter was too much, and this spotlight that was on her had her clowning.

"Why are you so embarrassed when Brazil shows her unique personality, baby?" Gunner whispered as he walked us to the car. "I love it, and the public loves it too. Let her be herself. It's okay."

Maybe he was right, but I couldn't help how I felt. That child of mine needed to take it down a notch.

"You're right, babe," I replied with a smile as Gunner took me into a hold and kissed me.

Brazil had to tease. "Oh, Lord! Here y'all go." She giggled.

"Girl, get in the car."

"Okay, Mom." Brazil opened the door and climbed in, then buckled up while I said goodbye to Gunner.

"I'll see you back at the house."

"Be safe."

"You, too."

The butterflies danced in my stomach as I got in the car and pushed the start button with a smile. Brazil just had to say something sassy.

"Mom, seriously? So, you're really about to just drop me off at Daddy's?" She smacked her lips and huffed. "You know I wanna stay with you, right, Mom? I haven't seen you in a long time. I miss you, and I miss Gunner too."

"Don't you miss your daddy?"

"I do, but I'm used to him being away. He's strong, and he'll be okay if I stay with you, Mom. Call him and tell him that you don't want me to go."

"Seriously, Brazil?"

"Mom, I wanna stay with you."

Sick of arguing with my seven-year-old, I cut it short and told her that she was going. It wasn't up for debate. That shut her up. She didn't say a word until I pulled up at the address that Braxton had sent me.

"Daddy lives here?" Brazil questioned as she clicked her seatbelt off and sat up to look out the window. "His house is almost as big as ours, Mom."

"Yeah, and I'm sure you have your own room. Don't you wanna see it?"

Brazil got out as soon as I parked, then ran all the way to the door and rang the bell like crazy. I had to run up there and stop her.

"Hey, baby girl," Braxton greeted.

Our daughter leaped into his arms, hugged him, then asked where her room was.

"Don't you wanna see your puppy first?"

"*Puppy*?" Brazil yelled and jumped up and down. "You got me a puppy, Daddy?"

"Yep, and he's in the back yard in his doghouse, waiting for you. Go check on him and think of a name for him while I talk to your mama."

When Braxton led the way to the back door, I followed him so that I could get a better look at his house. It was pretty nice.

"Thank you, Daddy!" Brazil yelled as she ran outside to play with the puppy.

Closing the screen door, Braxton turned to me and shook his head. "Even after seeing you fuck that nigga like that, I still love you, Oaklyn."

"Do we have to go there?"

"I just want you to know that I'll fall back and let you find yourself. I'll be right here when you're ready to work on us again. I'm not giving up on you. I'm not giving up on us," he mumbled.

When he entered my personal space, I became nervous. The strange feeling made me uneasy.

"What makes you think I would ever get back with you, Braxton?"

"Because the love we share is forever."

"Yeah, I used to think that too, but not anymore."

"You don't love me?"

"Braxton, stop. I don't wanna talk about it."

"I love you, Oaklyn."

"*You love her*?" a female voice snapped from behind me.

Instantly spinning around, I came eye to eye with a beautiful, dark brown-skinned woman. Shaped like a Barbie, she wore expensive clothes and jewelry, and had long, single braids.

"You hear me, Braxton? Do you love her?"

"Teagan, stop that shit."

"No, I'm not gonna stop shit! Do you love her?"

On the verge of tears, Teagan rushed toward Braxton with her fist cocked back. I moved out of the way and peeped out the window, checking on Brazil, who was busy with the puppy.

"All this time you've been spending with me, all the love we make, and you wanna run back to this fat bitch?"

"Okay, maybe I should leave and take Brazil with me. I don't want her around all this madness," I huffed. "I knew this was a bad idea."

"No, wait," Braxton insisted and snatched away from Teagan. "This chick was just leaving."

"What?" she shrieked and went after him again.

"Get the fuck out, Teagan! My daughter is here, and you wanna come up in here being disrespectful by acting like this?"

"Braxton, I love you, and you over here beggin' this big bitch—"

"Whoa!" I warned while pointing my finger in her face, nearly touching her nose. With a second strike under her belt, she didn't have room for a third. This was my last and final warning. "Watch yo' fuckin' mouth."

Boldly grabbing my hand, Teagan bent my finger backward until it popped. *Strike three!* Without notice, I punched that bitch with my left. She had me fucked up if she thought she could put her paws on me with no repercussions.

"Get this big bitch off me, Braxton!" Teagan hollered and balled up on the floor to try to protect herself.

My baby daddy didn't make a move. He just stood there, letting me stomp this bougie-ass female until she screamed that she was pregnant. Equipped with that bit of pertinent information, I backed off, huffing heavily.

"That bitch is lying," Braxton insisted.

Forget what he said. I wasn't about to take the chance of catching a case if I made her miscarry.

"Bitch?" Teagan whined loudly. A bloody mess and crying, she struggled to get up off the floor.

Feeling badly for her, I extended my hand to help her, but she slapped it away. If I didn't have a heart, I would've punched her ungrateful ass in the face again.

"You fucked with the wrong one! Both of you!" Teagan hollered, snatching up her designer handbag and limping down the hallway. "And Braxton, you will be sorry if I lose this baby. My family will be coming for you." Angry and distressed, Teagan stormed out of the house and slammed the front door.

All I could do was laugh. "Boy, you sure know how to pick 'em."

"That ain't my girl."

"But that's your baby."

If I said I wasn't bothered by another woman having Braxton's baby, I would be lying. That shit hurt more than I cared to admit out loud.

"I'm sorry, Oaklyn. That girl don't mean nothing to me," he said, trying to convince me.

"Don't worry about how I'm feeling, Braxton. Worry about watching your back. You heard what Teagan said."

"What did Teagan say?" Brazil asked as she popped through the back door carrying the fluffy little black puppy.

"She didn't say a thing. She's gone."

"Is she coming back?" Brazil probed. "I'm just saying, if she does, I want her to bring me some of that ice cream she bought me last time."

"I'm about to go, boo. You staying?"

"Yeah, she's staying," Braxton gritted. "I miss my baby girl."

Brazil laughed and ran over to give me a hug. She wanted to stay. That puppy definitely did the trick.

"What are those scratches on your face, Mom? They look like the ones I had when I got in that fight with Amy. You remember that?" Brazil started. "Were you and Daddy in here fighting?"

"Girl, no," I said, thinking of a lie. When I couldn't come up with one quick enough, I did what I did best. I changed the subject, then got the hell out of there.

Troubled by what Brazil had insinuated, I sat in the car and called Koola to tell her what happened. Since she had run off to California with her new boyfriend, who I had yet to meet, I had barely spoken to her.

"Girl, I'm glad you answered because you wouldn't believe who I just got in a fight with."

Shockingly, Koola let me get it all out before she started screaming. "That nigga Braxton is a fool, Oaklyn."

Yes, he was. A *whole* fool.

Chapter Twenty-nine

Braxton Carter

Hurt and baffled, I fought to understand what had just happened. First, the fight in my kitchen where Oaklyn beat the hell out of Teagan. She got her good, but immediately stopped after the pregnancy claim.

"Damn," I mumbled to myself and thought about the brawl having a different outcome. Guilt from having evil thoughts consumed me as I stood there and silently wished that Oaklyn would've kept right on beating her until she lost it. A baby with Teagan wasn't an option for me.

"Daddy, I got a name for my puppy!" Brazil hollered as she ran back into the house for the third time and instantly seized my undivided attention.

"What is it?"

"Wait, wait, wait. It is a boy, right?"

"Yes, Brazil. It's a boy."

"Okay, okay. I'm gonna name him Lucky."

"I like that. But why Lucky, Brazil?"

"Because I'm the luckiest little girl in the world," she yelled and threw her hands up in the air while she twirled around. I loved seeing my daughter so happy.

"Oh, yeah! Your contract got signed today. Congratulations, Brazil. A seven-year-old millionaire."

"I don't care about that money, Daddy. Mom can have all that. I just wanna play basketball, make videos, and have fun like a kid."

"Don't you wanna buy toys and stuff for yourself? Don't you wanna start a college fund or something?"

"I'm gonna get a scholarship to go to whatever school I want to because I know how to work hard for it, Daddy. And I don't need any more toys. I have everything that I could ever want," Brazil explained. "I have my mom and my daddy. I have my grandma, and now Coach Riley, and I have Gunner. You all make sure I'm loved and that I'm safe, and that's all I need. Oh, and my basketball, too."

That girl was too much, and I loved the way she expressed herself. The only thing that I didn't like was how she threw Gunner up in there. And who the hell was Coach Riley? I sure did ask.

"He used to play for the Phoenix Suns, and he also coached Gunner's college team when he played for the Oregon Ducks. Grandma knows all about him. That's her new boyfriend."

Her new boyfriend? When did Draya start dating again?

All this was too much, and so was Brazil. She needed to stay out of the grown folks' business. That was what she needed to do.

"Go check on Lucky while I get this call," I told her, then waited for her to go outside before I picked up the phone.

"What, Teagan?"

"I'm at the hospital."

"Okay, are you good?"

God, please forgive me for hoping that she lost the baby, but I know it ain't meant for us to have one together. Please don't punish me like that.

"You think I'm good after you let Oaklyn jump on me like that, Braxton? Then you humiliate me by kicking me out in front of her?"

"Teagan, my daughter is here, and you came over here starting trouble by putting your hands on Oaklyn. I can't have that shit going on around my baby girl while I'm fighting for joint custody right now."

"While you're worrying about protecting Brazil, your baby inside of me might not make it," she cried. "Come here and be with me. I'm scared, and I can't call anybody."

"Where's Eva?" I asked her because I sure wasn't about to go down there.

"I want you, Braxton."

"I have Brazil, and I can't bring her with me. You'll just have to call your mom or dad."

"If I did that . . . if my father finds out that I'm pregnant and you let that girl make me lose my baby, he'll kill you, and maybe that bitch, too."

"You act like yo' daddy a mobster or some shit. I ain't worried about him," I replied with a laugh. "You done lost your mind, Teagan."

"He is a mobster, and my family runs deep. You saw some of them at my surprise party. You know what it is, Braxton," she low-key warned me.

Remembering the gangsters who were there that night made me believe Teagan, but I still wasn't about to run up there. Them muthafuckas would have to come for me. "Look, I hope you feel better, but I gotta go. My daughter needs me."

"I need you, Braxton!" Teagan hollered to the top of her lungs. "Don't make me press charges on you and Oaklyn."

"Bitch, you trespassed onto my property. I didn't invite you over. You don't have a key. Your name ain't on the lease, and I damn sho' didn't let you in. I ought to press charges on you."

Teagan took over the debate by talking over me, using a never-ending run-on sentence. She probably didn't even notice that I hung up until minutes later. When she called back, I didn't even bother answering. I just ignored her and went outside to get my daughter.

"Brazil, you need to come inside and bathe. You ain't even seen your bedroom yet."

Rushing through the back door with Lucky in her arms, Brazil followed me down the hallway so she could check out her Portland Trailblazers-themed sleeping quarters. She couldn't stop applauding when she saw it.

"This is the best, Daddy. I went from living in the projects to having two rooms, one here and one at Mom's. Oh, yeah, and the one at Grandma's, but that's small compared to the other two. I'm so lucky. No, no, no. Like grandma says, *I'm blessed.*"

She sure was, and so were her parents. Oaklyn and I couldn't be prouder of Brazil. She was truly exceptional, and it saddened me that I hadn't spent much time with her the past few years. Regretfully, back then, I had put my career first. Not anymore, though.

"Daddy, this is *awesome!*"

"You have your own matching bathroom, too." I showed her.

Brazil couldn't wait to take a bubble bath in her soaker tub. "Can you watch Lucky for me, Daddy?" she questioned as she tossed him into my arms.

"I guess so." I laughed and went right outside to put him in his heated doghouse, then went back inside.

While Brazil enjoyed herself playing with the basketball hoop that I had put up over the tub, I chilled in the living room and called Oaklyn. I wanted to make sure that she was okay.

Unlike all the other times I called her, she answered on the first ring. "Is Brazil okay?"

"She's cool. She's in the tub," I replied. "I was calling to check on you."

"I'm fine, and you ain't gotta worry about me. Worry about the baby you're having and that girl's daddy, who she said would kill you," Oaklyn clowned. "Matter of fact, maybe I should come get Brazil just in case she comes back acting up and brings her Mob family with her."

"Now you're clowning, Oaklyn. She ain't coming back over here. She knows better," I lied because I didn't know what Teagan was capable of.

Thrown for a loop by the discovery of her family Mob ties, I wondered if I should take Brazil back to Oaklyn. If something were to happen to our child, she would never forgive me. Hell, I would never forgive myself. Placing all my worries on the back burner, I focused on Brazil. She needed to feel my presence and know that I would always be there for her. In the past, I hadn't made it clear. To reconnect on a father/daughter level, I spent my evening watching movies and eating popcorn and chocolate with my baby girl until she passed out.

That gave me a chance to call the hospital to see if any of Teagan's stories were actually true. I needed to know.

Chapter Thirty

Teagan Hoffman

Braxton had it coming if I lost this baby because even after I told him that I was pregnant, he still didn't make a move to help me. It was like he wanted that big bitch Oaklyn to stomp the embryo out of me, knowing she was nearly twice my size. Upset, shaken, and alone, I lay in that cold hospital bed, feeling betrayed. How could Braxton act that way after sharing all of those intimate moments with me? The way I fucked and sucked him on demand had to count for something.

"Please let this be Braxton," I whispered as my cell rang in my handbag.

Disappointment swept across my face when Eva's full name popped up on the screen. Initially, I thought about letting her call go to voicemail, but I quickly changed my mind because I needed someone to talk to. Since Eva already knew that I was pregnant, I didn't think it would be a big deal to reveal what had happened over at Braxton's. Well, my version, of course.

"You were over there fighting?" She gasped loudly. "Teagan, are you and the baby good?"

"I'm waiting now to get an ultrasound."

"And Braxton's not there with you?"

"No, I'm here by myself."

When Eva offered to come, I gratefully accepted. "I'll see you soon."

"On my way," she assured me before hanging up.

Just as I put my phone away, the tech came in and gave me an ultrasound. At twelve weeks, she couldn't see much, but she did tell me that everything looked good. *Great news!*

"Stay put, Ms. Hoffman. We're just waiting for a few test results to come back before we can release you," the tech explained. "The doctor will be in to check on you shortly."

After the tech quickly disappeared out the door, I was left all alone again for the next thirty minutes. Where the hell was the doctor on duty? Crammed up uncomfortably on the firm mattress, I fidgeted with irritation. I didn't want to be there by myself with no one to talk to.

Right as I began to cry, up popped Eva. "Are you okay?" She gasped as she ran into the room, panting nervously.

"I should be asking you that."

"I'm okay. I ran up the stairs. That's why I'm breathing hard," she explained as she walked over to the side of the bed and checked my IV. "Good. They got fluids pumping into you to make sure you and the baby are hydrated," Eva acknowledged with a raised brow as she read the bag.

"What's wrong, Nurse Banner?" I teased her because she worked as an ER Nurse at Kaiser Hospital on Sunnyside.

"I was just checking to see what they were putting in you," she teased and bent down to give me a hug. "Wait, that girl did that shit to your face?"

"Bitch, please. You should see hers," I exaggerated. "I'm glad you're here, though. Can you get me some ice water?"

"Coming right up."

Eva dashed out of the room and came back within minutes with a big plastic cup of ice with a little water. I really appreciated her help.

"This is good, and I was thirsty. Thanks, Eva."

"Anything for you, boo. Anything to save your life."

As I set my cup on the side table, I wondered what Eva meant by that. I tried to ask her, but I suddenly became extremely drowsy. I don't know what came over me that quickly, but I couldn't fight the sleep that eventually knocked me out.

Unaware of how much time had passed, I woke up disoriented, with a massive headache and an upset tummy. Swiftly bending over the side of the bed, I released everything that I had eaten in the past six hours.

"Why is my stomach cramping? It feels like I'm starting my period," I grunted as the doctor walked in.

My parents entered behind him. How did they even know where I was?

As soon as that question popped into my head, a silent bell sounded off. The disturbing alert held me in disbelief. Refusing to grasp the facts in front of me, I anxiously scanned the room in search of Eva. She was nowhere to be found, and that didn't sit well with me.

"How . . . how?" I stuttered while staring at my mother.

After looking over at my father, she bowed her head and remained quiet. Never had I witnessed her behave this way.

"Mom?" I blurted out while glancing back and forth between the physician and my mother. "You're not gonna tell me what's going on? Is my baby okay, doctor? Tell me."

"I'm sorry to inform you, but while you were out of it, you began convulsing and bleeding. We had to do a DNC, and that's why you—"

This was not happening! It couldn't be. One minute, I'm looking at my baby's heartbeat on the ultrasound, and the next, I wake up bleeding? Something wasn't right.

"We found several drugs in your system. . . ." The doctor went on until I interrupted him again.

"I don't do drugs! Not even Tylenol, and I haven't even had a drink since I found out I was pregnant," I shouted. "Something ain't right. Someone did this to me. Someone made me lose my baby!"

I was throwing an all-out fit. The doctor excused himself and left me in the room with my parents. Neither of them looked happy.

"I'm telling you, Papa, somebody made me lose my baby," I hollered. "Where's Eva? She was the only one here."

"You didn't know yo' girl was a snake?" Amari spoke as she joined us.

Sweat began to form in my armpits and back when she crept closer to me with an evil look. As we locked eyes, she explained to me how she had used Eva. She only got close to her so that she could pump her for information.

Thinking back to what Eva had said before I passed out, I realized that she only did it to save my life. Was I in danger? Was my own family out to destroy me?

"Where is she? Where is Eva?"

"Why you wanna know where she is? The bitch ain't loyal," Amari scoffed.

"And you know what happens to anyone who crosses our family," my father added with an intimidating stare.

"Does that include me? Because I damn sure could've died with my baby."

"It's called sacrificing," Amari sneered. "The same thing your li'l friend did."

"What? What are you even talking about? Where is Eva?" I repeated.

Amari whipped out her phone and shoved it in my view. The sight before me would haunt me for the rest of my days. Poor Eva's sliced neck choked me up. All of the flesh and blood spewing from the wound broke me down.

"You killed her?" I gasped, ready to throw up again.

"Look, Teagan, the doctor went to get your discharge papers. You are coming home with us, and Amari will get your car home," my father clarified. "We will discuss all of this when we get there."

"I'm not going anywhere with you guys. You're all a bunch of murderers," I hissed. "Just get out!"

When no one moved, I began hitting the call button to get some help, but nobody came. That made me realize that my family had the staff on lock, too. Nowhere was safe for me. When they killed my baby, they should've just killed me, too, because now I had nothing left to live for.

Nothing.

Chapter Thirty-one

Gunner West

Two weeks later . . .

The day came for Camille's thirty-day evaluation and release hearing. My attorney urged me to appear and make a statement in order to make certain she was charged with a Class A misdemeanor for violating a restraining order. In Oregon, it carried a fine of nearly seven thousand dollars, along with up to one year in prison.

Hopefully, that will be long enough for her to get some mental counseling, I thought.

From what Detective Monague told us, Camille claimed that she had nothing to do with her sister, Janille, coming to my crib to try to kill me and Oaklyn. She said that Janille got angry after the story about me and Oaklyn went public, and everyone went against her. Although that story sounded believable, Monague explained how he had proof otherwise. According to video obtained from various businesses and a few neighbors who had the Ring camera installed, Camille and her sister were both seen at my parents' house, as well as out at Wilson High School, where I coached the boys' varsity team. That bit of information bugged the hell out of me. Thinking of all the times that they may have been watching me. For what, though? What were they up to? The thoughts of what crimes Camille might be capable of committing were disturbing. If her sister got killed because she was crazy enough to come for me, then what would Camille do?

"Damn," I chanted lowly while staring out the window at the two squirrels chasing each other up the tree.

Deep in thought, I stood there fidgeting until Oaklyn entered the living room, calling my name. "Gunner, are you ready to go?"

"Yep. Let's get this shit over with so we can get on with our lives." I sighed and embraced Oaklyn. "I'm so sorry for getting you caught up in all this mess. This shit is wild."

"No need for apologies, Gunner. You have no control over other folks' actions. That girl and her sister are responsible for this. Not you."

"Yeah, but you could've easily run off when Camille's sister tried to kill us, baby." I added a kiss and a smile before I went on. "You stuck by my side, and that screams volumes for your character. I'd be a fool to ever take your love for granted like the last man. I'll cherish that shit and you, too."

Oaklyn held me tightly. "Thanks for loving me, babe."

"Always and forever," I whispered and released her after another quick kiss. "Let's go."

On the way to southwest Portland, Oaklyn and I spoke about Brazil and how she had kept up with her studies during all the chaos. It actually took a team effort to make that happen. With the help of Draya and Coach Riley, Brazil had been focused and had even toned down her sassiness—just a little.

"Dang, this is where they're keeping her?" Oaklyn inquired while frowning at the large brick building, which we slowed down in front of. It appeared to be pretty old and a bit run down.

"You know you don't have to come in here with me, right?" I checked with Oaklyn when we entered into the west side of the parking garage and grabbed the nearest vacant spot.

"I wanna be in there for you, but if you're gonna be uncomfortable with my presence, I can wait in the lobby or something."

That simple exchange of words led to a mutual understanding. Together, it was. Hand in hand, we entered the building, filled with confidence. There were no more worries with Oaklyn by my side. She stood beside me for the entire hearing.

The evidence presented before the court consisted of factual information that my attorney had never shared with me before. With all my focus on him, I listened to him give a full background report on Camille and Janille. My face dropped and shock ran through me as he spoke about how the sisters were raised by their aunt in California, who abused them until they were taken away and separated in two different foster care homes. Two years later, at the ages of twelve and thirteen, Camille and her sister found each other, and three days later, their aunt was found dead. According to the reports, homicide didn't have enough evidence to link the girls to the murder, nor could they find them. Once again, they had disappeared and didn't pop back up on the grid until they both reached eighteen, ten years before I even met Camille.

"That's crazy." Oaklyn gasped lowly as we all sat around the long conference table and listened until he finished. He left the whole room quiet.

"Gunner West?" the judge announced.

Not prepared to speak after learning about the rough childhood Camille and her sister had, I asked for a few moments to drink some water and regroup mentally.

"Okay, I'm good." Once I cleared my throat, I began with how I met Camille, and then I rambled on about how things were during the first several months we were together. Everything was great between us, until things suddenly changed overnight. One day, we loved each other, and the next, she hated me, all because she couldn't go with me to a training camp where I had to teach. When I told her that I would be gone for several months, she flipped. She told lies on me, she broke my windows out, and even threatened to kill me. I explained that I didn't hate Camille. In fact, I felt sorry for her. Maybe if I had known about her past, I would've been a little more understanding. Just maybe.

"All I want is to feel safe," I said, wrapping it up. "The only way I see that happening is if Camille gets the help she needs. Whether that means she gets it in prison or the mental ward, so be it."

My testimony and all the evidence should've been more than what was needed to put that woman away, but they still let her have her last word, saying it was standard procedure. Whatever.

"You may speak, Ms. Rollins."

The once-beautiful Camille took the stand looking pitiful with no makeup, puffy eyes, messy hair, and a face full of rage. Looking like Beyoncé on drugs. The invisible daggers she shot my way stung, but I couldn't pull myself to look away. It felt as if she had some type of evil spell on me.

"I just wanna say, I love you, Gunner, and I have loved you since the day that we first met. I'm sorry for the way that I acted when you pushed me away, but you hurt me, and I went to that reporter with those lies because I wanted you to feel the pain that I felt."

Camille's demeanor went from evil to angry in a matter of seconds. Right before my eyes, she had turned into a totally different person. "You wanna know what's messed up, Gunner? It's messed up that it didn't even seem to faze you when you sued me. You took all my money and tarnished my name. Then, for you to flaunt another woman around in the media. . . . Yes, I got beyond mad, but not as enraged as I became when your family killed my sister. My only sister, Gunner. She was the only one who loved me. The only person I had left, and you knew that shit. You did that shit to punish me. But why? I swear . . . I swear, I hope you drop into hell with gasoline drawers on. If I could send you there today, I would, and whenever they let me out, know that I will. That's a fucking promise, Gunner. A fucking promise!"

"That's enough!" the mental health court judge yelled to security, and they got right on it. "Take Ms. Rollins out, right now!"

The tall, white, stocky guard hurried over to Camille with his handcuffs out, but before he could slap one on her wrist, she suddenly grabbed his gun and struggled to get it out. As they tussled for less than two seconds, she somehow took the safety off and released a single round, hitting the security guard's foot. For this small hearing, he was the only law enforcement officer in the room. It took another ten seconds for other cops to come busting in.

"Get *the* fuck back!" Camille cried out as she waved the weapon around, then landed her aim on me. "You took my heart and my sister's life. You gotta go!"

Just as she tapped the trigger, gunfire erupted. To protect Oaklyn, I pulled her to the floor and covered her with my body.

"What the hell?" she whispered as the room grew quiet.

"She's dead," I heard a male voice announce.

To see what was happening, Oaklyn and I slowly got up and peeked over the table. "They killed her?" she questioned.

"Yes, I don't think they had a choice, baby. She tried to kill me." The words that came from my lips made it real. Camille tried to kill me. First her sister, and now her.

"Clear! It's all over, and y'all can rise," the officer with the southern drawl announced. "But before you go, we are going to need to take a short statement from everybody. After you've done so, you are free to go."

Going out into the hallway, we gave a recap of what we saw and then got the hell out of there. No need to stick around and be reminded of the tragedy. As we walked to the parking garage, I called my parents and told them what had happened while Oaklyn did the same thing with her mother. As soon as we both finished our calls and got in my truck, we looked at each other and took a deep breath. When we released in unison, Oaklyn spoke first.

"Gunner, you know that right there made two dead bodies within a month. I can't take it anymore. I gotta find a release." She sniffled. "Two senseless deaths. Two women . . . two sisters. Mental illness is real, and no one deserves to go through something like that. Everyone deserves help, even Camille and her sister."

"I hear ya," I mumbled as thoughts of my ex being shot invaded my mind. That woman in the courtroom was not the Camille I knew and once loved. The devil now had a hold of her and made her unrecognizable.

"You know what? Since Camille didn't have family, let's make sure she and her sister are buried properly. I'm not saying we have to give them a funeral or anything, but we can pay for someone else to do it. We can also donate some money to a mental illness charity in their name. It would make me feel better to know some good came out of it."

"Oaklyn Jones, always looking out for folks. Girl, I tell you. I don't know anyone with a bigger heart."

"That can be both a blessing and a curse." She laughed, then looked at me. "You know what I need?"

"What's that?" I asked.

"I need a getaway."

"*We* need a getaway," I corrected as I hopped on the highway.

"Glad you feel that way, because I have a surprise at my house. I wasn't going to give it to you today after everything that happened at the hearing, but now, I really think that it's the perfect gift to bring joy to both of us."

Although we had just witnessed Camille losing her life, I couldn't help thinking that Oaklyn's surprise was a few rounds of stress-relieving lovemaking. If it was, I was with it, and after I sexually exhausted her in the bedroom, I planned on giving her the ring that I had been holding onto for the past two weeks.

To prevent spoiling her surprise, I decided to hold off on mine until she did her thing. I didn't want to steal the spotlight, but I did want to know what she had up her sleeve. "So, you just ain't gonna tell me anything?"

"Can't you wait five more minutes, babe? Dang."

Those next five minutes, I must've asked Oaklyn a dozen times to tell me her secret. She didn't budge, though. She held onto that shit until we got back to her place and went inside.

"Here it is," she cheered and pointed down to a set of designer luggage.

Sure, it was nice and all, but I didn't understand the sentimental value behind it. My confused look must've snitched me out because Oaklyn started laughing.

"What's so funny?" I wanted to know.

"Maybe I should've given you these along with the suitcases, huh?" Oaklyn teased and drew out airline tickets to Jamaica. "I even got my passport."

When she whipped it out and jumped into my arms, I about melted. Nobody had ever done something like that for me. Hell, I had always been the one planning and paying for trips.

"I ain't never been there before either," I confessed shamelessly. "I always wanted to go, though."

"Me too, and I can't wait for you to see where we're staying. The pictures got me so excited! I *love* the water, and I can't wait to go, babe."

"I can't either, and thanks so much, baby. This is something that we both need."

After we hugged, kissed, and celebrated with an intimate moment, I wanted to give her the ring, but I didn't. Something kept telling me to wait until we were on our trip. That way, maybe I could make the proposal more memorable.

One more week to wait. One week to prepare.

Chapter Thirty-two

Oaklyn Jones

A Week Later . . .

Thank goodness the ongoing drama had finally died down and enabled us to concentrate on Brazil and her first two sets of photo shoots for the next week or so. Considering all the offers that started rolling in once her athletic pics circulated all over the world, I could confidently say that her career got off to a great start. Exhausting, yet rewarding.

With the vacation getaway beginning the following day, Gunner and I had to take care of last-minute things. My house needed organizing, and Brazil needed to get back to my mother's, wherever that was. Ever since Coach Riley had come into her life, she had been staying between his two properties and her house. Not one complaint came from my mouth, though, because I thought she and Coach made a good match. Truthfully, I had never seen her so happy. My mother laughed more often, she smiled more often, and she seemed more passionate than before. I couldn't be more excited for her. She deserved it all and so much more.

Caught up in my thoughts about my mother re-entering the dating pool, I wondered if she would ever consider getting married. She used to say that it was out of the question once she went through that bad breakup with my father, and I could definitely relate to that shit. After not getting my happily-ever-after with Braxton, I just about gave up on that beautiful fairytale life. Then here comes Gunner, like a knight in shining armor to save this ghetto butterfly. Although our road became rocky early in, the good still managed to outweigh the bad in our fairly fresh relationship, and we remained solid. Together, we stood strong. Grateful to Gunner for helping me feel alive and renewed, I prayed for him every day. I prayed for his safety, his livelihood, and his soul, then thanked the Lord above for all his gifts, especially the gift of love.

Spinning around with a smile on my face, I caught Gunner sneaking up on me. When he unexpectedly lunged my way and I flinched, we both burst out laughing, then he hugged and kissed all over my lips, face, and neck to make up with me.

"Baby, you know I didn't mean to scare you. I just wanted to come tell you that I'm about to go," he announced and gave me one last peck on the cheek before he left my place to go jog two miles to his house.

As the door slammed behind him, it created a thunderous boom that echoed throughout the quiet house. The sudden noise caused me to jump again. "Ugh!" I grumbled and calmed down.

That incident with Camille still had my nerves bad. I even sprang from the sofa when my cell rang on the table beside me. Who was calling me now?

Ring . . . buzz . . . ring . . . buzz . . .

"Here we go," I mumbled to myself, then smirked when I saw who it was. "What's up, Braxton?"

"Hey, Oaklyn. I didn't wanna bother you. I was just calling for a couple of things. First, to let you know I dropped that custody shit. I know you're a great mother, and we've all been through enough. I really don't wanna fight with you, Oaklyn. I want what's best for you and Brazil."

"I want what's best for you too, Braxton, and I appreciate you dropping it."

When I finished thanking him, I questioned him about Teagan and the baby. Once he began to tell me about how she was in the hospital suffering a miscarriage, I didn't even want to know the story behind it. When he tried to tell me, I cut him off and asked him about the other reason he called.

"Oh, yeah, I wanted to know how Brazil's doing. I see she's been busy working and going to school like a little adult. I'm so fucking proud of her," he said. "I'm sorry I ain't been around like I'm supposed to. I feel bad about that shit, and although there ain't no excuse good enough for not spending time with my daughter, I gotta tell you that I've been busy negotiating a music deal."

"That's great, Braxton. I'm happy for you," I genuinely replied.

"Thanks, Oaklyn. It's a great opportunity for exposure, and they're offering more money than I've ever seen in my life. It would set me up for a long time. The thing about it is, if I sign this deal, I'll be overseas for an entire year doing a European tour opening for a major group," he explained. "That means that I won't see Brazil for a while. I don't even know how to tell her."

"Well, we both have passports now, so it would be awesome if you surprised her with two tickets so that I could bring her to come see you once you get settled . . . and maybe catch a show. She would love that, and it would take the sting off when you break the news to her."

"Now, that sounds like a plan. I'm about to call her now so I can tell her about my deal and congratulate her on her new ads. I'll talk to you soon."

When our call disconnected, all I could say was, "Wow!" Braxton and I actually had a civil conversation. No arguing whatsoever. This man seemed to finally be maturing—hopefully.

Comfortably dressed in my ripped jeans, fitted shirt with Brazil's ad logo on it, and the pink, yellow, and blue Jordan's Gunner got me, I went and retrieved the keys to the Benz from the hook in the kitchen. When I pulled the keyring down, I thought about buying a new car. I really wanted one, but it would have to wait until after the trip to Jamaica. Right now, I had to run out and take care of a few things.

The excitement that filled me had me flying from place to place, and within five hours, all my errands were complete. Now, back in the comfort of my own home with time to spare, I planned on using every minute wisely. Going down my checklist, I made sure that our bags were properly packed and that we were checked in for our flight. Lastly, I called the resort to make sure they had everything in our overwater villa that I ordered to be delivered. I wanted this trip to be extra special for both me and Gunner.

"Baby, I'm back," he sang out from the living room. His sincerity and humor always made me smile.

"You're so silly."

"You like it."

"Nah," I teased as Gunner came to shower me with affection. "I love it."

"Oh, shit, my baby loves me," he yelled out while hanging onto my waist with one hand. "Everyone hear me? Oaklyn Jones loves me!"

"I sure do. Now, let's get a good night's sleep. We gotta get up early for our flight."

Gunner ignored every word I said and followed me to the shower. He put it on me in there, on the bathroom counter when we got out, then in the bed when we called ourselves going to sleep. Shit, my eyes didn't close until after midnight.

Waking with a smile three hours later, I beat Gunner out of the bed and had everything ready before I got him up. Using my right hand, I leaned over and shook his body until he shivered under the sheets. Coming from beneath them, he groggily yawned, stretched, then opened his eyes and saw me dressed. In a comical panic, he leaped from bed and ran around like a chicken with his head cut off to get himself together. I couldn't stop laughing.

Gunner's humor lasted throughout the two flights, layover, and trip to the resort. Oh, but when we were escorted over a small ramp that led into an enclosed, heart-shape bridge where our bungalow was located . . . nothing but magical moments.

"Oh my God!" I shrieked loudly when we entered the private villa and the concierge brought our bags in. While I graciously tipped him, Gunner bypassed me to check the place out first.

"No fucking way! You see these glass floors, baby?" Gunner shouted and grabbed my hand.

Mesmerized by the ocean life beneath me, I stood frozen while he ran off yelling about a hammock, an outdoor shower, and the soaking tub with an amazing view of the horizon over the ocean. It all sounded good, but I still couldn't take my eyes off the different colorful fish swimming just below my feet. The clear floors gave me the illusion that I was walking on water and empowered me in a refreshing way.

"Are you good, baby?" Gunner checked with his arms wrapped around my wide frame.

"More than good, boo. I'm great. This shit is amazing." I gasped. "I can't wait to go to dinner tonight and wear this new dress I bought."

"Well, I think I gotcha something that you can wear with that dress, baby," he teased while rocking me in his arms.

After he broke the embrace, he backed up a bit, then extended his hand to me. Gladly grabbing it, I allowed Gunner to escort me out to the suspended patio. Once we stepped into the open space, the incredible view of the horizon just over the ocean stole my breath. I got so caught up in it that I didn't realize that Gunner was speaking to me until he cleared his throat.

"That thing I said that I had to go with your dress," he repeated as I spun around and saw him on one knee.

There could only be one reason for him to be down there. Could it be? Was it?

Oh my God! My insides danced and shouted as Gunner drew out that silver box and popped it open.

"You could sport this tonight and forever if you agree to make me the happiest man on this earth. Would you do that, baby? Would you be my wife? I mean, you already got my heart in a chokehold, so it would only be fair to make an honest man out of me, Oaklyn. What you say?"

The waterworks began, and the salty kisses followed as I jumped on him. Although his size and strength went unmatched, my weight immediately knocked him backward onto the patio floor.

"Yes! Hell yes! I'll be your wife for the rest of your life."

"To have and to hold me?" He laughed as he helped me up to place that huge diamond on my finger.

When he hugged me, everything felt right. God did answer prayers.

Chapter Thirty-three

Braxton Carter

Losing Oaklyn by far was the toughest lesson that I ever had to learn. It pained me to see her in love with another man who would be helping raise our daughter, but it hurt even more knowing that I was the one to blame. Time after time, she forgave me when I knew that I didn't deserve to be forgiven, and I ran with it. I took her love for granted. After all the good Oaklyn did for me, I repaid her how? By giving her nothing but the blues, filling her with disappointment and upsetting her with my constant betrayal. I would never forgive myself for that shit.

With no way to change the past, my only choice was to let go of my childish ways, release the bitterness, and grow up. To be a better man and a better father. A year out of the country, away from everyone, would allow me to do just that. It would give me the necessary time to work on myself.

As I sat there and silently repented, I thought about Teagan and Oaklyn fighting at my house and how I didn't do shit to break it up. That fucked my head up too. Unaware of Teagan's current condition, I realized that I hadn't heard from her since she called me back crying, talking about the possible miscarriage. She had hung up so fast that I didn't get a chance to question her about it.

Curious to find out what had happened, I dialed her up, but unfortunately, the recording stated that her line was no longer in service. Did she change her number? What was going on? Thinking that I could reach her on one of the social network sites, I hopped on the blue app and typed in her name, but nothing came up. With the assumption that Teagan had me blocked, I went to her homegirl, Eva's page.

"What the fuck?" I gasped as I read dozens of posts telling Eva to rest in peace. "This chick got killed?"

To check the validity of the posts, I did a Google search and found several articles about her murder. One said that Eva's throat got slashed, and another talked about how they had no suspects yet.

"Eva is dead, and Teagan is nowhere to be found. What the hell happened?" I chanted lowly to myself as I decided to go over to Teagan's.

The ride over there took twenty minutes. During that time, I thought of ways to apologize to her and let her know about my plans to move out of the country for a while. She deserved an apology and explanation before I left. Once I gave it to her, I could leave there with a clean slate and a clear conscience.

"Damn, she's selling her house?" I frowned when I drove up in her winding driveway and spotted the FOR SALE sign in her front yard.

With no way to contact Teagan, I used my last option: email. Sitting in my car, I opened my Gmail and attached her contact info, then typed up a long, heartfelt letter. I apologized and confessed my feelings for her. I let her know that I had met her at the wrong time in my life, and if things had been different, maybe it could've worked.

In the middle of typing, Brazil called from her new cell phone, so I saved my message to Teagan in the Drafts folder and answered.

"Hey, baby girl."

"Daddy," she cheered. "I'm going to be in a commercial. We get to start filming next week when Mom and Gunner get back."

"Where did they go?"

"Mom took Gunner on a surprise vacation to *Jamaica*," she blabbed, making Draya fuss at her for telling her mother's business. "Nana, it's just my daddy."

"So, if she wanted anyone to know, she would've told them," Draya countered.

"Maybe Mom forgot, Nana."

While my daughter and her grandmother debated playfully, jealousy invaded my mind. I couldn't believe that Oaklyn took that nigga to an exotic spot out of the country. We were in a relationship for ten years and had barely been to Seattle, California, and Arizona together.

"Are you gonna come to headquarters and watch them film the commercial, Daddy?"

Sad to say, I had to break the news to Brazil about my leaving that weekend. She acted torn up at first, but when I took Oaklyn's advice and promised to send for her and her mom, she quickly changed up.

"You know I got my passport, Daddy?"

"Yes, your mother told me."

"We are gonna have so much fun when we come," Brazil spoke happily. "Maybe we can even bring Gunner. I think he would love to come."

"See, now, little girl, that's quite enough. You're running your mouth a bit too much," Draya clowned and took the phone from Brazil. "Braxton, I don't know what's gotten into your daughter, but she'll call you after her bath."

Laughing at both of them, I hung up and thought about Brazil's request. Damn, that shit crushed me, but it also made me realize that she had to be close to Gunner to ask me some shit like that. With mixed emotions about the whole situation, I went down to the studio and did what I did best. I released it all in a new song I wrote.

Just as I finished and removed my headphones to set them on the stand, I looked up and saw my boy Chachi standing on the other side of the glass. He had this huge grin on his face.

"What's good, boi?" I greeted him as I came out of the booth.

As we pounded fists and bumped shoulders, I questioned him about the extra-wide smile he was wearing. "What's up with that, Chachi? New pussy?"

"Nigga, please!" he clowned and flashed his jewelry. "I got me a sugar mama."

"Ooohhhh, so you got you some *old* pussy," I teased, making him bend over laughing.

"You got fuckin' jokes, Braxton."

"You've been M.I.A., and you came in here cheesing. I knew it was something." I chuckled.

"Fuck what ya talkin' about. That shit you was blowin' in the booth was some fire. Lay that shit down and sell that shit today."

Chachi hyped me up, and when we finally calmed down, I filled him in on my new deal and my leaving. After that, I told him about Oaklyn and Teagan fighting, then about the baby.

"She having a kid by you?"

"That's what I don't know," I explained.

As I stood there and told him about Eva being murdered, and then Teagan disappearing, he had a million and one questions. Questions that I had no answers for. "That's what I'm saying, man. She said she lost the baby and then vanished. I don't know where she is. Now, I found articles on Eva's murder, but I couldn't find anything on Teagan's disappearance."

"You think she had something to do with her friend's murder? Or do you think that the people that murdered Eva took her?" Chachi probed.

"Shit, you got me." I sighed, wondering what had really happened.

"Hey, maybe you can call her father. Didn't you say that he was the one who hired you for Teagan's surprise party?"

"Somebody named, Amari Hoffman sent the payments for the gig. I think that's Teagan's cousin. The one I met at her house. I don't think they get along, though."

"You got her number?"

"Yeah."

"Call it and tell her that you're looking for Teagan. Tell her it's about business or something," Chachi suggested.

"Bet. I'm about to do it."

Grabbing my phone, I dialed her up. Amari answered on the second ring.

"Who is this?"

"This is Braxton Carter. I met you over Teagan's—"

"I know who you are, but I don't know why the hell you're calling me," she replied nastily.

"I wasn't trying to be disrespectful by dialing your number to get in touch with Teagan, but her number is changed, and—"

"Let me tell you something, *Braxton*." She cut me off. "This family don't think you're a right fit for Teagan, so I advise you to let it go. There's no more baby to tie y'all together."

"I saw that her best friend got murdered. I just wanted to make sure she was okay."

"I said stay the fuck away. It's over. You keep that little studio and whatever else Teagan gave you and go on with your life."

Before I could get another word out, the line went dead. That crazy bitch hung up on me. Aware that I would get nowhere by calling Amari back, I sat there and opened my Gmail again to finish typing Teagan's letter. When I finished, I hit send and then followed her cousin's suggestion. I let it all go.

Chapter Thirty-four

Teagan Hoffman

How did I even get to this dark place in my life? A place where only God could provide the light I needed. With no chance of Him coming to rescue a wretch like me in this hour, I began to give up hope. After being as disobedient as I had been, He had probably written me off anyhow.

"Teagan, your father wants you downstairs in the den," my mother announced through the closed door of the guest bedroom.

My jaw clenched and my body trembled as I rose from the bed. The toxic mixture of love and hate that I had for my parents began to take a toll on me. Reminding myself that it would be all over soon, I blew out a sigh of relief and closed my eyes. Saying a quick prayer, I asked for forgiveness, because when I left there today, our lives would never be the same. Never.

"Teagan!" My mother repeated herself in a more elevated tone.

"I'll be down in a minute."

"Are you done packing? The driver will be here to get you in the next half hour to take you to the airport."

Ignoring every word my mother said, I silently went over the plan I had set up this past week while my parents had me locked up in that house. My father may have taken my phone, but I still had my tablet stashed in the bottom drawer in the closet. With a little help from an old friend, I was able to obtain everything that I needed for my next move. It took a lot of courage to do what I was about to do, but I was up for it. Revenge may not have been the answer for some folks, but I disagreed. Some things you couldn't let slide, especially murder. The blood of my baby and best friend Eva were on Amari's hands, and my parents' as well. They were the whole force behind it, and they wouldn't go unpunished.

Instead of issuing them the death sentence, I killed a majority of their finances by scheduling all of their offshore account balances to be transferred. Every penny would go to MAMA (Mothers Against Murders Association). Their cash stash of over ten million dollars that they kept in the basement was put in a box, taped up, and set outside with the rest of the bulk trash. I arranged for that to be picked up as soon as I left. Sending a text with a simple one-word message would get both of the jobs done. It was all about timing.

Just like in Amari's case. After finding her guilty, I put my plan in motion for her, too. If only she came to me instead of destroying my life. All behind a code. Well, fuck that code, and fuck her. She had to die.

"Teagan, come on down now. The driver—"

"I'm coming, Mom."

Forcing a fake smile, I popped out of the room and pretended to be devastated about being sent to South America to live with my grandmother. Little did my parents know I had tickets to go in the opposite direction. Who the hell did they think they were, anyhow? I wasn't a kid. I didn't have to do a damn thing but stay black and die, but not tonight. It wasn't my turn just yet.

"You hear me, Teagan?" my mother asked, snapping me out of my silent rant.

"What did you say?"

"Your father is waiting to talk to you before you leave," she reminded me as I followed her down the stairs and into the den.

With his legs propped up on the ottoman and the remote in his hand, Papa looked up at me and ran down a bunch of rules. After two minutes in, I stopped listening because he wasn't the boss of me.

"Where's Amari?" I questioned. "I wanted to say good-bye to her."

"Isabella just cooked lunch like she always does at this time, so Amari is probably in there eating."

Strolling down the hallway in that direction, I suppressed the sneaky grin on my face and entered the kitchen. "I'm about to leave."

"Bitch, bye," she taunted as she stuffed some garlic bread in her mouth.

While wishing she choked half to death, I dug into the bottom of the cooler and pulled out the last two cold ones. This particular brand was Amari's favorite.

"Yo' sneaky ass don't wanna share?" she sneered.

"Bitch, you can have one, but you ain't gotta talk to me that way," I shot back and handed her one, tucking the other in my handbag. Then I hit the button on my tablet to set a five-minute timer. When she went to crack it open just like I anticipated, I smiled and walked into the living room to get my bags that Isabella had brought down. With only minutes to spare, I gave my parents a hug, goodbye, then casually walked out the door with one minute left. As the driver opened the door for me, I climbed in, then watched him toss my bags in the trunk, including the box I had set curbside—his payment for helping me.

Thirty seconds remaining—

My timer chirped as soon as we got through the gates. That meant that the poison that I had injected into the bottle of beer the night before had turned lethal. One sip of that shit and Amari was dead. Without a care in the world, I sent the final text to my banker, then tapped on the glass separating me from the limo driver. When he opened it, I asked if he had gotten everything I needed.

"It's all in the bag on the floor, ma'am."

Anxiously lifting it onto the seat beside me, I unzipped it and found the cash, credit cards, passport and ID with a new identity, a ticket to Spain, and an untraceable cell—everything required to start a new life with no family, no friends and sadly, no Braxton.

Attempting to block out the pain of the past, I drew out the phone and powered it on. Since I didn't have any contacts, I couldn't call anyone. Social media was out of the question and would get me caught up, so I couldn't download any of those apps. The only safe thing to access was my email.

Waiting until I got to the airport and boarded my flight, I sat down in my first-class cubicle and got on my phone before we took off. That only gave me minutes to scroll through my messages.

"Wait, what?" I gasped when I saw that Braxton had sent me an email. As I slowly read through the heartfelt letter he wrote, tears of relief and sorrow flowed through me. That man did care about me after all, and that was all the closure that I needed. Choosing not to respond, I reclined in my seat with a peaceful smile, closed my eyes, and thought, *one day, maybe one day our paths will cross again, Braxton. It just can't be right now.*

Sleep took over quickly, and within a few hours, we landed. Then I had to take a second flight. I slept through that entire one, too, and when I woke up in Madrid, relieved that no one knew my location, I had a new attitude. It all started when I got off the plane, made it through customs, and spotted all these people raising personalized, handheld signs. I nearly walked right by my private tour guide because I was too busy checking him out. He was fine! Glancing down at the sign, I read it twice before realizing that I was now going by the name of Leilani Lopez. Damn, I had to get used to that.

"Hey!" I greeted him and flashed my passport. "You're here to pick me up, right?"

"Yes, señorita. I'm Armando. I'll be your host for the next two weeks," he announced with a strong accent. So fucking sexy. Everything about him was, and I couldn't take my eyes off him. Okay, I know I said that I wasn't about to jump into another relationship, but I didn't say anything about not jumping in another man's bed. Shit, I had to have some fun and make some new friends. Why not start now?

Not wasting another moment, I began to get to know Armando during the ride. I found out that he actually owned the company that he drove for, but they were short drivers, so he came himself. He also told me about all the other businesses he owned. By the time we arrived at the house that I had leased, I knew all I needed to know about Armando, and I was confident that I wanted to be his friend—his intimate friend—but I didn't make a move on him until the second day.

After getting a little taste of this African American loving, Armando went from working for me to taking care of me within a week. For once, I wasn't the one forking out all the dough, and it felt amazing. At last, I was free, I was safe, and I was happy. Nothing else even mattered. Absolutely nothing.

Chapter Thirty-five

Gunner West

End of the Summer . . .

Through tragedy and death, the sun still managed to shine on my special day, the day I got to marry my best friend, Oaklyn. Everyone that we loved showed up to celebrate our union, along with over a hundred guests. Front and center were my parents, Draya, Coach Riley, Koola, and her new boyfriend, Shamhad.

Don't let me forget Brazil. As always, she unintentionally stole the show when she skipped down the aisle tossing rose petals onto the gold carpeting while an R&B wedding song played throughout the church. When Brazil reached the front of the sanctuary, she grabbed the mic and began singing along with the music. The precise melodic notes that belted from that little girl's mouth shocked me and the rest of the guests as well. Who knew she could sing like that?

Unbothered by the attention she received, Brazil sang on, while my eyes stayed glued to the door, waiting for my bride to waltz through the entryway. Now, I had been known to shed a few tears in my years, but never in front of a bunch of folks, half of whom were strangers. When they suddenly stood and gasped in unison, my eyes fought through the crowd to see her.

"Wow!" I gulped when I first got a glimpse of Oaklyn. My chest pounded anxiously as she approached me, then my view became clearer. Not even the tears could distort the breathtaking vision before me.

"Thank you, Jesus," I chanted loud enough to make the guests erupt in chuckles. While they were laughing, I happily cried and didn't care who saw me. Hell, I didn't even bother to wipe my face because I knew it wouldn't do any good.

"I'm blessed, baby. I'm truly blessed," I whispered to Oaklyn when she finally approached the podium in a form-fitting white dress that beautifully accentuated her plentiful curves.

"*We're* blessed." Oaklyn giggled and took her place next to me as the music died down. She seemed so calm and relaxed, while I struggled to keep still. I could barely keep up when the pastor spoke about holy unions. All I knew was we both said our vows, kissed, then jumped the broom.

Finally, I was able to exhale and enjoy the reception, our guests, and our abundance of gifts. Once we opened them and said our goodbyes, we headed to Oaklyn's and consummated the marriage.

"I love you, Mrs. West," I repeated with kisses as we cuddled in bed.

"I love you more, husband." She giggled and wiggled.

"Oh, so much has been going on that I forgot to tell you. My house sold a few days ago. When the funds drop, we'll buy a new spot."

"I was thinking about that too, babe." Oaklyn grinned. "Maybe I can donate this one to someone who really needs it."

The size of her heart constantly amazed me. Never had I met a woman like her.

"The wedding and reception were amazing, but we better try to get some sleep. We have an early one," Oaklyn reminded me.

"It was perfect," I mumbled with my eyes closed as I slowly drifted off.

When that magical day ended, a new one began that very next morning. Off to the Virgin Islands all of our loved ones went. It was something like a week-long, group honeymoon.

The first six days we were there, I made sure to do something special for Oaklyn. Each morning, she had a surprise waiting for her when she woke up. From a spa day to a rack of new dresses to enjoying an intimate breakfast on the beach as the sun rose, I spoiled my wife like crazy.

In the afternoons, we always spent time with Brazil. Allowing her to choose the activity meant that we were all in for a surprise. She had us ziplining in a tropical jungle, snorkeling with the stingrays and sea turtles, kayaking across the island, hiking to a waterfall, along with checking out several popular beaches. Some days, we were drained by dinnertime. Part of the evening was reserved for family.

"I can't believe that I'm Mrs. West." My wife gasped and twirled around with her eyes on her ring, the same as she had done the entire six days we had been there. "Everything happened so fast that it's hard to believe it's real," Oaklyn continued.

"It's real, Mom. I was there and saw you, say I do and get that ring and kiss Gunner!" Brazil giggled as she entered the living room of the suite. "That makes you my stepdaddy. My grandma told me that."

"Yep, that's what it means." I laughed and tickled her.

"Well, I know I already got a daddy, Gunner, but can I call you Pops like you call your father?" Brazil asked, making me emotional, but I held it down and paused that shit.

"Of course you can," I told her. "I would be proud."

"Me too," she replied and gave me a hug. "I love y'all."

"We love you, too," Oaklyn and I chanted at the same time.

That moment right there, I would remember for the rest of my days. Brazil was something else, and I got lucky to get her as part of the package.

"Are you guys hungry?" I asked, breaking up the emotional moment. "Draya, Coach Riley, Koola, Shamhad, and my parents are meeting us at the seafood restaurant on the south side of the main resort. It's our last night here, so let's make sure not to be late."

"We won't be," Brazil yelled on her way back to her private bedroom of the suite.

Within the next hour, we were finally ready to go and meet everyone at the restaurant. Dressed in the matching short outfits that Oaklyn had bought for the trip, we walked over to the seafood spot hand in hand. This time, Brazil wasn't the only one getting all the attention. This time, it was all about family.

"Look at y'all coming in here looking sharp as a tack." Pops greeted us.

Showing love, we all hugged and then took a seat at the table. Draya and Coach Riley were the last to join us. That surprised me because all week it had been Koola and Shamhad showing up late.

"Look at the stragglers," Pops joked.

"They probably been upstairs—" my mother started but quickly stopped midsentence when she looked over at Brazil, whose eyes were locked on her.

"Glad you could join us," Oaklyn teased.

As she hugged Koola, the fellas and I pounded fists with Shamhad. Even though I didn't know too much about him besides him owning several food trucks, he seemed like a pretty cool dude.

"Sorry about that, everybody," Koola apologized and took a seat beside Oaklyn.

During our meal, we shared stories about our time there on the island. We talked about the activities we engaged in, shopping at all the small shops, and of course, the delicious food.

"Anyone interested in having some dessert?" my mother questioned.

"Gladys, I gotta go to the bathroom. Can you order me a slice of cheesecake, baby?"

"Gerald, go ahead on. You know you're lactose intolerant," my mother clowned. "You already done ate those cheesy lobster bites. I pray you're not going in there to tear those folks' bathroom up."

There they went, always creating a scene, always making everyone laugh. But they were the best parents, and I wouldn't trade them for the world.

"Y'all are too funny," Koola cracked.

"Get married and stay together as long as me and Gerald. You'd stay having jokes too." My mother giggled.

"That's the goal," Oaklyn blurted out and grabbed my hand under the table.

"It sure is," I agreed with a smile.

Whatever I had done to deserve a wife like Oaklyn, I promised God that I wouldn't mess it up. Never would I take her love for granted. Never.

Chapter Thirty-six

Oaklyn Jones-West

When we came home from visiting both the U.S. and British Virgin Islands, we were exhausted and in need of sleep. All I could think about was that Brazil had one week before she went back to school. I hadn't gotten her clothes, shoes, nor supplies, and she still needed to film her second commercial. With pressure like that, I would think twice before signing another endorsement contract, and three times before deciding to have another child. Gunner may not have mentioned it out loud, but he sure had been dropping hints about knocking me up.

"Mom, Daddy called and said he bought the tickets for you to bring me to visit him in Italy," Brazil hollered as she busted in my room without warning. It made me mad at myself for buying her a cell phone, and even madder that she didn't knock on my door before rudely entering. After reminding that girl endless times, I would think she would get it.

"What did you forget to do before you just barged in here?"

"Sorry, Mom." That little smarty pants had the nerve to run out of my room, close the door, then knock. When I didn't answer her, she started yelling. "Mom! It's me! Your daughter! Brazil!"

"Girl, come in," I said.

"Mom, seriously? You did me like that?" Brazil paused in place and folded her arms across her chest.

"I'm just tryna figure out why you did all the dramatic stuff when you already bust in here and said what you had to say."

"You didn't let me finish, Mom."

"What is it, Brazil?"

"Daddy got our tickets to go to Italy for Christmas!" While my daughter jumped for joy and twirled around in circles, singing "We Wish You a Merry Christmas" and catching every note, I tried to think of a way to tell her that I wasn't about to spend my first holiday without my husband. No way would I leave him behind. Silently debating on how to respond to her without hurting her feelings, I thought hard to come up with a reply, but I had nothing. Absolutely nothing.

"Ah . . . ah, I don't know about that, Brazil."

"You didn't let me tell you the best part, Mom."

"What is it, Brazil?" I repeated for the third time.

"Daddy bought an extra ticket for Pops!"

"What? Braxton got Gunner a plane ticket, too?"

"Yep, all round trip, and we even get to go to his show." Brazil cheered again. "Backstage passes and everything, Mom. Do you believe this? I'm so happy."

"Me too," I confessed as I hopped up and joined in on the celebration.

Excited about getting another stamp on my passport, I waited for Brazil to run out of the room before I really acted up. Dancing from the bed to the bathroom, I anxiously retrieved my cell and called Braxton to thank him for being so thoughtful. This kind gesture showed his growth, and I appreciated the effort he made to accept and include my husband in this trip. It took a real man to do some shit like that after everything that had transpired.

"Hey, Oaklyn," Braxton greeted me when he answered the phone. "I guess Brazil told you what we talked about, huh?"

"About the tickets? Yes, and thanks a million, Braxton."

"No problem, and congrats on the marriage," he said with a smile.

"Thanks, Braxton."

"I take it that Brazil didn't mention anything else."

"About what?" I questioned curiously.

"About her performing with me while she was here. I saw the video of her singing at your wedding, and I couldn't believe it. I must've watched it a million times," Braxton confessed. "That little girl of ours continues to amaze me. First basketball with Gunner, and now singing just like her daddy. Extraordinary child she is. Slick, too. Did you know she could blow like that, Oaklyn?"

"I mean, she sings all the time in the car, but never loud. It's like she studies the melody and the lyrics, then adds her own twist to it. She's been doing it for the last couple of years," I explained. "I guess I didn't make too much of it, just like with the basketball."

"Damn, Brazil has so much going for her, and I just wanna be a part of it, Oaklyn. Please don't deny me this one thing. Just one song," Braxton pleaded.

"If she wants to do it, then I won't stop her. I just hate all the attention she's getting. I don't want her distracted from her studies."

"Oaklyn, it'll be during Christmas break, and my manager will take care of everything."

"Okay, I'll talk to Brazil. I need to make sure all of this won't overwhelm her."

"She already told me yes, but y'all discuss it and let me know."

"I sure will, Braxton."

"A'ight, cool, but one more thing. Did Brazil mention the song she helped me write for the commercial, or the dance we're supposed to learn?"

"Oh, shit! No, she didn't." I gasped and shook my head.

"I'm not surprised." He chuckled. "I'll let you go, Oaklyn, but make sure you go talk to Brazil so she can fill you in."

"Will do, Braxton. I'll talk to you soon."

When we hung up, Brazil knocked on my door like she had been on the other side of it eavesdropping during the entire conversation. That child of mine.

"Come in, girl."

"Hey, Mom." She waved and grinned sneakily, peeping her head inside my room before fully entering.

"Hey, Brazil."

"So, are you gonna let me sing one song with Daddy?"

"Do you want to?"

"Yes! I wanna sing in Italy with my daddy. That would be *amazing*, Mom."

"Okay, I guess you can then."

Brazil cheered on her way out of my room but paused before leaving. Turning to me, she smiled and asked for another favor.

"What is it?" I smirked playfully.

"I need you and Pops to do a TikTok video with me. We can practice here, so we can be ready to film next week."

"What?" I shrieked as Brazil asked me to check my email.

"It's for my next commercial, Mom. They already have all of our clothes for us to wear with their brand on it, and—"

"Wait, wait, wait! Who is *all* of us?"

"Well, you, me, and Pops will do the dance together. Nana and Coach Riley will do it together, and Daddy will be filmed in Italy while he does the dance and sings. Then they'll put all of our videos together, and it'll be epic! And you know what else, Mom?"

"What?"

"We all get paid, *and* we're promoting a positive message, *and* we're donating some of the money we make to the less fortunate, like we used to be. We can even help some of our friends back in the projects where we used to live."

"Who came up with all these ideas, Brazil?"

"I did. We have something unique."

"Is that right?"

"Yep!"

"What's that, Brazil?"

"We have what people call a blended family."

"Where did you hear that from?"

"From Nana. I told her all about the idea, and she wrote it up for me and sent it to the company. They loved it, Mom. They loved my idea." Brazil giggled and explained everything before she busted out in a song and dance.

"Family over everything. Family over everything. It doesn't have to be blood that connects us; it's more about those that protect us; the ones that love us; the ones that put no one above us. . . . Come on, Mom! Get up and do the dance with me."

Brazil and I must've practiced for the next hour. I could barely breathe when we finished, but I bet I had that damn dance down.

"One more time, Mom," Brazil instructed as she pulled me back up from the chair next to my bed and began dancing again.

"Oh, shit! Are we learning a new dance?" Gunner laughed as he walked in on our last round. That man jumped right in and had those steps down after fifteen minutes. It was so fucking cute!

"We can teach Nana and Coach Riley tonight when they get here for dinner," Brazil explained like she had everything under control. "I already called them, and they said they'll be here by six."

"And who's cooking?" I raised my brows and stared my daughter down, trying not to laugh.

"Nobody. I'm using the app that Pops installed on my phone. Uber Eats. They have everything, and he said I can—"

"Oh, he did, did he?" I smiled and glanced at Gunner as he slid by me and went into the bathroom.

"Yes!" Brazil shouted happily and clapped her hands as she headed out of my room. "I need to decide what to order."

As my door closed, I yelled out to Gunner, "You know that's your bill, right?"

"I put the one with a thousand-dollar limit on it."

"A thousand dollars?"

"She ain't gonna do that much damage. Besides, she don't know how to check out." Gunner smiled and kissed me to hush me up.

After he finally released me, I told him all about the trip and the video. When he didn't look surprised, he admitted that Brazil had already told him.

"I guess everybody knew but me, huh?"

As soon as I began pouting, Gunner held me close and loved all over me until I giggled. Squirming out of his grip, I looked up at him, held his hands, and smiled.

"What is it?"

"I don't even wanna say it, babe."

"What?" Gunner pressed. "Just say it."

"I don't wanna jinx anything."

"I don't believe in that shit. Just say it, pray about it, then watch it manifest into reality."

"Okay, then," I replied with my eyes still glued to his. "This is so perfect. Life with you is so perfect. Brazil and I are lucky to find you. You walked into our lives at the right time and showered us with all the love that we didn't know we needed. You changed me, and I feel so blessed."

"As I do," Gunner blurted out. "You, Brazil, and even your mom. Y'all accepted me, loved me and my family, and made me feel whole again. I didn't think that was possible after all the failed relationships I've been through. You showed me how it felt to be truly in love, and I couldn't have picked a better partner."

"Stop it! You're making me cry." I laughed and wiped the steady flow of tears leaking down my face.

"Shit, me too."

Chuckling together as we both went into the bathroom to freshen up, I couldn't stop silently thanking God. Truthfully, I never would. Unsure of where the road would lead us next, I became eager, knowing that I would travel it with my family, the ones who truly loved me. Unconditionally!

Epilogue

Braxton Carter

Winter Wonderland . . .

If the sound and stage manager, Sofia, hadn't been near me when I watched Oakland get married to Gunner on my cell, I probably would've let the tears roll. It took seeing that shit for me to finally get it and let her go. As much as I hated it, I knew I had to.

Seeing right through my facial expressions, Sofia came to comfort me, catching me in a vulnerable state. I lowered my walls and shared all my past insecurities. When I finished, I noticed she had become just as emotional as I was. Opening up to Sofia that day started a friendship between us that quickly escalated into an intimate relationship. Thankful to God for sending her to me, I promised myself not to make the same mistakes I had made with Oaklyn. No way would I lose another woman I loved to arrogance and selfishness. No way. Now, here we were, a few months later, and the winter holidays had arrived. Sofia and I had a bunch of plans, including the concert two days before Christmas.

"So, are you taking the ticket package over to the hotel?" Sofia asked after I mentioned that Oaklyn and her family had arrived in Milan and finally settled into their hotel suites.

"Yeah, you're coming with me, right?" I pressed, hoping that she would agree.

"You want me to?"

"Hell yeah! Why wouldn't I?

"Because me being there might make things awkward," Sofia replied, walking up on me to steal a kiss.

"Not at all. If you're gonna be a part of this blended family, I suggest you come with me."

"Have you even told them about me, Braxton?"

"Nope, but I'm ready to introduce you today. Come on."

"I don't need to change?"

"No. You look damn good in that dress."

Hand in hand, we left the apartment and went over to the hotel. Parking in the front, I dialed Oaklyn up to let her know that I had arrived. Traveling inside, we waited in the lobby for everyone to arrive so that I could give them their tickets and backstage passes. While Sofia sat in one of the plush chairs and scrolled through her phone, I stood there and hopped on mine to watch the commercial that we all did together. The incredible reaction following our display of unity was unbelievable. Brazil's idea literally went viral, and our concert tonight was sold out because of it. Hundreds of people posted on social media that they were attending just to see Brazil, a few celebrities included! This made me one proud father.

"Hey, Daddy!" I heard my daughter yell from behind me.

Putting my phone in my back pocket, I spun around to spot everyone coming my way. Seeing them all together and so happy warmed my heart.

"Hey, y'all," I replied with my arms out.

Brazil leaped right into them and squeezed me. I could immediately feel the love. "Daddy, I missed you."

"I missed you too, Brazil." I smiled and greeted every-one. "Everything you need tonight is in this envelope. It includes the info on the car service picking you guys up and dropping you off. That way, nobody has to worry about parking."

"Thanks so much," Draya shouted, then gave me a hug before formally introducing me to her new man.

"Nice to meet you, Braxton." Coach Riley smiled.

"Nice to meet you, too," I replied, then brought all focus to my lady. "Oh, and I want you guys to meet Sofia."

"Daddy, is that your girlfriend?" Brazil shouted with a huge grin.

"Yes, she is."

"She's so beautiful," Brazil cheered and ran to hug Sofia.

"So are you, love." My girl giggled as she stood back up and held my hand.

"Okay, take this. You'll need it for the show." I stuffed everything back into the envelope and passed it to Oaklyn.

After giving them details about how everything would go that night, I left them and went to the arena to get ready. All of my clothes were there, and I had a full bathroom in my dressing room. While Sofia did her job backstage, I took advantage of the food they provided for me, then went to shower and change. Sitting on the stool in front of the mirror, I slid into my shoes and then stared at my reflection. Now seeing a humble man before me, I smiled and wondered why I couldn't accomplish this shit years ago. Knowing that treading into the past could set me back, I took a deep breath and released it slowly.

"All good things come with faith and works. I deserve better because I'm better," I chanted as I heard a knock at the door. Expecting to see either Oaklyn and Brazil or Sofia, I swung it open and got the shock of my life. I couldn't even get a word to come out.

"Hey, Braxton." Teagan spoke with a smile and a new glow about her, but I still felt threatened because of what had happened to Eva. I didn't know what the deal was.

"Ah, hey, Teagan."

"I swear I came in peace," she assured me while holding her hands in the air. "I got your email, and thanks. I really needed that for closure, and it helped me move on. I just wanted to let you know that I hold no ill feelings toward you and only wish you the best."

"How did you know I would be here?" I questioned, thinking that she had flown all the way from the States to see me.

"I kept up with your European tour, and I don't live far from here."

"Wow!"

"Don't look so surprised. I've been through a lot these past few months, but through it all, I found myself, and I found my soul mate. I'm truly happy, and I hope you are too."

"You must be asking because you heard about Oaklyn getting married to ol' boy."

"Yes, I did. Are you good?"

"Yeah, I'm good."

"That's all I wanted to hear." She smiled and motioned for a hug.

My body immediately tensed up, but when I held her in my arms, a peculiar calmness swept over me. I couldn't quite explain it, but it felt comforting.

"Thanks for stopping by. I'm glad you came and that you're doing good," I said when I let go of her and stepped back.

"Me too." Teagan grinned and patted my shoulder. "Take care, and if anyone asks, you haven't heard from me nor seen me."

"My lips are sealed," I responded as I took my fingers and pretended to zip my mouth closed before escorting her to the door.

As she left the room, I smiled too. Everything felt so right.

"Come on, Braxton. It's time," my manager yelled out through the intercom, causing me to clear my head and pump myself up for my performance.

Exiting my dressing room, I heard my song playing and the crowd cheering. This concert would be like no other.

"Brazil!" they shouted over and over.

Instead of bringing her out at the end of my show like we had planned, I ended up calling her to the stage right away. She stayed up there through two of my songs and then tapped out, sweating and all. All of this was like a dream come true. Even if I couldn't have Oaklyn, sharing Brazil with her was all the love I needed.

Feeling complete, I ended my set, then went to spend some time with my family, the blended group of people that I had grown to love and respect—Sofia included. For me, that was a big deal. A very big deal!

"Can you answer some questions?" my manager asked as security held the press back.

"Sure," I agreed as they directed all the questions toward Brazil.

"Do you plan on pursuing a singing career like your father, or will you stick to basketball like your pops?" the first guy asked.

"Why can't I do both?" Brazil questioned.

"How does it feel to have two famous dads?" another guy probed.

"I feel blessed," she hollered and threw her hands up. "I love them both, and they're both *great!*"

Before they could ask anything else, security escorted us out the rear exit. That was the only safe place to go.

"Do you have to leave, Daddy?"

"I gotta go to my next city, baby girl. I'll see you soon, though."

"For New Year's at our house," Brazil pressed. "You and Sofia?"

"We wouldn't miss it for the world," I promised.

Even if I had to skip a performance or catch a red-eye flight, I wouldn't let my daughter down. Only death could keep us apart, and I didn't plan on dying anytime soon—Lord willing. Only He had the last say.

The End!